SEEDS OF CHANGE

THE GRAND HUMAN EMPIRE

BOOK 4

JOHN WILKER

EDITED BY
CHRISTINA SHORT

Rogue Publishing

CONTENTS

For my Wife, Nicole

You're about to embark on a fun adventure!

When you're done reading, I hope you'll take a minute to leave a review!

If you liked the story and want more, joining my newsletter is a great way to get free samples, and exclusive short stories.

If you like supporting things you love by sporting merch or buying direct, well you're in luck! I've launched a shop, take a look. **Use, discount code "Osprey" and you'll save %15!**

PART 1

CHAPTER 1

"This is so boring!" Jax hissed. He and Naomi were sitting in the *Osprey*'s cargo hold, the loading door wide open, their legs dangling over the edge.

Beyond the *Osprey*: the massive landing bay of the dreadnought *Goliath* flagship of the Nemesis fleet, now the home base and flagship of the Resistance.

Jax watched as crewers below them maneuvered cargo modules from below the *Osprey* to a stack a hundred yards away. "They got new uniforms." He looked at her. "How do they have new uniforms?"

She sat her beer on the lip of the hold. "Why would I know?"

Before Jax could answer, one of the crewers below them shouted up. "Ready for the next load."

Jax sighed. "Copy that!" He looked over his shoulder. "Ready?"

Behind him, Baxter said, "Of course. I got this shiny new body just so I could shove cargo modules around."

The *Osprey*'s cargo arm retracted into the hold. Baxter set about securing the next load onto the hook.

Jax tilted his head toward Naomi. "Blame her. She took the job."

"You had other prospects?" Naomi retorted.

"Not being tangled up with them." He jabbed a finger at the crewer waiting below.

The woman looked at him. "What?"

He waved her off.

Baxter silently transmitted to Skip, the *Osprey*'s managing Sapient Intelligence, that the load was ready. The cargo arm lifted the pallet of crates a foot off the ground before extending to its full three-meter length beyond the edge of the hold.

Across the bay, a group of crewers was working with a half dozen of the massive ship's droid complement. Jax watched the group. "Weird. You don't see that much anymore."

"What?" Naomi asked. He nodded toward the scene across the cavernous landing bay. "Ah. Yeah." She turned to Jax. "Maybe it won't be so uncommon if they succeed."

Jax made a rude noise. "The Indies got their clocks cleaned. What makes you think Commander Tight Pants and his ragtag—"

"They have uniforms," she interrupted.

"—Ragtag, but well dressed, all matchy matchy followers have any better of a chance?"

She shrugged. "You like things the way they are?"

He shrugged.

"If it helps," Rudy said as he rolled into the cargo

hold from the spiral staircase and the common deck above, "they pay well, and we were close to broke."

Below them, the crewer woman shouted to her colleagues. Jax and Naomi watched as droids and humans gathered around the cargo modules, divvying them up to be moved to different parts of the landing bay before moving to cargo holds throughout the massive ship.

The *Goliath* landing bay was a hive of activity. The *Osprey* wasn't alone; two other cargo haulers were parked in the bay. Unlike the *Osprey,* the other two ships were Resistance vessels, cold and empty after being unloaded. The massive dreadnought had served as the Resistance's mobile command center ever since Jax and Naomi had called them in when they found the Nemesis fleet three months ago.

Rudy rolled over next to the pair. "They've done a remarkable job getting the *Goliath* in working order in such a short period of time." Making his smart material rollerball adhesive, he tilted to look down below the lip of the cargo hold. "New uniforms?"

Jax groaned and took another sip of his beer.

Naomi clucked. "You act like this is the worst thing ever. We haul some totally innocuous stuff from one place to another, get paid better than most jobs this size, and get to sit and relax while others do the unloading."

Jax shook his head, waving his free hand to take in

the enormous hangar. "And if the Imperials show up? I don't mean now, but while we're on approach or departure? Sure, we scrub our idents, but still. Valerian Co-op Infiltrators aren't exactly common." He sighed again. "We're too involved. This isn't our fight, and if we get snatched up, you know they—" He waved his hand again. A droid a hundred paces off noticed and waved back. "They won't be swooping in to bail us out."

From behind them, Baxter said, "They might."

Jax's face made it clear what he thought of the likelihood of that.

Naomi stood and looked over her shoulder. "Two more bundles, plus the time to sort and such. Come on." She offered her hand.

Jax finished his beer and took her hand. "You good overseeing this?" he asked Baxter.

The matte black combat droid made what might be a rude noise but said nothing. Jax shrugged, dropping his free hand to Rudy's rust-red head. "Let's see what they've done to this old ghost ship." He looked at Naomi. "Wonder if Martin is still aboard?"

The trio took the stairs from the cargo hold to the small boarding chamber and the lowest part of the ship. The boarding ramp was already extended by the time they reached it.

Jax flagged down a crewer. "Hey, we're gonna wander around a bit. Let Baxter know if you need us."

The woman looked around, her pale blue eyes squinting. "Who's Baxter?"

Jax opened his mouth, then closed it. "Never mind."

To Naomi, he whispered, "I hate that none of these people know who we are."

She stared at him. "You just got done complaining that we were too tied to the Resistance. Now you're mad they don't know you. Make up your mind."

Jax smiled. "I'm deep and complex."

"You're neither," she retorted as they reached the hatch leading deeper into the ship.

The trio passed one of the small cleaning droids. Jax slowed, watching it work its way down the corridor. "I remember when those things were trying to kill us."

"Good times," Naomi said, eyes glued to her gPhone.

"What's up?" Jax asked as they rounded a corner that would take them toward the massive ship's internal spaces and the central bank of lifts.

Naomi looked up. "Oh, nothing. That guy I went out with last week. Being a bit of a creeper."

Jax leaned over to glance at her device's screen. "Oh, my." He looked up. "Definitely some wow factor there. Take it you didn't ask for that?"

She looked at him. "No woman asks for that pic, ever."

They passed two crewmembers deep in conversation about who knew what.

She shook her head. "No kidding, but the guy isn't doing well with my 'I travel for work and can't answer quickly all the time,' thing." She swiped at the string of messages. "Nineteen since we left Kelso, culminating in this wonderful view of his manhood." Sliding the device back into her pocket, she continued, "As if I might forget what it looked like or that being reminded would make me reply more promptly. Dudes can be such creeps."

"No argument." Jax nodded. He added. "It is impressive though," Naomi said nothing.

The lift doors slid apart. A young crewmember stepped back to make room.

"They're everywhere," Jax whispered.

Rudy was the last to enter the lift. As the door closed, he said, "So, it is not okay to send images of your genitals to people?"

Jax and Naomi groaned in unison.

The rest of the lift ride was painfully silent. Neither Jax nor Naomi could bring themselves to turn to look at their lift companion. The doors slid apart, and Jax shoved Rudy out.

"You guys are too easy to mess with," the nav droid chuckled as he rolled toward the ship's central core.

"Oh, look. New tree." Jax pointed. The ship's core was a multi-level terraced space meant to give the crew a compartment that wasn't low ceilings and corridors.

In the center was a wide circular planter. The last time Jax and the others were aboard the *Goliath*, it was home to a long dead oak tree. Now it was home to a very alive, very lush, and very healthy...maybe also an oak tree.

"Wow," Naomi said. The trio moved to the planter's lip. Looking up at the easily three-story tall tree, she asked, "How do you think they got it in here?"

"Secret of the Resistance," someone said from behind them.

They turned to see a tall blonde woman standing before them. The rank stripes on her sleeve marked her a lieutenant commander. Jax's eyes went wide as he looked up to meet her gaze. She was objectively stunning.

"Close your mouth," Naomi whispered.

She offered her hand. "I'm Commander Collins—Stephanie Collins." She shook each of their hands. "I understand that's your VC Infiltrator in the hangar?"

Jax was still staring. Naomi elbowed him, then said, "That's us."

The lieutenant commander nodded. "Those are great little ships. Fast, hard to track, great for sneaking around."

Jax finally regained his composure, shaking his head. "Yeah, Commander Tight—er, uh, I don't know his name—talked us into running cargo for you all."

Collins nodded. "As we grow, keeping up with supplies is getting harder and harder." She smiled. "Folks like yourselves are invaluable members of the—"

Jax raised a hand. "We're not part of the team."

Collins nodded. "You could be."

Jax shook his head.

"You can't think the system, as it is, works? The emperor makes his friends richer," she continued. "Corporations are grabbing up resources left and right, all with Abernathy's blessing. Individual citizens' lives are getting harder and harder."

Jax stared at her.

"Would it be so wrong to be part of something larger

than you? Something that was trying to make everyone's lives better?" Collins said.

"At the possible expense of our own lives? Yes." Jax pushed Rudy. "I think it's time to head back to the hangar bay. Baxter probably has the last two loads moved off. We can take off."

Collins stepped back. "I understand. You know how to reach us if you change your mind." She looked at Naomi. "Either of you."

"Tell Martin we said hi," Jax said, heading for the bank of lifts, Rudy rolling behind him, hot on his heels.

Naomi lingered briefly. "Nice to meet ya," she said to Collins before moving to catch up with Jax.

In the lift, she turned to him. "You sure went from wanting to get into her pants to—"

"I think they are called trousers," Rudy offered. Naomi held up a hand, bio-circuits glowing blue. Rudy's head spun a full 360 degrees as he rolled to the opposite side of the lift.

Jax shrugged. "I hate salespeople."

"I don't think she—"

"Can't we drop it?" he said as the lift doors slid apart. "I'm not looking to join up and I don't need any more friends."

Naomi regarded him for a moment. "Because you have so many? Friends, that is?"

"I have enough." He turned to face the lift doors.

Commander Mark Roberts, leader of the Resistance, was waiting for them at the base of the *Osprey*'s boarding ramp. He smiled when he saw them enter the hangar.

"Jax. Naomi. Good to see you both." He looked down. "Hi, Rudy."

Rudy slowed just enough to say, "I like the new uniforms," before rolling up the ramp.

Jax eyed the tablet in the commander's hand. "You handling accounts payable now?"

The big man smiled. "I just wanted to make sure I saw you two before you took off." He held the tablet out.

Jax produced his gPhone, opening his banking app and holding the device up to the tablet. "What'd you want to see us for? We met your saleswoman already. And passed."

The commander tipped his head. "Can't blame us for trying. You two...four...have proven to be incredibly skilled. You'd be invaluable assets to the cause."

Jax's gPhone beeped. He put it back in his pocket. "Pass."

Commander Roberts held up his hand. "Just think about it?"

"Nope." Jax pushed past him, heading up the boarding ramp.

Naomi looked up the ramp after Jax, then turned to the commander. "He's an asshole. Comm me when you're ready for another supply run." She reached up and patted his shoulder as she headed up the ramp. "Oh," she added over her shoulder. "The uniforms *are* nice."

The big man stepped back as the ramp rose, folding before it sealed against the hull. He shook his head as he turned, catching the optic sensor of one of the bipedal droids that served as crew for the big ship. "Let's clear this area. Right now, they're leaving."

The droid nodded and wirelessly summoned several others. Behind him, the sound of the *Osprey*'s lift engines powering up was audible over the din of the busy hangar.

Inside the *Osprey*, Naomi was following Jax up the spiral staircase that connected all four decks of the small ship. "You know, you can at least be nice. You don't have to agree with their politics to treat a customer with respect."

Jax stopped on the common deck, making his way toward the small kitchenette. Naomi followed as Rudy continued up the center of the staircase in a specially designed column of null gravity that ran up the center of the staircase.

From the overhead speaker, Skip announced, "Captain, I've got the lift engines spinning up. We're cleared to depart when you're ready."

"Thanks, buddy," Jax said, opening the refrigerator and grabbing a beer. He looked over the door to Naomi, who shook her head. He took a sip. "It's not that I don't respect them. I do. Hell, I wish them all the luck possible. Fuck the Empire. I just don't want any part of it." Naomi opened her mouth, but he continued. "The Empire cost me my parents. I can't risk them taking anything...or anyone...else." He turned and headed back to the staircase.

Naomi didn't move. She knew about his parents, of course. Before she inserted herself into his life over a year ago, she deep dived his life. She knew his parents had been prominent Indies, that they'd died in the last major battle in the war. That he had been raised by his adoptive aunt, the current governor of the independent space station, Kelso station.

Jax dropped into the pilot's chair. The displays before him came to life: diagnostics, reactor power levels, comm channels, and more.

Rudy was already plugged into his station. "Where are we heading?"

Jax slipped his beer into the cup holder bolted to the console before him. "Uh...Good question." He pulled up a nav chart on the larger display in front of him. "We'd get into Kelso too late." He swiped the screen a few times, looking at the entries for systems and stations between Kelso and this stretch of nowhere that the Resistance was currently calling home.

Naomi came up to the stairs. She decided to let the topic from downstairs go. "Where to?"

Jax looked over his shoulder, tapping the screen. "Thinking a pit stop at Valhalla. Grab a bite to eat, a dozen or two drinks." He waggled his eyebrows. "Find some...entertainment."

She made a face.

"What's that face for?"

Naomi hunched her shoulders. "It's just, well, the last time I was on Valhalla, there might have been an incident."

Jax turned his chair around. "Incident?"

"More like a run-in."

"A run-in? With?" Jax leaned forward.

Naomi scowled at him. "It was nothing. Just that..."

"Spit it out!" Rudy barked, startling Naomi and Jax.

Naomi leaned away. "Someone needs to recharge." She turned to Jax. "It was nothing. Forget it. It's fine. Let's go to Valhalla."

Jax turned back to face forward. Glancing at Rudy, he said, "Came on too hot, man."

CHAPTER 2

Clinton Morris stepped off the shuttle and looked around. The shuttle terminal was bustling; commuter shuttles entered one side of the hollowed-out asteroid station and departed the other.

Freeground station occupied the interior of a five-kilometer-long asteroid in planetary system P5X-232. The system lacked habitable planets but made up for it in a higher-than-average number of large asteroids rich in rare metals.

After mining one of the large asteroids to exhaustion, the company that owned the lease established a permanent presence in the system to save costs. That was how Freeground started. After the mining company went bankrupt, the station fell into disrepair, then found new life as a weigh station between several more populated systems after a few smugglers—and probably worse—stumbled on it and brought it back online. The Empire seemed ambivalent to its existence for reasons no one knew.

Clinton shifted a sturdy case from one hand to the other, reaching into his pocket to grab his gPhone. He checked it and then headed off toward the ramp that went up out of the hangar space to the open residential section above.

The case was specially designed by whomever ran the courier service. Once locked by a client, only the client could unlock it. When it arrived at his apartment, his handler had made it clear that it could stop a blaster bolt, but he'd lose his job if he put that to the test.

He stopped at the customs checkpoint. He did not know whom that woman behind the window worked for, given the station's nebulous ownership and affiliation.

"Reason for your visit?" she asked, hand scanner held before her.

He held his gPhone out, letting it beep, acknowledging that it had shared his ident with her system. "Business. I'm a courier."

She looked him up and down. "Bit scrawny for a courier."

Clinton reared back. "How do you know what a courier should look like?" To the best of his knowledge, few people even knew the organization existed.

She shrugged. "Well, really, you're too scrawny for most jobs." She winked. He scowled. "What's in the case?" she asked.

"Nothing, yet," he replied.

She shrugged. "Welcome to Freeground." Grumbling, he took the stairs to the level above. The main commerce zone.

At its widest, Freeground measured nearly two kilometers. The cavernous commerce section had multi-story buildings running down its center, where the ceiling was tallest. Shorter buildings filled in on either side as the cavern walls rounded on their way down. Four narrow lanes ran the length of the station, bisected by four cross streets.

Standing at either end provided a weird perspective of pyramidal design to the space.

"This place is gross," Clinton said under his breath when his shoe slid on something dark and greasy.

"What's that?" a rangy spacer leaning against a nearby building asked. The man was in a pale blue jump-suit that looked like it had been around the system a few times.

Clinton looked up. "Nothing. Sorry." He increased his pace toward the Hotel Excelsior. Nothing about the exterior said excelsior, but maybe they focused on the inside. He glanced over his shoulder. The spacer was staring at him.

He crossed the street after a bulky cargo van rumbled by. Watching the vehicle rumble up the street, he real-ized he hadn't seen a single grav-lift-enabled vehicle since arriving. Even the power loaders in the cargo and ship-ping levels below were wheeled, tracked, and bipedal.

The Hotel Excelsior was the next block up. Clinton sighed. The sooner he could get out of this backwater hollowed out potato of a station, the better.

Being a courier had seemed like a great way to see the Empire. That's what the recruiter had said, at least.

The Hotel Excelsior occupied an entire block. As far as Clinton could tell when researching the station, it was the only hotel on Freeground. The closer he got, the more he was convinced nothing good came from being on Freeground station.

Clinton stopped just inside the lobby. Unlike the open space outside that was lit by meters-long light strips bolted to the rock overhead, the lobby was all black paint and black lacquered wood-type materials lit only by dim ultraviolet lamps.

Once his eyesight adjusted, he spotted the check-in desk tucked into the opposite wall. He looked at the skeletal man behind the counter.

Artificial gravity was so ubiquitous that seeing someone raised in less than 1g was startling. Long, thin limbs, head slightly larger than average, on a long thin neck. "I'm meeting people..." He pulled out his gPhone, checking the contact details his handler provided. Looking up, he said, "Granum Husk?"

The low-gravity-raised clerk looked at his terminal. "Top floor. McGregor suite."

"Thanks." He looked around. "Lifts?"

The man pointed.

Clinton was going to have some words with his handler. He was new to this courier gig, but this seemed like hazing. His first job had been equally unappealing, and he was sensing a pattern.

Growing up on Terra Nova, Clinton wanted nothing more than to see what was beyond the capital planet's orbit. Now, standing in the lobby of a two-star, at best, hotel in a hollowed-out asteroid that was abandoned by its corporate owners and now was run by...well, he wasn't sure who was in charge...He was rethinking some of his choices.

While he waited for the elevator, he messaged his handler. The only reply was, *Suck it up and get the job done. Pussy.*

"Wonderful," he whispered. If he ever got a chance to meet the mystery person on the other end of the encrypted messages, he'd punch him or her in the face.

When he accepted the contract to become a courier, knowing he'd never meet his handler or another courier, he knew what he was getting into, but it still felt weird. Being a loner growing up helped. Sort of.

The top floor of the Hotel Excelsior was the fifth floor. Hollow asteroids had little space for tall buildings. The lighting on the residential floors was only a little brighter than the lobby, thankfully not black light. The builders had mirrored the hallway to make it feel wider than it was. It made Clinton nauseous.

Doors lined both sides of the hallway until either end was reached. The McGregor suite and its identical twin on the opposite side, the Finnian suite, spanned the width of the building. Their doors were at each end of the hallway.

Clinton pressed the announcer button next to the door.

Jefferson Sanchez was sitting at his desk, the large floor-to-ceiling window behind him showing the pale blur arc of Farndale.

He was reading the latest loss prevention report from one of the smaller towns' dirt sides. An employee had tried to sneak a few vials of experimental life extension treatment out of their lab. Apparently, she had been hoping to set up a side hustle moving the new treatment on the black market. They had caught her, of course. His team down on the planet was good. He trained them. Sighing, he looked up from the tablet at the view beyond. He hadn't been down to the planet in a while. He should visit his parents.

They still lived in the coastal resort city of Sea View.

"Mr. Sanchez." His assistant, Barry, interrupted his reverie. "I've got someone from agri-tech out here." The screen built into his desk flickered to life, showing a company dossier on the woman outside with Barry. A small inset window showed a live feed from the camera above the door. Barry was sitting at his desk smiling at the visitor.

She was a senior researcher and team lead. Had shuttled up to Station 1 from Farndale. Her workspace was in Blithe, one of the smaller research campus/towns on the planet's largest continent. Not the one his parents lived on.

He tapped the icon on the glossy surface of his desk, opening a channel to Barry. "Send her in."

Monika Jones walked in a moment later. Jefferson stood, offering his hand. She shook it.

After gesturing for her to sit, Sanchez asked, "What can I do for you, Ms. Jones?"

Her eyes were glued to the floor. She looked up, rubbing her neck. Her discomfort wasn't surprising. Sanchez's department was in charge of loss prevention, which in modern terms often meant hunting down current and ex-employees to recover stolen intellectual property.

When she didn't immediately answer, he cocked his head.

"I believe we..." she started. She cleared her throat once, then once more. When Barry had announced her earlier, Jefferson gave her dossier a quick read. Been with the company for almost ten years. Rose up the ranks of her division moderately fast.

"Yes?" he pressed.

"I haven't heard from two of my people," she croaked.

Jefferson reached over and keyed his terminal awake. Jones' dossier was still on the screen, so pulling up a list of her direct reports was a single tap. "Who?"

"Leonard Berkowitz and Malcom Delacourt," she answered. It was obvious she'd been practicing throwing those names out.

Sanchez started with Berkowitz. The employee photo in the dossier's corner showed a bald white man in his mid-fifties. He'd been with BioTek for only three years. A senior researcher in the agri-tech division. He was one of Jones' direct reports.

He swiped back up to Jones' department and tapped on the other name. Malcom Delacourt. He was younger than the other, dark-skinned, hailing from New Cairo. Been with BioTek for six years. He worked for Berkowitz now, but prior to that, he was a researcher in the genetic resilience department. Sanchez flagged that for further reading later and looked up. "When was the last time you saw them?"

"Last Friday," she said. She was intentionally not meeting his eyes. He was used to that. Few employees were comfortable around Loss Prevention and Recovery, the official department name. "They took a cryo-transport case from the lab. I don't know why or what's in it."

Sanchez tapped the icon for Barry. "Barry, we're going to be a while. Order lunch." He looked at Jones. "You should clear your calendar for the day."

Looking into the luxury suit from the open door, Clinton smiled. "Hi. Mr. Husk?" He shifted the case to his right hand, extending his left.

The man that opened the door, a middle-aged man of European descent, nodded and shook his hand. He stepped aside, ushering Clinton inside. He leaned to look past Clinton down the hall before releasing the door control.

Clinton walked into the suite's lounge area, spying

another man, younger, in his twenties, bald, his hairless dark-skinned dome glistening with sweat. Clinton smiled. "I'm your courier."

The first man joined the other. "Thank you for coming. Were you followed?"

Clinton raised an eyebrow. "To Freeground? You're joking?" The looks on the two men's faces gave the impression that they weren't. The two men who stepped out of the side room, pistols in hand, confirmed it. Clinton shook his head. "No, I wasn't followed." He looked at the two armed men. "Are we expecting friends?"

The older man shook his head. "Can't be too safe."

The younger one exhaled. He gestured to the lounge. "Please have a seat."

Clinton followed the two men to the seating area. He looked around. "Look, guys. I'm here to do a job." He gestured to the two armed men. "I don't know what—"

The older man patted the air. "We understand." He pointed over his shoulder. "They're just here as insurance." He turned to his colleague and nodded.

"Insurance?" Clinton pressed.

"Our employer is..." The older one looked to the younger. "Let's just say, powerful."

The younger man reached behind the chair he was in and pulled out a metal case. It was featureless: no lights or status displays. The thing was almost entirely blank except for a small panel in the center of the top piece. Clinton couldn't see what, if anything, was on the small indentation from where he was sitting. He could see that this case would fit inside his much more rugged case, so that was good.

He leaned forward. "What's in the case?"

The younger man smiled. "Better you don't know. Your handler said that would be okay." He looked at Clinton, who nodded. He continued. "The case is the job. It needs to get to our colleagues intact. Unopened." He spun the case around and slipped it closer to Clinton, who saw that the indentation did, in fact, have a small screen. It was showing two status displays, what looked like power and...maybe temperature? "There's an internal power source that will keep the case sealed and viable," the man offered.

Now that Clinton could see the display, he saw that there was a power readout, what looked like a battery indicator for a backup power cell. A few blinking icons that didn't mean anything to him.

He said, "Okay, looks fine. I assume my handler explained how it all works?" He put his case on the coffee table next to the other case. Popping the lid open, he lifted a thick metal cable out of the way. "Once your case is in here and I lock the cuff, only the unlock code will open the case and release the cuff."

The younger man nodded. "We're ready. I'll send the code to our friends." He had a gPhone in his hand.

The lid of Clinton's case had a slight indentation in the center meant for a gPhone. Clinton put the two men's case inside his, closed the lid, and gestured to the indentation.

The younger man placed his phone on the lid. The screen lit up. Clinton reached for the cuff.

The younger man watched his phone. "Looks like the randomizer sync is done."

Clinton looked at the screen and saw the same. He clicked the cuff around his wrist. With a soft clink, the cuff locked, and the case beeped. The man's phone screen flashed a message that the sync was complete.

The older man opened his mouth, but the suite's door announcer beep interrupted him.

CHAPTER 3

The two armed security men looked at each other, then at the two men across from Clinton, then finally at the door.

As the first man reached the door, he looked at the small security panel and its camera view. He reached for the icon to activate the intercom when the door exploded inward.

Blaster bolts flew down the hallway, striking the wall next to where Clinton and the others sat. He screamed. The two men screamed. The armed guards shouted and returned fire.

"What's going on?" the younger man screamed, looking at Clinton. He snatched his phone from the top of Clinton's armored case. The display near the handle blinked green. *Sync complete* scrolled across.

"Why the hell should I know?" Clinton replied from a crouch behind the chair he was sitting in a moment ago.

More gunfire filled the short hallway as the two guards fell back, taking up positions in the lounge. One of them turned. "Four men, all armed!" He leaned around the corner to return fire but fell to the ground instead, a molten glob of bone and skin where his face used to be.

The younger client rushed over to grab the man's gun, firing frantically down the short hallway. A shout of pain came back, followed by another. He turned. "I got —" A bolt caught him in the side, burning half of his torso away. As he spun, another blast hit him in the chest.

The older man crawled to Clinton. Without a word, he slapped the cuff around Clinton's right wrist. A light on it lit up.

"Hey, what the fuck—" Clinton protested.

The remaining guard grunted, a blaster burn on his leg. He leaned out and squeezed off two shots. They must have hit home, because two distinct voices cried out as the guard fell to the carpeted floor.

The older man looked at Clinton. "You have go to the —" A bolt struck him, flinging him away from Clinton, who was staring openmouthed at the spot the man had just occupied.

Clinton spun as the shabby spacer from the street earlier limped into the room. "Wha—You?" he stammered.

The man grinned. "I knew you'd lead to something interesting."

Clinton looked at the man, then the surrounding corpses. "What the hell?"

The guard with the ruined leg grunted as he rolled over. The dirty spacer spun, firing wildly. Clinton ducked and scrambled around behind a chair. A bolt from the guard's weapon struck the spacer in the chest as one of his shots struck the guard in the neck. The guard made a choking noise before falling silent. Clinton peered over the arm of the chair. A plume of acrid smoke was rising from a scorch mark on the seat of the chair, inches from his head.

"Oh, shit," he whispered, not that anyone was alive to hear him. The dingy man from the street was lying in a crumpled, smoking mess. What had that moron been expecting? Clinton wondered as he stood. "I gotta get the hell out of here." He moved around the chair, the case on his wrist banging against it. He held the case up. "Shit." He looked at the case and the metal cable linking it to the cuff around his right wrist. The case's screen displayed *LOCKED*.

He looked around, spotting the younger man. Using his unencumbered hand, he frisked the man, looking for the gPhone he had used to sync the lock codes with the case. He found what was left of it in the man's chest pocket. A blaster bolt had melted it into the fabric of the jacket. He made a face as he realized some of the sticky bits weren't the jacket but the man's flesh. "I hope your friends got the sync codes," he told the body.

The pile of bodies in the short hallway caused Clinton's breath to catch. "Fuck." He whispered, stepping over one of the spacer's accomplices, an Asian man that had barely made it into the suite before catching a blaster bolt in the chest. He reached down and grabbed the man's pistol, slipping it in his waistband.

He made it to the hallway, looking around. The floor was empty, or the other occupants had enough sense to not open their doors. There was no way that the gunfight that just ended had escaped notice.

He reached the stairs as the elevator in the center of the hallway dinged, announcing its arrival. He slipped into the stairwell, easing the door closed as he heard the sound of several men and women whispering to each other as they made their way to the charred ruin of the door to the McGregor suite.

The lobby was no different from when Clinton arrived. The low-gravity man at reception was still there, though he stared open-mouthed at Clinton. "Uh. They were..." He pointed up.

Clinton nodded. "Yeah, send housekeeping up there." He rushed to the door. The street was no busier than it was before.

The transit hub was busy. Clinton wondered if there was ever a slow time at this godforsaken hollowed-out potato of a space station. He dropped the pistol into a trash bin just outside the customs kiosk.

The man behind the transparent barrier looked up. "Not here very long."

Clinton held up his right hand, the heavy-duty case secured to it. "Job's done. No reason to be here any longer than necessary."

"It grows on ya," the man said, looking at his terminal.

"So does fungus."

The man grunted and waved Clinton through. "Come again."

"Never," Clinton said, already a few steps into the terminal. The ticket booth was up ahead.

A droid occupied the ticket booth. It turned at Clinton's approach. "Greetings. Destination?"

Clinton looked at the display behind the droid listing the upcoming departures. He turned his attention to the droid. It canted its pale blue head. "Valhalla," he said.

The droid clucked. "Very good. Valhalla. Just yourself?" Clinton nodded. "Any luggage?"

"Nope." Clinton watched the droid work the terminal. It was basically human shaped; two arms, one head. His curiosity won out, and he stood up on his toes to lean forward. Two legs.

"Are you okay?" The droid's bright yellow optic sensors whirred as they focused on him, now that he was leaning much closer.

"Oh, sorry, I was just...never mind."

"Very good." The droid turned back to its terminal and raised an arm. The fingertips were glowing. "Your gPhone?"

Clinton held his phone out. The droid tapped the screen. "Your shuttle departs in ten minutes. You should hurry."

"Thanks."

"You two good? Need anything?" the waitress asked as she slowed down near the table Jax and Naomi occupied.

Jax looked at his beer and chugged the last third. "I could use another." He grinned. Naomi clucked.

The waitress smiled. "Another New Dallas Dark?" Jax nodded. She turned to Naomi, who shook her head, holding her own half full pint glass up. "Be right back." She looked at Jax and winked.

Naomi nodded at Jax's empty glass. "You branching out?"

"Huh?"

"Thought you were all about that New Terra Lager life?"

He shrugged. "Yeah, I dunno. Saw the tap handle and just made a game time decision." She raised an eyebrow. "What?"

She looked across the room at the waitress leaning over a table with a pair of women and their two children. Naomi turned to Jax. "She said she really liked the New Dallas Dark." She shook her head.

"Hate the—"

Naomi reached out and put a finger across Jax's mouth. "Shhh."

He reared back. "Gross. Your finger tastes like a mozzarella stick."

She licked her finger. "You're right."

Jax rolled his eyes as he wiped his mouth. He was about to say something when the waitress returned. She deposited a fresh, frosted pint glass full of dark brown ale in front of him. "Here you go." She winked again.

Naomi sighed loud enough to draw the waitress's gaze. She coughed. "Sorry, cheese stick stuck in my throat."

The woman smiled and turned to leave.

"Hater," Jax said before taking a sip of her beer. "This is pretty good, though."

"Why doesn't this place hire cute dudes?" Naomi complained. She made a show of looking around the bar. Their waitress had two colleagues, one on the floor with her, one behind the bar. The bartender was a middle-aged woman with an eye patch. The other staffer working the floor was a teenage boy.

Jax pointed to the young man, eyebrow raised. Naomi frowned. "I'm pretty sure it'd be illegal."

Jax shrugged, turning his gaze back to their waitress, who was at the bar waiting for the one-eyed bartender to finish making a martini. "Who orders a martini in a TGI Friday's?"

Naomi shrugged. "I got a message from Michael."

Jax turned his attention back to her. "Who?"

She leveled her gaze and stayed quiet for a moment. "New Terra," was all she said.

His eyes lit up. "Oh, your coffee guy."

"Coffee guy," she repeated before taking a sip that finished off her beer. "Anyway. He said he's got a new varietal hybridization he thinks I'll like." She held a finger up to silence him. "He's thinking about franchising, maybe starting with Kelso."

"Like open our own coffee shop?" Jax leaned back, taking a sip of his beer. "I don't wanna run a coffee shop."

The waitress arrived before Naomi could reply. "Ready to order some food?"

Valhalla, and Thorston City, specifically, was about ten or twenty steps up from Freeground. Clinton looked around the arrivals area of the spaceport. Being an Imperial-controlled colony, there were shock troopers covering the wide tunnel entrance that led to customs and the exit. He got in line behind a heavyset woman in a business suit.

The trip had been uneventful, thankfully. The few people on the shuttle out from Freeground were more than happy to mind their own business during the entire trip. That suited Clinton just fine. He needed the time to think.

The line moved fast, Imperial efficiency at its best. The street outside was a wide, well-lit thoroughfare that connected the port to the main downtown core of Thorston City.

He pulled his gPhone out and looked at it. He thumbed through a few news feeds. Unsurprisingly, there wasn't any news about what happened at the hotel in Freeground.

He pulled up the encrypted chat app that connected him to his handler.

"Sir!" someone shouted.

Clinton tensed. Looking up, he saw a woman walking toward him. He slid his phone back into his pocket.

"Yes?" He thought he would get further than this before being caught.

"Have you heard the good news?" Up close, Clinton could see that she was in a rough-spun dress with a white top. Her hair was in a tight bun.

He rolled his eyes. "No, thank you." He held up a hand to stop her from offering him a pamphlet. She frowned and turned away.

He looked around. He needed some place to lie low, figure what was going on. A few blocks up the way, he spotted a TGI Friday's. "That'll do."

The bar area was sparsely occupied. He grabbed a seat at the bar, nodding to the bartender. "Something strong, please."

She nodded.

He pulled his gPhone back out, thumbing it on and loading the handler/courier chat app.

He tapped out a message and waited.

"Here you go," the bartender said, sliding a glass in front of him. He reached for it with his free hand but stopped short as the courier case slammed into the underside of the bar. She quirked a pale red eyebrow. "Quite the lunchbox."

Clinton sighed, putting his phone down to pick up the drink. "Long story." He downed the drink. "Another, please." She nodded and turned around. He looked at his phone. Nothing.

Picking it up, he went back to the app. He tapped another icon, the icon he was told to use only in an emergency.

He pulled the small commset out of his pocket, slipping it into his ear. The call connected. Clinton opened his mouth, but the voice on the other end cut him off. "Ditch your gPhone. Never try to contact me or the organization again." There was a pause. "Sorry."

"What the he—" Clinton started, but stopped when his gPhone beeped. The connection was closed. He looked at the phone. The icon to initiate a call was grayed out. "Damnit," he hissed, slamming the phone down on the bar.

The bartender returned with his drink. "Having a rough day?"

He sighed, downed the drink. "You've no idea."

She shrugged. "Lay it on me, String Bean."

CHAPTER 4

"Two baskets of cheese sticks and now a burger?" Naomi said, poking at her salad.

"And?" Jax asked around a mouthful of hamburger. According to the menu, it was actual beef, even. Not the vat grown stuff common on the stations and outer colonies.

She picked at her salad. "Just saying. That vest only hides so much."

Jax stopped chewing. "What do you mean?" He looked down. His free and nongreasy hand went to his midsection.

"I mean, you should take better care of yourself." She took a bite of her salad. "You're not nineteen anymore. You can't live on fried things and beer." She made a show of looking him up and down.

He went to take a bite of his burger and looked at it. It smelled and tasted so good. Perfectly medium rare. Seasoned just so. He sat it back down on his plate. "I hate you."

"You'll thank me next time we're being chased and you don't have a heart attack."

He grimaced. "The idea is to not be chased."

Angling her head, she asked, "Have you met us?"

"I feel like the chasing quotient has increased since you entered my life."

"You're welcome."

Staring at his half-finished burger, he said, "It's shameful we have faster-than-light wormhole travel but haven't figured out how to make burgers not fattening, or invented a workout in a pill."

"Perhaps if the Ganymede aliens had left a few on their ship, we'd be there." Another bite of salad. "Salads are tasty. Just sayin'."

"No, they aren't." Before she could reply, he snapped his fingers. "By the way, don't think I've forgotten. You owe me a story."

She quirked an eyebrow.

"The   incident-not-an-incident-but-more-like-a-run-in."

"Oh..." She reached for her drink, her eyes never breaking contact with Jax, who refused to blink. "Fine," she said, her glass thumping the table more than intended.

At the table next to them, two women that Jax assumed were on a first date, were looking at them. He smiled. "Too much salad." They turned back to their conversation.

Naomi sighed. "A year or two before I met you, I was lying low here in Thorston City, actually."

"And..."

"I'm getting there!" she snapped. "I pulled a job and just needed to not attract attention. So, I got a room over in the business district. I was minding my own business." She looked at his expression. "What? I was!" She took a bite of her salad.

Jax eyed his now not-quite-warm-enough-to-enjoy burger and sighed. He took a swig of his beer instead.

"So, I was at a bar having a drink and this guy comes up to me." She shook her head. "He wouldn't take no for an answer." Jax nodded knowingly. Men had changed little, even with the advent of wormhole travel, Sapient Intelligences, and artificial gravity.

"He kept pushing until finally I'd had enough."

Jax grinned. "And?"

Naomi shrugged. "And I broke his nose." She chuckled. "Maybe his arm? I didn't really linger. Turned out he was the governor's son."

"Oh..."

"Yeah."

There was a loud thud from the bar. Jax figured the cute redhead was slamming pint glasses. Naomi looked over his shoulder.

He took a sip of his beer, about to dig into the gritty, bloody details, when he noticed that Naomi still wasn't looking at him. He waved a hand. "Hello?" Her gaze was firmly over his shoulder. He turned in his chair, following her gaze. "Damn." He spied a tall new addition to the bar's patrons, talking to the bartender. The guy was holding a drink in his left hand and a weird briefcase in his right.

Jax turned back to see Naomi glaring at him. "I saw him first."

He held up both hands. "Hey, that's not very progressive of you. You don't know how he rolls."

She tilted her head. "I get to find out first." She nodded over Jax's shoulder. The bartender was placing a salad before him. "See, he doesn't eat mozzarella sticks."

Jax waved a dismissive hand. "Maybe he had a whole plate of them for lunch and wanted something a little lighter."

He turned his head enough to see the man at the bar. "I bet he had a long day at the..." He rubbed his chin. "Bank?"

"Consultancy," Naomi countered.

The man at the bar was in a modern cut, bespoke suit.

Jax nodded. "Yeah, he has a kind of consultant-y look about him." He stared for a moment, then turned. "Maybe his significant other threw him out? Looks like he slept in his suit."

The waitress arrived. "You didn't finish your burger."

Jax frowned first at the waitress, then the burger, then Naomi. "Yeah, lost my appetite."

"Want anything else?" She leaned on the table. Jax looked up. Was one of her buttons undone? "Before my shift ends, in ten minutes."

He leaned back. "Well..." Naomi pulled a face. He

gave her a tiny shrug and inclined his head toward the bar.

Naomi inhaled and released a sigh that would fit in with a stage production. "I'm going to hit the bar." She stood.

The waitress smiled at Jax.

Naomi set her empty glass down, nodding to the bartender. The woman returned the gesture. She turned to the right. "Hi." She smiled.

The man looked over, then turned back, then turned again, eyes wider. "What?"

"Hi," Naomi repeated. She offered her hand. "Naomi Himura."

The man continued to stare at her. She moved her offered hand. He adjusted in his seat and moved to shake her hand. The case attached to his right wrist slammed into the bar again. "Fuck," he hissed. "Sorry." He leaned away to make room for his left arm to come up. He elbowed Naomi. "Sorry."

"Woah." She leaned back and put her hand on his arm. "It's cool. It's cool." She smiled. "You look like you've had a rough night."

"Try, rough few days." He took a sip of his drink.

She looked over her shoulder at Jax, only to see the table empty. She frowned. He better not have left her here. She turned back to her new friend. "So. What do you do? You're some type of consultant?"

The man frowned. He stabbed a forkful of salad. "No. Not a consultant." He looked at her. "What makes you think I'm a consultant? For what?"

Naomi shrugged. "Your suit." She smiled. "Looks business-y."

"Business-y?"

"That's a word. Or mostly one, anyway. But yeah, you look like a guy who tells business people how to business."

"How to business?"

"You're part parrot, too?" He frowned, and she smiled. "So, what *do* you do?"

"So, what time do you get off?" Jax asked after breaking off the kiss.

The waitress, Jessica, exhaled. "Eight." She bit her lower lip. "There's still ten minutes left on my break." She pulled him close.

Jax leaned in. "I'm Jackson, by the way."

She closed the last distance between them. "Don't care."

Just as their mouths touched, someone said, "Ahem."

Jax and Jessica turned to see a man in a red polo shirt, a few years younger than Jax, standing before them. "Jess, I think your break is probably almost over."

She nodded, her hand on Jax's chest. "Sorry, Tom." She looked at Jax. "Eight." She exited the small hallway that connected to the kitchen, rounding the corner back into the main dining room.

Jax looked at the younger man. "Hi."

Tom smirked and said, "I think your burger is getting cold, sir."

Jax nodded. "Don't want that." He followed Jessica into the dining room.

He stopped short.

CHAPTER 5

Three men, far too well-dressed for a TGI Friday's bar, were standing just inside the door. He ducked back behind a pillar next to a table in the main dining room. The family at the table all looked up.

He looked down. "Sorry, I'm a private investigator. My client thinks his wife is cheating on him with his dentist." He looked at the husband and winked, tipping his head back toward the bar.

The wife looked at Jax, then at the husband. "Todd?"

Jax turned back to the bar as an argument broke out behind him about Todd knowing what that weird man meant when he winked.

"Stephanie, I don't—"

"Don't you—"

The three men were scanning the room. They weren't local security, that was for sure. Maybe Imperial security? Why would imps be in a Friday's? Could they be on to Naomi? That had to be it.

One of them looked at the bar, then his gPhone. He patted his friend's arm, nodding toward where Naomi and her new friend were parked at the bar. Their backs were to the door. Naomi didn't know they were in the room, that she was in danger.

"We gotta stop eating at Friday's. Goons keep showing up," he whispered. He looked around. No fire alarm to be seen.

The trio of well-dressed men reached the bar, spreading out to surround Naomi and the handsome lunchbox-carrying guy. The one nearest lunchbox guy said, "Excuse me, sir. Were you on the shuttle from Free-ground that arrived earlier today?"

Naomi frowned. "And who's asking?"

The man near her said, "BioTek corporate security."

"Bio who?" She adjusted in her seat so that she was facing the man she was speaking with.

Behind her, Clinton sighed. "Shit."

From across the room, someone shouted. "Brandi-Lee?" All five people at the bar turned. Actually, most of the bar and some of the dining room turned. Jax was stomping in from the dining room. "Brandi-Lee! I knew it. I knew you were sleepin' around!"

He had affected an accent that Naomi had never heard him use before. She leaned around the third man, the one standing behind her and the man who still hadn't even given her his name. Making eye contact she mouthed the word, *what*.

The man next to Naomi held up a hand. "Sir—"

Jax continued toward the bar, ignoring the suited men. "This him? This the man you been sleeping 'round with? This pencil-neck?" Jax looked at the man next to Naomi. "You like sleeping with other men's wives, asshole?"

Clinton's mouth hung open. "I, uh...what?" he stammered.

The man nearest Clinton and Naomi turned to Jax. "Sir, you need to calm down." The man that was behind the pair at the bar was next to his colleague, both forming a human wall between Jax and Naomi.

"I'm gonna kick your ass!" Jax shouted, then added, "Nothing to say for yourself?"

Clinton looked at the raving lunatic on the other side of the two corporate security men. He looked at Naomi, whom he realized was hyper-focused on the two men before her.

Jax screamed, "I loved you, Brandi-Lee!" He leaped at the two men in front of him. He did his best to make it look like the man next to Naomi was his target. As the two men moved to intercept him, he lashed out with a savage chop to the biggest of the two's throat.

As the man Jax struck staggered away from the group, Jax moved as fast as he could, shifting his balance to lunge in toward the other man nearest him. He landed a punch that was meant for the man's face but landed on his shoulder as the man saw it coming and adjusted his stance at the last minute.

Naomi, still on her barstool, planted her foot between

Jax's opponent's legs with as much force as she could muster. The corporate security man grunted and pitched forward. Jax grabbed his suit jacket and hurled him into a table of what looked like a freighter crew enjoying a night out.

The table collapsed, sending drinks and the three men and one woman occupying it, scattering amid shouts of surprise.

The man nearest Clinton looked at the chaos, then at Clinton, his hand moving to what was likely a stunner tucked under his jacket. Clinton lashed out with a rabbit punch, catching the man by surprise as blood spurted from his nose. The man reached for his damaged nose, the stunner forgotten.

Jax watched that exchange, then grabbed the man's shoulder, spinning him in place. He landed a blow to the man's midsection, forcing the air out of his target.

By now, the four freighter crew were on their feet kicking the man that had destroyed their table. His friend, still a bit pale and hunched over, fired a stun blast at the spacers, scattering them, allowing his colleague to get to his feet.

Jax leaned over to Naomi. "Are these guys after you?"

She pushed him away as one of the corporate security men lunged in with a fist aimed at where Jax's head would have been. She elbowed the man in the face, then threw a knee to his midsection.

"Me? What? No. Why would you think that?" She ducked a jab and let a kick fly that glanced off the target's raised knee. She and her opponent traded a series of fast, vicious blows. A punch to the chin sent her staggering.

Jax moved in with a right hook that sent the man sprawling, crashing into an empty table, the occupants already engaged in what he now saw was a bar fight in the extreme sense.

He glanced at Naomi, wiggling the fingers on both hands. "You know."

She sighed, dodged a kick, and pointed. "They want him." She was pointing at an empty chair. "Where'd he go?" She shoved one of the freighter crew aside and pointed toward the dining area and large crowd standing around watching the fight. The man she had been speaking to was tall enough to be seen over most of the heads in the crowd. "He's going that way." She pointed. Jax looked over just as someone tackled him to the ground.

The door to the street burst open. "Everyone, stop!" an electronically amplified voice shouted. "Thorston City Security!" the voice added.

The various brawlers, now over a dozen, slowly separated from their opponents and stood around.

Jax tapped Naomi's shoulder and canted his head in the direction Clinton had been going. The diners in the main dining room were slowly migrating back to their seats. The pair fell in with them, keeping low.

Jax spotted the family from before. "Later, Todd."

The man made a rude gesture.

Naomi increased her pace. Over her shoulder, she said, "We gotta find that guy."

"What guy?"

"What do you...? The guy from the bar. The guy I was just talking to."

"Oh. That guy." He frowned. "Why?"

Jax and Naomi leaned out of the narrow alley behind the restaurant. The local security forces had everyone from the bar standing in a line on the sidewalk. They were talking to the three suited corporate security men.

Jax looked at Naomi. "Corporate security?" She shrugged. "And they didn't want you?" She nodded. "They wanted that rando?" Another nod. He leaned back to look at the gathered crowd. "Well, good thing they're not after us." He pulled out his gPhone. "Skip we're—"

"Going to find out what's going on," Naomi interrupted.

Jax looked at her. "What now?" He leaned against the wall. "Why?"

"He needs our help. He doesn't have anyone." Naomi pulled him back down the narrow alley. "Those three corporate goons wanted him." She spread her arms. "You know that can't be good."

"For him." Jax was shaking his head. "You don't even know his name." He couldn't fathom why Naomi wanted to get involved in whatever it was that was going on here.

"Jax, you didn't talk to him. That guy has been running. From what, I don't know. I don't think he has anywhere to go, or anyone to call."

He looked up at the night sky. "Shoulda just gone

home. They have beer and cheese sticks on Kelso." He looked at Naomi. "What's in this for us?"

"Does there have to be something? In it for us, I mean?"

He shrugged. "Yeah. Kinda an important part." She shot him a look. He knew the look. In the short time that they'd been working together he saw it a lot. He sighed. "How do you propose we find him?"

She smiled. "Let's see what our friends out there are saying." She produced a gPhone that wasn't hers.

Jax grinned. "You lifted one of their phones?"

She shrugged. Bio-circuits in her fingers and hand pulsed pale blue. The screen of the phone lit up, code scrolling across it.

From the speaker, a man's voice said, "—Dangerous. The sooner we find him, the sooner your colony is safe."

Another voice, likely one of the locals, said, "We'll get patrols out right away. I've got my staff scrubbing all the security cams in a two-kilometer radius."

"BioTek appreciates your support, Commander."

"Of course. If what you said is even half accurate, I want that terrorist off this planet as soon as possible."

Naomi looked at Jax. "That dude wasn't a terrorist."

He waved a hand. "Uh huh."

After slipping out of the bar when that maniac started his rampage, Clinton took off in the first direction he saw. He was heading further into the downtown core of Thorston

City. He wasn't familiar with the city, but knew he had to put distance between himself and those security men. And that angry lunatic and his wife.

BioTek. He looked around. He had no idea where he was. BioTek made sense. Those guys on Freeground must've worked for the mega-corp.

He reached a wide intersection. Plenty of people were still out and about, many exiting an entertainment complex. The latest *Space Rangers* holodrama had been released a week or two earlier. Looked like it was still drawing crowds. Clinton planned to see it when this job was done. He shook his head. He'd have to catch it when they released it for at home viewing. If he lived that long.

Clinton looked back the way he'd come, spotting the red and blue lights of a local security ground car. He ducked down the street next to the entertainment complex. The alley smelled of stale popcorn. He turned and looked around, then headed for the complex lobby.

The lobby of the entertainment complex was a large four-story affair with escalators moving people up and down between the levels. Auditoriums formed a U-shape around the lobby on all four levels.

In the open space above everyone's head, two holographic characters from the *Space Rangers* movie were striking poses.

"Ticket, sir."

Clinton turned. "Excuse me?" He came face to face with a freckle-faced young woman, her tight, curly hair done up in a knot atop her head.

"You got a ticket?" She waved her hand to take in the

lobby and auditoriums hung off each level. "You know, for a vid? This isn't a bar. You gotta have a ticket."

He sighed. "I just need to catch my breath."

She eyed him skeptically. "Ten minutes."

He nodded. "Thanks." He pulled out his gPhone, opening the maps app.

CHAPTER 6

From the food court tucked just inside a Spacer Wares down the block from the TGI Friday's, Jax and Naomi huddled over his gPhone. "Rudy, Baxter, I need you two to hook Skip up to the spaceport data bus. We need to hack the city's security net."

"So, your night went well, then?" Rudy quipped. He disconnected from the station he occupied on the bridge of the *Osprey*. He rolled to the staircase and the open null-gravity tube in its center.

Jax looked at Naomi, who shrugged while smiling and sipping her soda. She said, "It's important."

As Rudy made his way to the cargo deck, Skip, the *Osprey*'s Sapient Intelligence, said, "I'll do what I can." He added the reply to the ship's speakers so Rudy and Baxter could hear.

Jax added, "Once you're in, we'll need you to keep the authorities busy."

Rudy met Baxter in the hold. He slowed down enough to signal the huge matte black combat droid before continuing to the lowest level of the ship, the small boarding area. "Give us a few minutes," Baxter's deep voice rumbled.

The boarding ramp unfolded as it lowered, hitting the permacrete with a thud.

Rudy rolled down the ramp, using what scanning systems he had to ensure there weren't any spaceport personnel around the ship. He rolled under the ship, sending, *Do you know where the nearest umbilical hub is?* over the ship's wireless network.

Twenty meters to the west, near that hideous New Cairo mid-size, Skip replied. Rudy saw the umbilical hub. There was a hub in the middle of every four landing pads in the small- and mid-sized ship section of the spaceport.

On an Imperial world like Valhalla, droids were at best tolerated in limited cases. More often, they were outright banned. Even after years of Imperial rule, and the dropping of the old "Droids are the cause of all of our problems" rhetoric, the grudges, real—or more often, imagined—lingered.

Rudy moved as fast as his little smart material roller-ball would allow. He grabbed the data umbilical and headed back toward the *Osprey*. He was almost there when the umbilical snagged and he flipped over, slamming to the ground.

From the ramp, Baxter said, "Smooth." He stalked over, picking up Rudy and the umbilical, giving the latter a sharp tug to free it from the dispenser.

Rudy made his rollerball adhesive and levered back upright. "What're you wearing?"

Baxter stopped. "A cloak."

"I see that. Why?" Rudy caught up with the combat bot as the much taller droid plugged the data trunk into the *Osprey*.

Baxter spun slowly, the cloak spreading out, covering his massive frame top to bottom. "Imperial world. This way, we can move around freely."

Rudy's head spun a full 360 degrees, his optic sensor whirring. "Dressing like the Dread Pirate Roberts is the plan?"

Baxter turned, saying nothing, his crimson optic sensor swishing back and forth. "I could throw you, probably, across the spaceport."

Rudy rolled back to the ramp, giving his much larger companion a wide berth.

Over the wireless, Skip sent, *I am in. Thank you.*

Rudy motioned Baxter back aboard the ship.

Jax looked at his phone screen. The maps app was showing an intersection. He looked at Naomi. "Let's go." They crossed the street.

"You know where we're going?" Naomi asked.

"No. I thought you did," he said. They stopped, both looking around. The downtown core of Thorston City was a maze of towers that kissed the clouds, connected by walkways. Landing pads jutted out into the sky. Several buildings had more than one, looking like flowers with offset petals.

Jax toggled to the maps app on his phone, swiping

and pinching until he said, "Oh." He looked around and gave Naomi a weak smile. He pointed back the way they had come. "That way." She sighed.

Back aboard the *Osprey*, Baxter was standing in the cargo hold. Wirelessly, he said, *You're sure?*

I am. Chen-Sun Tea Emporium, Skip confirmed. *I hacked the local security infrastructure and traced him from the restaurant to the tea shop. I do not think it was his intended destination.*

Baxter turned toward the stairs leading down to the boarding room. *And local security?*

The equivalent of a chuckle came across the shared network. *I sent them across town. To an adult entertainment complex.*

Baxter sent, *Jax would be proud.* He grabbed his cloak and headed down the stairs. *Do you have any thoughts on how best I should exit the spaceport?*

As a matter of fact, I do. Sending coordinates now, Skip answered.

Baxter descended the boarding ramp, scanning in all directions. The spaceport was as busy any other port. Thankfully, most spaceport personnel had better things to do than watch parked ships, and most spacers didn't loiter once landed. He made his way to the indicated section of the spaceport's ring wall in a matter of minutes, dodging the occasional ground crew.

He was standing in what looked like an abandoned mechanical bay.

The previous tenant went out of business a year ago, Skip informed him.

Baxter made one last scan to ensure no one was

anywhere nearby, then deployed both of his shoulder-mounted railguns. A quick scan of the duracrete, then an adjustment to the power level on each gun, and he was ready. The sound of the zip-crack of the railguns firing was lost in the noise of the busy space port.

Five minutes later, Baxter was stepping through a rough tunnel in the spaceport's wall. The railgun rounds shattered the enzyme-bonded stone enough for him to easily clear the rubble by hand.

Looking in the window of the Chen-Sun Tea Emporium, Jax said, "Yup, he's in there." Naomi nodded and turned for the door. "Woah, woah. Where are you going?"

"In there. To talk to him."

Jax shook his head. "Cuz that went so well the last time."

"What's that supposed to mean?" Naomi's hands found resting places on her hips.

Jax mimicked her pose. "Well. Let's see. Last time, you sidled up on him, corporate security showed up, I had to bail you out, we got a full-blown ruckus out of it, and then your new beau ran away. Oh, and now we're dodging that same corporate security force." One of his eyebrows quirked up. "I miss anything?"

Her look could have frozen a sun, but she gave the smallest possible shake of her head.

Jax grinned. "I'll be right back." He moved to the door. She made a rude gesture.

The tea shop wasn't very busy at that time of night. Jax looked around, counting customers: only eight, mostly couples enjoying a non-alcoholic nightcap. Jax wasn't sure who looked more miserable, the guy they were looking for or the woman at the bar nursing a steaming mug big enough to fit a softball.

He sat down opposite the man with the super weird lunchbox strapped to his arm. "Hey."

The noise that came out of the man's mouth was not at all masculine or even potentially human. He looked at Jax, squinting. "You're that madman from the Friday's." He held both hands up in front of him. "I wasn't sleeping with your wife. I just met that woman."

Jax grinned and leaned back, hand on his heart. "She's not my wife. She's my business partner. That was all an act."

"An act?"

"Yup. And you're welcome."

Clinton tilted his head. "For what?"

Jax waved his hand. "Getting you out of that mess at Friday's. Those corporate security goons—they were there for you, man, not us." He offered his hand. "Jackson Caruso."

Clinton stared, finally taking a deep breath. "Clinton. Clinton Morris." He offered his hand, the metal case knocking against the table, sending his teacup clattering to the floor. "Gah!"

Jax's gPhone beeped. He pulled it out and looked at the screen. *I'm outside.*

"So, what's your deal?" Jax leaned in. "You've got that lunchbox thing. Corporate assholes want you. You steal something?" He nodded his head to the case. "Steal that?"

Clinton followed Jax's gaze. "This?" He raised the case. "No. I'm a—"

Jax's gPhone rang.

Naomi was camped out on a bench outside the tea shop. Stupid Jax, going in there talking to the sexy briefcase guy while she was sitting on a bench playing with her phone.

A message arrived. *I'm outside.*

She looked up and around. *Where?*

If you could see me, it wouldn't be covert.

Naomi sighed. Jax was exhausting enough. Now he had Baxter acting weird.

She closed her eyes, inhaled, and leaned back on the bench, thinking they should have just gone back to Kelso station. Opening her eyes, she nearly yelped. Down the street, walking toward her, was a quartet of well-dressed men, three of whom she recognized. Behind them, six uniformed Thorston City security officers were following.

She grabbed the earbud from her phone, tapping it as she secured it in her ear. "Skip, you said you were sending the cops in the wrong direction."

"I am."

"Then why am I looking at four corporate security

and six local cops marching right toward me? Me, Jax, and the man we're trying to help."

"You do not know his name?" Skip asked.

"Is that the important bit right now?" she retorted, a hand moving up to massage her forehead.

"I do not know how they found you." A pause. "Oh, I see. They must have discovered my intrusion. Very clever."

Naomi tapped the device in her ear, hanging up. She didn't need to look at the screen to find Jax's details. The bio-circuitry that ran the length of her finger along the back of her hand and up into her sleeve glowed blue as she accessed her gPhone's operating system with a thought. The screen flickered, lines of code scrolled, and then Jax answered. "They're here," she said.

Standing, she sighed. "I hate this part." She strode off toward the group of men coming her way. "Why is it all dudes?" she wondered under breath.

As she closed the distance, she took a deep breath, then another. "Gentlemen! Gentlemen, could you help me?" She waved both arms frantically. "Some hooligans mugged me!" She spread her arms to stop the group. "They took everything!"

"Ma'am, please," one of the four BioTek men said.

Naomi turned her face, hoping the other three from earlier wouldn't recognize her. "I saved for years to come on this trip and they took everything!" she wailed.

By now the six local security men had formed up around her and the corporate men. One of them offered his hand. "Ma'am. We can call someone to take your statement."

"But what am I to do, now?" she drawled. Stupid Jax and his fake accent had her doing it too.

"Wait, a minute?" one of the BioTek men said.

Naomi coughed, stepping between two of the locals. "You know, good sirs," she said.

"You were at the bar," the same BioTek man said.

"Well, I should go." She shoved the two men she had stepped between into the crowd as hard as she could. They collided with their colleagues and the BioTek men amid shouts and curses.

She bolted, her gPhone in her hand. Her fingers, pulsing blue, connected her call.

"Incoming!"

In the teahouse, Jax swore. He looked at Clinton. "You're gonna get us killed." He inclined his head. "They're co—"

Clinton shoved the table at Jax as he stood up. He darted toward the rear of the shop.

"Hey, wait!" Jax shouted.

Clinton didn't slow down. He shoved the back door open and slammed into a matte black wall of armor. It clutched his shirt as his legs flew out in front of him, driving him to the ground.

He opened his eyes to see a bright red dot swishing back and forth across a matte black and mostly feature-less metal face. "Hello, we're here to save you. You're welcome."

Jax spied Naomi darting past the tea shop window a moment before the door burst open, causing the small shop's patrons to all stop what they were doing and look up.

Jax turned, smiling at the BioTek man in the doorway. Behind, he could see three more dark-suited men and several uniformed local cops outside.

The man in the door entered, scanning every face in the room before settling on Jax. Outside, the rest of his team was spreading out in front of the building.

The other tea house patrons watched as the well-dressed man walked to Jax's table and sat down. "You were in the restaurant." It wasn't a question.

Jax smiled. "A man can't get a nice earl grey after dinner?"

"Earl grey isn't an after-dinner tea," the man replied.

"Says you." Jax turned to make eye contact with the server. "Another earl grey, please." He turned to the man, smirking.

The man opposite him sighed. He removed his gPhone, an expensive ruggedized unit. "You're in over your head." He held the phone screen out. Clinton's picture was staring back at Jax. "You saw, yes?"

"What'd he do?"

"Does it matter?"

"Kinda. Shoplifting is serious and all, but—"

The young man working the floor slowed down as he passed the table, depositing a steaming hot cup of tea. "Don't knock this one over," he said.

Jax took a sip of his tea. Coughed. "Shit, this gross."

He set the cup down. "That Star Trek guy is out of his damn mind."

The BioTek man sighed again. "Are you always this exhausting?"

Jax tried the tea again, coughed. "So, is there, like, a reward?"

The man opposite him leaned forward. "I'm sure we could work something out. BioTek is very serious about recovering its property."

"That lunchbox of his?" The man nodded. "What's in it?"

Out back, Clinton stood up. "Who, who the hell are you?" He was looking at a nearly seven-foot-tall figure in a dark black cloak. The only thing visible was the demonic red light swooshing side to side.

The figure said nothing.

Clinton blinked, leaning forward. "Hello?" He looked up and down the darkened back alley behind the tea shop.

Naomi came around the corner. "Oh good, you got him."

Clinton turned. "What the hell is going on? Who are you people? What do you want with me? Why is your husband or business partner or whatever in there? Who's he with?" He jabbed a finger at Baxter. "Why is this, whatever it is, standing here? Why did it attack me?" He threw his hands up. "Why is it wearing a fucking cape?"

"It's a cloak," Baxter growled.

Naomi turned to the big combat droid. "Really?"

Baxter spun. "Time to go."

Naomi nodded, gesturing for Clinton to get a move on. She pointed the opposite way that she came from.

Baxter stalked ahead of the pair.

Bringing up the rear, Naomi said, "We're gonna have to talk about your fashion choices, Bax."

Inside the tea house, Jax leaned back in his chair. "Damn, that's a lot of money." The man across from him nodded. Jax's phone beeped. After glancing at the screen, he said, "Well, this has been fun." He stood.

The BioTek man held out his phone, swiping the screen in Jax's direction. "In case you'd rather cut to the chase...We'll get what's ours, either way. It just depends on whether or not it benefits you."

CHAPTER 7

Jax watched the BioTek executive leave the tea shop. He looked at the teacup before him and groaned. "So gross." He looked at the server. "Check."

The man came over and swiped on his gPhone, sending the bill to Jax's phone. Jax looked at the screen, then up at the server. "For tea?"

"Two teas."

"Two gross teas."

The other man shrugged.

Jax paid the bill. "Done."

As he left, the server waved. "Come again."

Three blocks from the teahouse, Jax turned a corner next to a Galaxy Goods and stopped short in front a massive wall of what looked like canvas or maybe a cotton blend standing over six feet tall. "Christ!" he shouted, stumbling back.

Naomi and Clinton appeared from behind the mass of cloth. The former said, "We gotta get to the spaceport."

"Agreed." Jax leaned to the side, looking at Clinton. "Good luck out there."

Naomi rushed forward to punch Jax in the shoulder. It hurt more than he would ever admit.

Before Jax could do or say anything, both his and Naomi's phones beeped. Baxter spoke before they could look at the devices. "They're heading this way." He turned to look west. "We should go. That way."

Despite his disguise, Baxter was insistent that they stick to alleys. He and Clinton were up ahead, getting ready to cross the street.

Naomi turned to Jax. "We gotta help this guy."

They crossed the street. Jax shrugged. "Not to, you know, repeat myself, but why?" He looked at his gPhone. Twelve more blocks to the spaceport. The spaceport didn't seem so far away when they were in the cab.

Naomi sighed. "He needs help. I don't know what's going on, but you don't get corporate security forces on you for nothing."

"Nothing beyond pissing off a corporation, you mean?"

She turned. "Why would a company as big as BioTek want to track down this one guy?"

"Stole that fancy lunchbox," Jax replied without needing to think about it. That weird metal case was kind of obvious.

Naomi shook her head. "Like I said, he's on his own."

"Still not seeing how that's our problem."

"I just have a feeling," she finally said, not knowing what else to say.

Jax shrugged. "Sounds profitable." She slugged him in the shoulder.

Up ahead of Jax and Naomi, Clinton looked up at the massive cloaked droid next to him.

"So, like, you guys...just rescue people and stuff?"

"Not usually."

"Oh. Then. Thanks, I guess."

"Wasn't my idea."

Clinton fell silent for a beat. He looked up. "Your cape is dumb."

Most spaceports were standalone rings several kilometers wide set on the outskirts of whatever city built them. As Thorston City had grown over the decades, it slowly absorbed the spaceport like a slow-moving lava flow overtaking a boulder. Now the spaceport was surrounded by Thorsten City. Low-rise residential and warehouse districts occupied most of the city around the port.

Baxter led the group through the winding alleys of the garment district, retracing his steps. The spaceport ring wall was visible above the buildings.

Jax pointed at a building ahead. "Hey, Bax, maybe we can stop in, get you a new cloak?"

Baxter stopped. "You do know that I can kill you in thirty-three different ways, without even deploying my guns?"

Clinton took a step away from the mountain of matte black metal and dark wool.

Jax tapped the earpiece linked to his phone. "Skip, there a back door into the port?" He turned to Baxter. "How'd you get out?" He cocked his head. "Please tell me you didn't go through the main lobby."

Baxter made a metallic grumble. "Of course not." A metal hand rose and pointed to a three-story building set right against the five-story wall of the spaceport.

"A rug distributor?" Jax asked. He pointed to the building next to it, the Wool Warehouse.

The combat droid didn't look at Jax, but said, "Thirty-three." He stalked toward the rug store.

Jax shook his head. "Skip, we'll see you in a few. Get the pre-flights started, will ya?"

"Affirmative."

Baxter held open the door. "This place went out of business several years ago." He followed everyone in, letting the door close behind him.

Clinton looked around. "You know, I could just lie low here. Figure out what my next steps are." He gestured to the stairs that led up to a loft space. "I could stay up there."

Jax, almost to the back wall and a two-meter-wide hole in the permacrete that made up the building's shared wall with the spaceport, said, "Lying low isn't really something you're good at."

Clinton frowned. "I'll try harder. Now that I know they're after me. I didn't know that the first time, you know."

"Uh huh." Jax leaned into the tunnel that Baxter had carved. He stood. "Dude, how the hell?"

Baxter did his best approximation of a shrug. "Skip helped me find an unoccupied mechanical bay that lined up with this currently unoccupied warehouse." He joined Jax at the tunnel entrance. "Not all of us bumble from one thing to the next." He entered the droid-made tunnel.

Jax made a face but motioned to the others. "Let's go."

"Seriously. I can just hide out here," Clinton tried again.

Naomi put a hand on his shoulder. "They'd find you in a heartbeat. You stand out. Not to mention, someone will notice Baxter's handiwork sooner or later. You don't want to be here when that happens. Come on."

The spaceport proper was as quiet as a spaceport ever got. Ships arrived at all hours, but most freighter crews would rather spend an evening planetside, either sleeping soundly and not worrying about a shipboard mechanical failure, or carousing around downtown.

A small ship, probably a personal shuttle or short-range commuter, came in overhead, its grav-lift engines humming. Clinton looked around, spotting a ship. "That looks fast."

Jax followed his gaze to a Bartleby 8900. "They are. That's not us, though." He pointed past the sleek, long-range recreational vehicle. "That's us."

Clinton craned his neck. "What? That?"

"Oh, boy," Baxter said from deep inside his cloak.

They reached the *Osprey*. "This thing?" Clinton gestured to the infiltrator before them. "It's a relic."

Jax tipped his head, hand on his hip. "Excuse me. The Valerian Co-op Infiltrator is a classic. Not, I repeat, not, a relic." He turned to the ship. "Skip, open up."

Nothing happened.

Jax turned to Clinton. "See what you've done?"

The lanky messenger shook his head. "I don't. Is it broken or something?"

Something in the *Osprey* made a grumbling whine type of noise.

Baxter turned to look back the way they came. "We've got company."

Jax threw his hands in the air. "Seriously?" He looked at Clinton. "*I'll lie low. They won't find me this time.*" He did his best imitation of Clinton's voice.

The other man glared. "How is this my fault? Your bot cut a big asshole in the wall."

Baxter said, "For what it's worth, they're coming from the main entrance."

Jax raised an eyebrow at Clinton.

Naomi finally said, "Children. Please." She turned to the *Osprey*. "Skip, please. He didn't mean it and I don't want to get shot. Lower the ramp. Please."

From a speaker near the ramp, Skip said, "He should apologize."

From the direction of the main entrance, someone shouted. Jax sighed and looked at Baxter.

The bot made a show of unclasping his cloak, and letting it fall to the ground in a puddle around him. His forearms whirred and clicked.

"No killing," Jax said, adding, "Imperial world."

Baxter made a clucking noise, then fired two shots. A large gray cube that was probably important to the operations of the spaceport exploded, sending the approaching group of security officers scattering to the ground. A loud popping noise came from a ship parked near the remains of the gray box: power feedback through the umbilical that connected it to the now flaming power transfer junction box.

"Subtle." Naomi sighed. She ran over to the data bus umbilical, still connected to the *Osprey*. One good tug, and it disconnected and fell to the ground. She did the same with the power bus umbilical.

Baxter fired again and another power transfer junction exploded, a bright orange ball of fire blossoming into the night sky.

Jax looked at Clinton, who looked back at him. The latter finally sighed. "I'm sorry, Mr. Ship. You're not a relic."

"Insincere, but I will take it." The boarding ramp unfolded. "Welcome aboard, Captain."

Everyone ran up the ramp as return fire finally pinged off the side of the ship. Baxter fired two more rounds, then made his way up.

Clinton, Jax, and Naomi ascended the spiral staircase. At the common deck, Jax pointed to the sofa. "You. Sit." He didn't slow down, making his way up to the bridge. Naomi spared Clinton a look and a shrug, following Jax.

Baxter joined Clinton a moment later. "Jax says, stay put."

Clinton looked around before collapsing onto the sofa. "I heard him."

Up on the bridge, Rudy was waiting. "So, this would be one more planet we're probably not welcome on?"

Nodding as he dropped into his comfortable pilot's seat, Jax said, "At least for a while." He picked at a piece of tape that was curling, then focused on the console. He flipped switches and toggled displays. "We ready to go?"

From the overhead speaker, Skip said, "We are. Pre-flight checks complete. Spaceport control has revoked our departure clearance."

Jax grinned, pushing the grav-lift engine's power lever up. "Too bad we didn't hear that part."

He glanced over his shoulder. "We're gonna need clean idents like yesterday."

"On it," Rudy and Naomi said in unison.

Handheld weapons fire was still pinging off the hull. The local security forces and their corporate minders had regrouped.

"Captain, they are attempting to override controls remotely," Skip reported.

Jax made a face. "You're not letting them, right?"

"I have not decided."

"Skip..." Jax warned.

"We are clear but should get off the ground. Fast."

"Oh, you think?" Jax put his hand on the power lever for the grav-lift engines.

"Uh oh. I've got multiple contacts, including an assault shuttle that is angling to block our lift vector," Skip warned.

"Hang on!" Jax shouted as he pushed the power lever all the way forward. The *Osprey* leaped off the perma-crete, leaving everyone's stomachs behind.

Naomi made a strangled noise behind Jax. Down below, something crashed into something else, then the sound of their new friend groaning floated up the staircase.

Jax continued to feed power to the grav-lift engines, raising the *Osprey* up and over the top of the spaceport's ring wall. The previously mentioned assault shuttle pilot must have regained their composure. It was angling back toward the *Osprey*.

"The shuttle is hailing us. It's local security," Rudy reported.

"Light armor and armament," Skip added.

"Well, don't answer!" Jax shouted.

"Is everything okay up there?" Clinton shouted.

"Fine. Everything is fine! Just fine!" Jax replied.

He angled the *Osprey* away from the incoming shuttle. He gave power to the atmospheric engines.

"We're now being yelled at in two languages," Rudy announced.

"Three planetary interceptors just appeared on sensors," Skip reported.

"Damn." Jax hissed. The shuttle was at best a nuisance, but planetary interceptors were fighter craft. Well armed and very fast fighter craft. He pushed more power to the engines. The *Osprey* leaped forward, leaving the assault shuttle hovering alone over the spaceport.

The *Osprey* roared out over Thorston City. "Interceptors will be on us in forty seconds."

"We can't fight them," Naomi said, focused on her console. "Blowing out of here is conspicuous enough. Blowing up security ships, not a good look."

"I know that," Jax said, adjusting their course. He reached over and toggled the ship's weapons systems off. In the same motion, he activated their meager countermeasure package.

"We are being targeted," Skip announced.

"Shields up," Naomi said.

"What if we shoot 'em down but don't blow 'em up?" Jax asked, reaching for the weapons console.

"Nope. Just get us out of here," Naomi said.

Jax huffed and pulled the twisted the controls, sending the *Osprey* spiraling up away from the city. The three interceptors made a wide arc, falling in behind the fleeing infiltrator.

"They are now behi—" Skip began.

"I know!" Jax interrupted. He reached over and pressed a control. Nothing happened. He looked over his shoulder. "Add chaff to the shopping list, please," he grated. So much for their meager countermeasures.

"Oops," Rudy said.

The bridge shook as the *Osprey* took fire. Something near the rear, over the staircase, erupted in sparks.

A scream came from the common deck.

Jax pushed the controls hard over, forcing the *Osprey* into a turn that brought it back toward Thorston City's downtown core.

"We're supposed to be leaving the atmosphere," Naomi said, her knuckles pale as she clutched the sides of her console. The *Osprey* twisted again as blaster bolts struck the rear shields. On a small sub-display, a wireframe of the *Osprey* outlined in green lines flickered. The green lines at the aft of the ship turned orange.

Jax pulled back on the controls, bringing the *Osprey* almost entirely vertical. He slammed the atmospheric throttle all the way forward into the notch at the top that was outlined in red.

The G-forces pushed him and Naomi into their seat backs, and if the ruckus down on the common deck was an indicator, Clinton was now somewhere inside the refrigerator.

"We will clear the atmosphere in thirty seconds," Skip announced. He added, "You did not lose them, you know."

Jax's full attention was on the view out the forward transparent titanium window. The twilight was giving way to the pitch blackness of space. He was doing his best to ignore the black spots swimming across his vision.

"Missiles. Missiles. Missiles," Skip warned in his purely informational tone of voice.

Jax glanced at the sensor display to his right. Three blips were on his tail, farther back than before, but now six smaller red blips were racing toward them. Most planetary security interceptors were agile in the atmosphere, and could hold their own in space, but sucked at getting between the two. Their missiles, however, would not struggle to exit the atmosphere.

Jax's mind raced. Without countermeasures, missiles were hard to shake. They would never get clear in time to open a wormhole if he did nothing. Watching the six red icons close on them, he had an idea. He pulled the atmospheric engine throttle all the way back, killing all thrust. The *Osprey* lurched as her momentum carried her forward. Jax didn't stop to appreciate the sensation. He brought the sub-light engines online.

"Captain?" Skip said.

Jax ignored him, watching the six red icons get closer. The *Osprey* had slipped into a tail-first plummet. The sub-light engine power indicator was flashing. He was pretty sure the operations manual had an all caps warning about powering up the engines without giving them an outlet.

"Jax?" Naomi said.

Jax closed his eyes and, with one hand, clutched the atmo and sub-light throttles, pushing them forward. The surge of drive plasma from the atmospheric engines and raw energy of the sub-light engines ignited behind the ship. The explosion tossed the *Osprey* forward at an angle, turning her nose over tail. Alarms wailed and the sound of metal groaning drowned out everything else. Jax slapped the emergency cut off for the sub-lights, then fought to bring the ship back under control.

On the tactical display, all six missiles were gone, consumed by the explosion. A few seconds later, the ship was back on course out of the atmosphere. Jax killed the atmospheric engines and slid the sub-light throttle up, slowly. He wasn't sure if that stunt had caused any damage.

Turning in his seat, he grinned. "See, it all worked out. We'll be far enough out for a wormhole by the time those little puddle jumpers climb out of the atmosphere." He met Naomi's flat gaze. "What?"

She pointed over his shoulder.

He turned back. "Well, shit."

Forty degrees off their starboard bow, a starship a half-kilometer long, painted pale blue-gray, was burning on an intercept course.

BioTek colors.

"Oh, hell." Jax adjusted their course. The large ship slid out of view to the right. He tapped controls and flipped a few switches, before pushing the sub-light throttles up a few more notches. Skip wasn't complaining, so Jax was as certain as he could be that he hadn't broken anything.

"We're being hailed," Rudy said.

Jax spared a glance over his shoulder. "Just plot us a course. If we can stay ahead of them, we'll be fine."

"Everything okay up there?" Clinton shouted.

"It's fine!" Jax shouted. He glared at Naomi.

Rudy broke the silence. "I've got a course."

"To where?"

"Does it matter? Somewhere without a big corporate cruiser. Isn't that enough?"

"Fair point." Naomi nodded.

"We're being targeted," Skip warned, adding, "Again."

"It's fine. We're almost clear of Valhalla's gravity well," Jax said. He reached over to power up the wormhole generator.

"Missile launch," Skip announced.

"Why is everyone shooting missiles at us?" Jax growled.

Skip said, "Ten missiles. Impact in eighty seconds."

"Ten seems a bit much," Rudy said. "Five would be more than enough to kill us all."

"Six was more than cheery," Naomi quipped.

"Three would probably do it, actually," Rudy said.

"Dude!" Jax snapped.

"They're high yield," Rudy said in a lower voice.

"Forty seconds," Skip said.

"I can see the tactical display," Jax shouted.

An alert started beeping. The bridge fell silent. Jax swore and pulled the throttle back from the notch with the red outline. The *Osprey* didn't slow down but was no longer accelerating at her maximum thrust.

"Missile impact in twenty seconds," Skip said. "If we survive this, remind me to send a sternly worded email regarding that maneuver you just executed."

"Will do, pal. I don't think you're gonna have the—" Jax started. Then the light on the wormhole generator flipped to green. He slapped the activation control.

A green-purple vortex swirled before the *Osprey*. The small craft leaped into the wormhole a split second before ten missiles streaked by.

PART 2

An hour later, after ensuring that nothing was going to explode, and that nothing had entered the wormhole behind them, everyone gathered on the common deck.

Jax looked around, spotting a dent in the refrigerator door. "Oh shit, you really did hit the fridge." He glanced over at their new passenger. "We'll add the new door to the bill." He continued down the stairs, heading for the wounded refrigerator.

Clinton and Naomi were on the couch, the former administering first aid to the latter's forehead. A pair of beers was leaving rings on the coffee table.

Of Baxter and Rudy, there was no sign, which suited Jax just fine at the moment. He grabbed a beer from the fridge and moved to the lounge area. Dropping into the overstuffed chair, he said, "So."

Naomi patted Clinton on the shoulder. He nodded, looked at Jax, and stood. "Bathroom?"

Jax pointed to the hatch in the forward bulkhead.

When the hatch closed, he looked at Naomi, repeating, "So..."

She grabbed one of the beers from the table and took a sip. "He needs our help."

"You've said. More than once."

"Still true."

He shrugged. "We don't even know what helping him looks like," Jax protested. "I say we dump him off at the least dangerous place for us to stop over at and be done. It's bad enough we're going to need new ident codes. Oh, and you know, Valhalla being burned and all."

She waved a hand. "Valhalla isn't all that."

Jax barked a laugh. "True, but we're running out of places to land that won't take a sizable bribe or fresh paint and new idents."

"You say all that like that's different from your regular life," Naomi replied.

Since meeting Jax a year ago, she'd watched Jax, and by extension herself, be chased off at least three colony worlds and one space station. When she hitched her future to Jackson Caruso, his weird hang-ups around family, friends, and connections to anyone that weren't his two droids were not obvious.

Jax continued, "It's bad enough we're tangled up with Commander Tight Pants and his band of rogues. Now you want us doing..." He threw his hands up, sloshing beer onto his shirt. He scowled. "...We don't even know what, to save Tall and Geeky."

"Why do you keep calling him that?" She sipped her beer.

"Have you seen his pants?"

"Obviously not as in-depth as you. Anything I should know?"

Jax glared. "No one needs pants that tight."

"Get over his pants." She took a sip, eyed the bottle, and got up from the couch.

Jax sat forward in the chair. "Every time we run supplies for the...them, we risk getting pulled deeper into their shenanigans. One stray Imperial patrol paints us, and every Valerian Co-op in the Empire gets hunted down and impounded."

From the ceiling, Skip said, "I don't want to be turned into a toaster."

Jax looked up. "See."

In the kitchenette, Naomi sighed.

"We're lucky those local Imperials weren't that competent and luckier there wasn't a big ship in the system."

The hatch to the small restroom at the front of the common deck opened. Clinton stepped out. Jax had forgotten the man was in there. What had he been doing?

The tall mysterious man with his rugged looking lunchbox thing took in the room. "Okay if I crash somewhere?"

Jax nodded and pointed to the short hallway aft that led to the crew berths. "First door on your right."

Clinton nodded his thanks and crossed the common area, saying nothing more until he reached the hallway.

He turned. "Thanks for getting me off Valhalla." He turned before either Jax or Naomi could answer.

Rudy appeared in the center of the staircase, rising from the cargo deck. Baxter clanked up the stairs behind him.

"Where's our guest?" the small rust-colored nav-bot asked.

Naomi hitched a thumb over her shoulder toward the crew berths. The droid bobbed, adjusting the density of his smart material rollerball. It was the closest he could get since his head only rotated. He rolled to a charging cradle set against the bulkhead that was home to the bulkhead-mounted entertainment screen. "So, what's our next move?"

Baxter moved to stand behind the chair Jax was in. The common deck wasn't what anyone would classify as spacious. The spiral staircase that ran from top to bottom between the three main spaces of the ship took up a fair bit of space.

Jax opened his mouth, but Naomi cut him off. "I'm trying to convince Jax that we should help Clinton."

"With what, exactly?" Baxter asked in his deep basso.

"Apparently it doesn't matter," Jax quipped. "We just save every damsel or..." He looked around. "What's the masculine of damsel?" He waved a hand. "Whatever. Apparently, we help every sad sack we can, no matter what."

"That does not sound like a solid long-term strategy," Baxter said.

"Or a particularly profitable one," Rudy added from his charging cradle.

Jax quirked an eyebrow and looked at Naomi as if to say, *See, I told you.*

She countered with, "I'm not saying we go out and be heroes or anything."

"Good. Do I look like a hero?" Jax interrupted.

Naomi crossed her arms. "Not even a little."

Jax nodded. "Exact—wait, what do you mean, not even a little?"

She made a show of looking him up and down before saying, "He's here, now. We invited him into our home."

"Ah," Skip said from the overhead speaker. "Thank you."

Jax and Naomi looked up at the same time, frowning. He turned back to her and said, "You did. Not we." He continued, "I'm not saying we space him. I'm saying we get where we're going." He looked at Rudy. "Where are we going exactly?"

Rudy's main optic sensor spun as he focused on Jax. "Nowhere in particular. I picked a spot near New Cairo. Will take us a few days." A pause while the droid checked his calculations. "We should drop out of FTL in the next hour or two to confirm our location and make course adjustments."

Jax nodded. "Okay. So, we get to New Cairo, wish him well, and send him on his way." He made a gesture, moving his flattened hand across his chest, raising as it went. "And we get the hell out of there before BioTek, and whomever else wants him, figures out where he is."

From behind him, Baxter said, "That is not what Thomas and Allison would have done."

The statement caught Jax by surprise. His mouth fell

open at the mention of his parents. Naomi's eyes widened as she looked first at the massive wall of matte black combat droid behind Jax, then at Jax himself.

Jax closed his mouth and craned his neck to look up at one of his oldest friends.

Baxter continued, "Your father did not want to get involved in the war. Your father, often, advocated moving your family from Kelso to one of the further out colonies."

Jax looked down and said, "I never knew that," under his breath.

Baxter nodded his head once. "After they died, Miss Singh suggested to Rudy and I that we not mention it."

Rudy chimed in, "Your mother was vehement that they could not sit back and do nothing. As Senator Stenson's influence grew, droids were being destroyed en masse, systems were falling to the Unity Caucus faster than anyone had thought possible."

The small droid added, "They signed up for the battle over Zeus."

Jax stood. "I need to think. I'll confirm our heading and check for messages." He moved toward the staircase. Reaching it, he stopped a moment, then went up without a word.

Naomi watched Jax go, then looked at the two droids. Neither said anything.

As much as wormhole travel had revolutionized space travel for humanity, it wasn't without its drawbacks. Namely, that a ship in a wormhole did not know where it was in real space. Ships tended to go a few hours, drop into local space to confirm their position, and open a new wormhole. That also gave the crew a chance to confirm their wormhole generator was functioning correctly.

The larger issue, which was also addressed by frequently dropping back to local space, was communications. Since no signal could escape wormholes, ships dropped out often to catch up on messages, make calls, etc.

Everyone agreed it wasn't ideal, but it was what worked.

Jax dropped into his pilot's chair at the front of the *Osprey*'s small bridge. The wraparound transparent titanium view screen allowed the wormhole to paint the bridge in swirling purples, greens, and oranges.

He consulted the various displays and readouts. After being reverse engineered from a crashed alien ship centuries ago, and mass produced, wormhole generators were commonplace. They did exactly two things: open a wormhole, allowing a ship to enter, and open the other end of a wormhole, allowing a ship to exit into normal space.

The swirls vanished as the *Osprey* exited the wormhole. The sensors began probing nearby space, as well as looking at all the stars in view to get a location fix. No nearby threats; location about where he expected them to be.

The communications panel lit up. One of the things

that everyone in the old Independent Systems Alliance had agreed on was the need for communication relays, placed every five or so light years in a grid, thousands of them in all. A ship exiting a wormhole accessed whichever relay was closest, downloading messages, news, travel advisories, anything they needed.

He reached over and tapped a control to bring up the comm log. The incoming call was live. That was unexpected. The caller couldn't have known when the *Osprey* would return to normal space. Jax raised an eyebrow. He had looked at another display seeing that the communication was coming from Farndale.

"Who's this?" he asked aloud.

"No idea," Skip offered.

"We flipped our ident when we left Valhalla, right?"

"Of course."

"So, who's calling?"

"You could ask them."

Jax looked at the ceiling. "I'm asking you."

Skip made a rude noise. "This is a guess. That corporate cruiser got a good read on our ident. Probably hacked it. Since I did not notice, that means they are good. Once they hacked our ident, finding our comm ID would be easy. We don't change that since the main ship ident masks it. Usually."

"I didn't understand most of that," Jax admitted.

Skip made no reply.

Jax eyed the comm system. "They had to set a repeating hail and just let it run."

"Yes, that is the most likely explanation," Skip agreed.

It was unlikely someone was sitting at the other end, just waiting for Jax to answer.

Jax sighed. "Let's find out." He pressed the blinking amber button. It turned green.

The display above the window came to life. A slowly rotating BioTek logo was the only thing on the screen. That mystery solved.

Jax was about to drop the call when a moderately handsome man in his early fifties appeared, replacing the BioTek logo. "Hello," he said.

Jax inclined his head. "Hi."

"I'm impressed. Your escape from Valhalla was something else. I don't know who you are. Your fake ident was good, and your comm ID is blank." He leaned forward. "That's illegal, you know." It wasn't a question.

Jax leaned back in his seat. "You weren't there."

The man shook his head. "No. I made the mistake of going for expedience, letting a local handle it. Not only did he fail, but he brought local Imperials into it, something I'm keen to keep from happening in the future."

"The future?" Jax repeated.

The man sighed. "Oh, yes. I'm afraid this isn't over."

Naomi was walking past the hatch to the room Clinton was in. He hadn't closed it behind him. She looked in to see him sitting on the lower bunk, staring at the bulkhead opposite him.

"You okay?" she asked, her voice low to not startle him.

He looked up. The case attached to his wrist was in his lap. "No?"

She stepped in, moving to the small work desk opposite the bunks. She turned the chair to face Clinton.

When he said nothing, she said, "So, what's the deal with that fancy briefcase?"

He shifted the case awkwardly, moving it to the bed next to him.

"You ever been to Terra Nova?" He looked up, meeting her eyes.

Naomi clucked. "Once or twice." He raised an eyebrow. "Story for another time."

He nodded. "I grew up there. Not Titan City. A suburb of a suburb. Middle class through and through." A sigh. "There wasn't anything to do, no place to go. I had good grades, few friends."

Naomi was beginning to wonder where the story was going when he said, "After college, I had no plan. Worse, no prospects."

She nodded. After escaping the Interface program and getting off Terra Nova, she'd been aimless for a while, her only goal survival.

Clinton continued. "I saw an ad. It was vague but promised adventure, free travel across the Empire, skills training, and more. I didn't know what a messenger was, but it sounded so... so cool." He moved his right hand, bringing the case back onto his lap. "These are custom made. Unhackable, unbreakable." He jangled the tether attached to his wrist.

"Each one of us is assigned a case, a handler, an encrypted gPhone, and an expense account. We never meet our handlers, and the case shows up at your house in an unmarked box as if it was shipped with your weekly order of snacks."

"Wow. Really? I had no idea," Naomi said. She moved her hand to the case, looking at Clinton, who nodded. She rested her hand on the top. Cold. She wasn't ready to expose her gifts to him yet, but even without activating her bio-circuits, she should have been able to sense any electronics within the case. Nothing. Withdrawing her hand, she asked, "And it's electronic? Something inside syncs with a gPhone and creates an encrypted key pair?"

He nodded. "That's my understanding. Honestly, all the training sims they sent were self-defense, Espionage 101, and the like. Literally nothing about the case outside of the fact it won't unlock until the phone from the other end of the sync call passes the right key over." He shook his head. "Technically, either phone can do the unlock, but the one the clients had on Freeground was slagged."

"You didn't bring it with you, did you?" Naomi asked. Even slagged, she might be able to dig into the phone and get the key code out.

Clinton shook his head. "No, why? It was worthless."

"No reason." She looked at the case, and the man attached to it. "What about your handler? Expense account? All that?"

He shook his head in resignation. "Burned. I was able to get a call in, he told me to run. The app uninstalled on its own after that, taking my expense account details with it. All I've got is what I had in my personal accounts." He looked at the hatch and the corridor beyond. "So, what's the plan? I heard some of your discussion while I was in the head. Sounds like your boss wants to toss me."

Naomi sighed. "Okay, one, he's not my boss. We're partners. Two, the matter isn't resolved. But yeah, he doesn't really do the 'good guy' thing very often."

Clinton leaned back, resting his head against the bulkhead the bed was mounted to. "This was only my second run." He sighed.

Naomi put a hand on his knee. "It's not decided. Jax may surprise you."

CHAPTER 9

Jax squinted at the man on the screen. "That lunchbox thing? Looks like it's secured to his wrist."

BioTek man nodded. He hadn't offered his name to Jax, and Jax hadn't asked because he didn't care. "I'm sure can work around that. Messenger tech is advanced, to be sure, but not impervious."

The man continued, "All I'm asking is that you hand him over. Outside of the Valhalla office, BioTek hasn't involved the Imperial authorities, and I'd like to keep it that way."

Jax opened his mouth, but the man continued. "However, if we can't find a mutually beneficial arrangement, BioTek will be forced to use all the resources at our disposal. I assure you, they're many and unpleasant, and that's before we include the Empire, who, as I'm sure you know, can be equally unpleasant."

Jax closed his mouth and nodded slowly. "Back on Valhalla, your underling mentioned a reward."

The man frowned. Jax thought he might have cursed under his breath.

"I'm sure something can be arranged."

"Something with a lot of zeroes?"

The man scowled, nodding.

Jax pressed. "And you don't want the, what was it? Messenger?"

"Nope. Just the contents of his case," the man assured him from a few hundred light years away.

"Let's say we meet. You can get the case off, we'll take him, you take it? Cut us a nice reward payment?"

"Yes," the man ground out.

Jax rubbed his chin.

The mute icon appeared in the corner of the display. From the overhead speaker, Skip said, "Captain, you are not seriously considering this?"

Jax glared at the ceiling as he reached for the mute icon on the panel. He looked at the man. "Here's what I'm thinking."

Jefferson Sanchez sat staring at the blank screen. He looked around the office he was sitting in. Unlike his office on Station 1 over Farndale, this one had no windows. The wall behind him could turn into a view from any of the hundreds of cameras lining the hull of the cruiser *Curry*, the flagship of BioTek's fleet.

He exited the office onto the command deck. He

eyed a young woman and nodded. "Good job breaking that fake ident. The comm ID you found was good."

The woman smiled. "Thank you, sir."

He took a breath, taking in the bridge of the most advanced ship BioTek owned. The *Curry* was a half-kilometer wonder, as advanced as anything the Imperial navy was sailing but more graceful in every way. She was primarily a small space station with engines. Unknown to anyone outside of BioTek was that she also had teeth. All ships carried defensive weapons: missiles and the like. The *Curry*, despite her smaller size, could hold her own against much larger ships—if she had to, of course.

He shook his head, clearing the daydream away. "Any luck on figuring out their real ident?"

She frowned. "Afraid not, Mr. Sanchez. Whatever they used to fake their identity, it was done well. Rolling encryption and adaptive—"

He cocked his head, waving a hand. "Not a problem. Who they are isn't important." He spied the ship's captain. "We have a destination."

The BioTek corporate fleet was treated as a business unit. The captain was the Senior Vice President of the *Curry* business unit. She gave Sanchez her full attention, a hand moving up to rake her fingers through her close-cropped black mane. "Where to, Mr. Sanchez?"

Sanchez joined her in the center of the bridge. Unlike in most ships, there wasn't a single command chair. Instead, that space was occupied by a conference table large enough for eight. The table's surface displayed a star map of most of the Empire, small dots representing

BioTek assets, assumed positions of Imperial vessels, and more.

He studied the map before using both hands to slide it sideways a bit, revealing another portion of the Empire. He pointed, looking up to meet the captain's gaze. "Here."

She nodded. "Never been. My kids are gonna be pissed." Smiling, she tapped the indicated star, bringing up a menu. She sent the destination to the helm station. The young man sitting there nodded to her that he had received their destination.

The manta-ray-shaped ship made a slow turn toward its destination. A deep thrum reverberated through the big ship.

Sanchez watched as the star field on the wide forward viewscreen was replaced by the swirling orange, purple, and green smudge that was the mouth of a wormhole.

As the ship dove into the swirling vortex of space-time, Sanchez turned and headed back to his quarters. How this simple retrieval had gone so sideways was beyond him. He stopped outside his quarters, trying to recall how many retrievals he had completed in his career. More than a hundred, for sure. All had their challenges, but none had been as difficult as this one, and it wasn't done.

The messenger hadn't struck him as particularly capable, but the spacers he had fallen in with must be professionals he hired after Freeground.

Jax opened the hatch to his quarters, sniffing the rich aroma of fresh brewed coffee. He padded down the short corridor into the kitchenette. Clinton and Naomi were at the small cafe table that served as the dining table.

When Jax had come down from the bridge the night before, both of them were already asleep.

Naomi looked up. "Morning."

He nodded to her, then to the coffee pot built into the cupboard. "Is that?"

"Yeah." She smiled.

"You said wouldn't share it with me."

She tipped her head toward Clinton. "We have company."

Clinton looked down at his steaming mug. "Am I missing something?"

Jax poured a cup, inhaling deeply. "She's got a bootie call on Terra Nova that's a coffee geek. She's running low and has been stingy of late." He raised his mug. The other two raised theirs. He grabbed a package of breakfast pastries and joined them at the table.

"So..." Jax said, then unwrapped a pastry from its silvery foil and took a bite.

Clinton looked nervously at Naomi, who said, "So..."

"We're heading to UniDis Four," Jax said. He took another bite. The strawberry ones were his favorite.

Clinton looked at Jax, then Naomi. "Uh. What?"

"UniDis Four? What the hell for?" Naomi sat her

mug down hard enough to send coffee sloshing over the lip.

Jax leaned back a bit. "I got a call last night."

Clinton visibly tensed, his knuckles white around his mug. He looked at Naomi. "Guess he isn't going to surprise me."

Jax held his pastry up. "What's that mean? Never mind, just hear me out. This guy, whoever—"

"Whomever," Clinton corrected, then held both hands up when Jax turned a glare his way.

Jax continued, "He works for BioTek. High up, I'm guessing. Said they only want the case. Not you." He let his expression go flat. "He made it clear they weren't going to drop this, and if they didn't get their way, they'd bring in the Imperial authorities." He looked at Naomi. "Remember what I said."

She nodded. "How'd they track us down?"

Jax looked at the ceiling. When nothing happened, he cleared his throat.

The overhead speaker said, "Oh, that is my queue, I guess. It is impossible to know if they cracked the *Osprey*'s true ident, but they obviously cracked the fake we were using. We are lucky that our comm ID is blank. Cracking our fake registry exposed the comm ID. Since it's blank, it will not lead them anywhere, but they can call us."

"So what?" Naomi said, her mug clutched in both hands. "We drop him off at an amusement park, that's that?"

Jax shook his head. "No, there's a reward."

Naomi was on her feet so fast the chair groaned

against its magnetic fastening. "On top of fucking him over, we're getting paid, and that's it. All good?"

Jax slammed his breakfast down, sending strawberry filled pastry scattering across the table and onto the floor. "Goddamnit, that's not what I'm saying!" He jabbed a finger at Naomi. "I already told you this was a bad idea, and now we're on the fucking cusp of being hunted by one of the biggest bio-pharma-tech-whatever companies in the Empire, and oh yeah, the fucking Empire itself!"

He got to his feet and stomped toward the lounge area.

Naomi looked down at Clinton. He was staring into his coffee mug.

From the lounge, Jax said, "The guy said he could get the case off you."

Clinton looked up. "I doubt it. That's not how it works." He raised his arm, the case hanging from his wrist. He shifted so that it was resting on the table. "They'd have to cut my hand off at the wrist."

Jax raised an eyebrow.

Naomi snatched a chunk of breakfast pastry and hurled it at him. "That's not an okay solution!" She stormed back down the corridor into her quarters.

Jax turned to Clinton, who was back to examining his coffee. Deeply.

Jax sighed. "It doesn't come off? Under any circumstance?"

Clinton shook his head. "The cuff, leash, and outer shell are a special alloy the messenger service had created. Harder than starship armor."

"Damn. And showers, going to the bathroom?"

"Awkward," the man said.

Jax moved through the kitchenette, grabbing his and Naomi's cups. He filled them and disappeared around the corner down the short corridor.

Naomi was sitting cross legged on her bed when a soft knock came. She sighed. "Come in, Jackson."

He poked his head in. "How'd you know it was me?" He came a little further in, brandishing the two now topped off coffee cups.

She shook her head. "Because Clinton isn't a selfish dickhead that owes me an apology, explanation...take your pick." She looked up. "And Rudy doesn't knock when he sneaks in to tidy up." She held out her hand, fingers wiggling expectantly.

Jax came in, holding out her mug. He sat on the far side of her bed. He frowned and pushed his hand into the mattress. He looked up. "Is this? Where'd you get this mattress? It's so nice. Mine isn't like this."

She sighed. "Of course, yours isn't. The mattresses on this tub are horrible, like sleeping on a poorly made bag of tumbleweeds."

He leaned back, stricken, his mouth hanging open.

She said, "I bought this one the moment we got back from Jebediah."

He looked around. "When? How?"

She glared. "Is my mattress really the topic at hand?"

Jax held up both hands, palms out. "Okay, I'm sorry."

Her head tilted. "For?"

He made a face. "Everything?" He stretched the word out uncertainly.

She took a sip of her coffee. Lowering it, she said, "You didn't talk to me first."

"About what?"

Another sigh. "Anything, everything." She waved her free hand. "Where we go, jobs we take. Whether we work with the Resistance or not. Whether to hand over an innocent man to a mega corp."

"Hey, that's not fair. You picked our last gig," he protested.

She shook her head. "No, I didn't."

"You did. You wanted to take the...You know, the cargo..." He frowned.

She nodded, dragging out, "Yeah."

His shoulders slumped. "Look, I didn't commit to anything. Just a meeting. Naomi, he's not," he raised a finger, "the Resistance is not," he raised another finger, "family. I don't owe him, or them, anything."

Up until the moment Naomi had inserted herself into his life, Jax had been on his own. Even his long-time friends on Kelso station, the place he'd called home his entire life, were never allowed to get too close. Even Sandor and the Delphinos were, at best, acquaintances. His relationships, even his brief fling with Steve Delphino, were, at best, what one would call short-lived.

"How can you say that? You gave the Resistance the Ghost Fleet."

He shrugged. "What was I...we...going to do with it?"

She scowled. "I know you weren't on board with my

being your partner, but I'd kind of assumed you'd warmed to the idea by now."

"I mean, sure. I'm fine." He pointed at her, then to himself. "This actually works better than I thought it would when I shot you in my room."

"You don't have to keep saying it like that." She took a sip of her coffee.

He made a face. "You know what I mean. We actually work well. The fridge hasn't been this well stocked in, well, ever."

She lowered the cup. "I know you did not just equate my value with the contents of the refrigerator."

Jax scooted towards the edge of the bed, away from Naomi. He said, "At the end of the day, my ship, my responsibility." He stood and left.

CHAPTER 10

Conference Room 1 aboard the *Curry* was directly forward of the bridge. The wraparound windows provided a view of the ship's wide gray-white bow and the expanse of space beyond.

Jefferson Sanchez was working at an oversized tablet when a chime sounded from the ceiling.

"Mr. Sanchez?"

He looked up. "Yes?"

"Incoming call from corporate."

He looked around the luxurious conference room, spotting the control panel for the room. He stood and activated the privacy mode. The wraparound windows shimmered as they became opaque and an LED strip around the door lit up red to indicate that it would not open under any circumstances until he deactivated privacy mode.

Dropping back into his seat, he said, "Put it through."

"Yes, sir," the officer said.

The ceiling beeped. "Mr. Sanchez, you're on with the board."

The segment of opaqued window at the forward section of the ship shimmered again, becoming a screen. A grid of twelve stern faces appeared.

Sanchez inclined his head. Calls from Farndale were never good. The board of directors for BioTek were scattered across the Empire most of the time. Getting them all together remotely was out of the norm. Getting them all connected to the corporate station over Farndale and then routing the call to the *Curry* was no small feat.

The chairwoman, a pale earnest woman in her seventies, looked right at him. "Mr. Sanchez. Report."

He cleared his throat. "We had eyes on the messenger on Valhalla but ran into a minor hiccup."

A board member, an older bald-headed man, coughed. "A hiccup?"

Sanchez cocked his head. "He was able to get off-world. He had help."

"Help?" the chairwoman repeated.

Sanchez again tipped his head. "Smugglers, I'm guessing. Maybe just run of the mill spacers in the wrong place at the wrong time. We haven't ID'ed them yet. We know they're in an old model Valerian Co-op job, but the ident was hacked, expertly."

Another board member opened her mouth, but Sanchez held up a hand. "If I may. We don't know who they are, but I was able to get in touch with them."

The woman leaned in. "And?" Her close-cropped white hair stood out in contrast to her dark skin.

"I've arranged a meeting."

The chairwoman's mouth quirked into a lopsided smile. "Do tell."

Sanchez folded his hands on the table. "We're enroute to UniDis Four now. We'll be there in," he glanced down at the large tablet, "two more days."

Another board member, possibly the youngest member, said, "And the plan?"

"Meet the smuggler—I didn't get his name—pay him a reward, get the messenger, and separate him from the case." He spread his hands wide.

On the window-turned-screen, eleven slow nods responded to the news. The chairwoman cleared her throat. "Excellent news, Sanchez. One small adjustment."

"Oh?"

"The contents of that case are too dangerous. We can't afford loose ends."

Another board member chimed in, "We lucked out on Freeground with those thugs killing our traitors. However, the messenger and these spacers he's hooked up with...they're involved now."

Sanchez looked right at the center of the cluster of faces, the chairwoman. "Ma'am. I assured the man we could separate the messenger from the case and—"

She raised a hand. "This isn't a debate, Sanchez. The contents of that case must either be destroyed or returned here to Farndale. No one can be allowed to know about this outside the company." She added, "We'll smooth over what we can on UniDis. Get it done."

Sanchez was quiet. It certainly wouldn't be the first time he had to take matters to the ultimate end in service to BioTek, but he never liked it. He told himself that made all the difference. He sometimes believed it.

At the end of the day, it didn't matter. He knew that. Stopping anyone that would harm BioTek was his job.

He nodded. "Understood."

The chairwoman angled her head. "Good. Report back to us when you reach UniDis Four. Remember, avoiding attention—particularly of the Imperial variety— is of the utmost importance."

Before he could reply, each of the twelve windows winked out until he was staring at the blank gray privacy filter on the window.

He tapped an icon on the surface of the table. "Captain, would you mind joining me in C-1?"

Clinton spent the two days of travel time to UniDis Four mostly in his quarters, which suited Jax just fine. Paying customers were one thing. Freeloading hard luck cases were another entirely.

Naomi had done mostly the same, having decided that she wasn't in the mood to fight or even discuss their next course of action with Jax. Rudy kept himself busy on the bridge while Baxter remained in his charging dock in the small engineering space on the cargo deck.

From the overhead speaker on every deck in every room, Skip announced, "We'll be exiting wormhole in ten minutes. Please square away whatever human problems you three are having and prepare for local space."

Up on the bridge, Rudy's main optical sensor whirred as it spun. Out loud, he said, "Someone is feeling plucky."

Over the wireless network that the droids and Skip shared, the ship's SI said, *I thought the silence would be nice. It was not. I'm not even physically there, and the last two days have been uncomfortable.*

Technically, you are physically here. We're inside you, Rudy shot back. Skip did not reply.

Jax and Naomi came up the stairs. "What was that all about?" the former asked as he moved to his chair at the front of the narrow space.

The speaker in the ceiling said, "What? Nothing. Six minutes to local space."

Naomi powered up her console, looking over everything. She pulled up UniDis Four. She had already looked at what the onboard systems had stored, which wasn't much. Once the *Osprey* exited the wormhole, all of the latest information on the resort planet would be requested automatically.

She looked up. "You ever been?"

Jax was silent for a moment. Finally, he said, "What?"

"UniDis Four," Naomi said, adding, "You ever go? As a kid or whatever?"

He chuckled. "Or whatever."

"Three minutes," Skip announced.

Jax said, "No. I didn't even know it existed until I was twelve or something. I think Auntie musta blocked any advertising or something. I was blissfully ignorant until the Delphinos told the whole school they were going.

Then when they got back, they made the teacher set aside like two hours for their multimedia presentation show and tell. It was gross." He blinked. "You?"

After a heartbeat or twelve of silence, she said, "No. My parents were always too busy, then I ended up in the Interface program, and well, they weren't big on field trips."

"Ahem," Skip said.

Jax reached over and pressed the control, cutting off the wormhole field generator. The green-purple-orange swirling vortex vanished as the *Osprey* shot out of the wormhole into the UniDis system. The massive gas giant orbited by the UniDis moons was directly ahead.

UniDis Four was meant to be the crowning achievement of the UniversalDisney mega corp, bringing all of their combined intellectual property to one place. UniDis Four was a mid-sized moon that required minimal terraforming. The dozens of islands that ringed the equatorial region made for perfectly contained theme parks dedicated to various brands.

That was the plan.

The Unification War broke out just before the grand opening. The park opened, no one came. It nearly bankrupted the company. The solution was to lease out the individual island parks to other brands. UniDis managed the infrastructure but only had one island park for their IP. The remaining islands were independently operated by other companies.

The *Osprey* was still a light hour out from the moon. Hundreds of ships of all sizes and shapes orbited the blue-green marble. Orbital habitats formed a metal ring.

Next to one of the larger habitats, half a dozen massive luxury star liners were lined up to dock.

"Damn," Naomi whispered. "Business is good."

"We are being hailed," Skip reported.

Jax didn't look over his shoulder, asking, "New idents in place?"

Rudy beeped an affirmative, adding, "Yup."

Jax nodded and looked at the comm system. A small display read, *Solario*. He turned. "*Solario*?" Rudy made a fist and bobbed it up and down, his version of a nod.

The comm system beeped, pulling Jax's attention back to it. He growled and flipped the switch. The display overhead came to life, and the face of a bored young man in a far too happy blue sailor suit with yellow and white highlights stared down at Jax.

The man composed himself and forced a smile. "Welcome to UniDis Four, the happiest planet in the galaxy." He grinned wider. "Do you have a reservation?"

Jax put on his own fake smile. "Hi. We don't, actually. Hoping we can book something now."

The younger man on the display bobbed his head. "Of course! I'm transmitting our pricing packages now, as well as coordinates for our temporary orbital parking, until you make your decision."

"Thank you so much!" Jax beamed. "Do we call you back?"

"No, I'm including the comm details for our sales

department. They'll handle getting you booked for landing, lodging, and park admission."

He waved. "Have a Potterific day." The screen went blank.

Jax adjusted their course, bringing the *Osprey* onto a flight path that would put them in a loose cluster with fifty or so other small- and mid-sized ships.

Naomi looked past Jax. "This is the temporary lot?"

Jax looked at the ships outside, all still powered up and holding position while they negotiated access to the moon below. "So, what're we looking at?"

"Parking lot," Rudy said.

"Right, but this is the temporary setup."

Rudy brought up a map of the local planetary system and its moons. UniDis Four was blue. Tucked into a Lagrange point between UniDis Four and the smaller third moon was a cluster of nearly two hundred ships.

"Woah," Naomi said. "How much is it to land?"

"A whole lot," Rudy said. She turned to the small rust-colored droid. His head swiveled to look at her, his big optic sensor whirring as it spun. "The orbital parking areas are a whole lot cheaper."

"So, how's it work?" Jax asked.

Rudy turned to him. "Park there. A tender comes to get you and ferries you to one of the space elevator complexes. Cheaper to shuttle over to the transport hub and take one of the mass transit shuttles down."

"How much cheaper?" Jax asked, easing the *Osprey* to a stop in the shadow of a charter shuttle painted, for some reason, to look look like a hippopotamus.

"I said, *a whole lot*. What do you think?"

"Fair," Jax replied. "Okay, we'll park and take the elevator down."

Naomi held up a finger, checking one of the screens before her.

"Jeez, they get you coming and going." She tapped her screen, and Rudy's map was replaced with a list of prices. "Lodging up on the orbital if needed. Lodging down there, which varies by island, and luxury level." She sighed. "Looks like it doesn't get cheaper than two a night, no matter where you stay." She groaned. "Oh, and of course the parking fee and elevator fee."

Jax shook his head. "How the hell did the Delphinos' parents afford this?"

Naomi snapped her fingers. "There's a community hostel in..." She looked up. "Sokovia?" She looked out the window at the array of ships parked nearby. "Thoughts?"

"We don't have that kind of money!" Jax said.

"Didn't you pick this place?" Rudy asked.

Jax spluttered. "Well...I just...I pulled up the nav chart and saw that we weren't that far from it, and...well, like I said, I've never been."

"That sounds right," Rudy quipped, his main optic sensor swiveling from Jax to Naomi, then to the staircase.

Clinton came up looking sheepish. "We're here, huh?"

Naomi nodded. "Just trying to figure out our next steps."

Jax ran a hand through his hair, then said, "Duh." He wiggled his fingers at her. "Could your—?" Her glare shut him up.

"Excuse me?" Clinton said, taking the last few steps up into the small bridge.

"Nothing," the other two said as one.

"Uh. Okay." He looked past Jax. "So, now what?"

Jax spun and slid his chair back into position. He tapped a few controls. As the communication display came to life, the face of a chipper young woman appeared. "Hi there! Ready to purchase your passes to the most magical place in the galaxy? The Hogwirts Express is ready to deliver you to any of our theme lands around the planet."

Jax canted his head. "Yes, I think we'd like to leave our ship up here and book passage down to..." He looked over his shoulder.

"West World," Naomi offered and shrugged to Rudy, who turned his optic sensor to her.

"West World," Jax repeated.

"Copy that, partner," the young woman drawled. "How many?"

"Five. Three adults, two droids." He leaned closer to the display overhead. "Droids are allowed?"

"They certainly are, sir! At UniDis Four, some of our most loved characters are of the Sapient Intelligence variety." She busied herself tapping something off screen, then looked back up. "Alrighty. I have you down for three adults, two droids shuttling down to the Wizarding World of Frontierland. I've sent over the parking instructions to move your ship to long term parking."

She tipped her head the other way, still beaming. "And with that, you are all set. One of our tenders will be arriving shortly to pick you up. Just let them know how to dock." She beamed. "Is there anything else?"

Jax shook his head. "Nope, we're good." Under his breath, he added, "And now broke."

After disconnecting from the sales office and moving to the Lagrange parking area, they heard from the inbound transfer shuttle.

Naomi ushered Clinton off the bridge. Rudy followed.

Jax watched them go, then set about putting key systems into standby. He tapped a few commands into his console, opening a secure communication interface. He tapped out a message, knowing that Skip would bounce it around as best he could, running it through more than one cypher to ensure that when it reached its destination the sender's ident would be impossible to find. He hit SEND, then said, "Holler when that tender arrives."

"Sure thing," Skip answered.

Jax reached the common deck as Clinton was exiting the head. He raised an eyebrow. "I hope you're a lefty."

Clinton raised his right hand, the case dangling by six inches of braided metal wrapped in low conductivity rubber. "I am, but it still sucks."

Jax wrinkled his nose and headed for his quarters.

Ten minutes later, Skip's voice rang throughout the ship. "The tender is arriving. Starboard side."

Jax reached the cargo deck as something was latching onto the hull with a dull metallic *thunk*. A light over the personnel hatch set in the starboard cargo door blinked green three times, then remained on. Good seal.

The hatch slid in, then to the side, exposing yet another twenty-something in blue, white, and gold. He waved. "Hi there, travelers. Ready to get your adventure on?" His gaze roamed the hold, settling on Baxter, all two and a half meters of matte black combat droid of him. He coughed. "I'm..." He looked around to the three humans. He settled his gaze on Clinton. "I'm not sure I can allow a combat droid into the park."

Jax waved a hand. "I didn't see anything in the rules."

The younger man produced a tablet from a holster on his side. "Uh..." He dragged out the last syllable as he gazed at the device. He looked up from the screen, blushing slightly. "Let me just confirm." He turned his back to the *Osprey* crew.

Baxter moved to stand next to Jax.

The young theme park planet employee turned back to the others. "I have great news. We have two choices."

Jax nodded. "Great. Lay 'em on us."

"We have an additional insurance policy you can enroll in. To cover any potential issues that might arise, him being a combat droid and all." Jax and Naomi nodded. He continued, "The policy, I'm afraid, isn't inexpensive."

"Oh..." Jax said. "The other option?"

The young man glanced at Baxter. "A restraining bolt."

Compartments on the backs of Baxter's forearms slid

open. One at a time, two-inch-wide segments slipped from the compartment. The segments were held together by a braided tungsten cord that ran through their center. Once the last segment slipped out, the cord snapped taut, pulling the segments into a single blade. "No. Restraining. Bolt," he growled.

"Oh my," the young park employee gasped, taking an involuntary step back.

"Oh great," Rudy whispered.

Jax put a hand on the big bot's arm. "Bax, chill." He looked up at the matte black face. The only feature, the swishing red optical sensor. When he was sure the droid was looking at him, he moved his eyes to Naomi.

Without a word, the twin blades lengthened slightly as the links disengaged from each other. Amid clicks and clanks, the pieces of the twin blades were pulled back into his forearms.

Jax smiled and turned to the young man at the hatch, now pale as a sheet. "We'll do the restraining bolt."

"Uh. Yes. Very good," he stammered. "I'll let the reception area on the surface know." He took a deep breath. "This way, please." He turned and led the way back through the docking tube to the UniDis tender that would take them to the space elevator complex.

Naomi fell in next to Baxter. She looked up. "I got you, big guy."

CHAPTER 11

"Ladies, gentlemen, and those that identify as neither, welcome to UniDis Four. This space elevator will take approximately thirty minutes to reach the surface. We'll be arriving at travel hub Eastwood. While you can depart the planet from any hub, your ship is nearest this elevator." The announcement continued with rules and regulations and current price promos and offers. Jax stopped listening.

He and the others were seated on level 2 of the three-story structure. Their level had a dozen or so other park guests scattered around the hundred-meter diameter elevator car.

When they boarded, an exuberant little girl introducing herself as Tammy said she and her family were from New Cairo, and she was so anxious to meet Donald Mouse.

The announcement continued, "Hub Eastwood is located in Brawndo West World. Atmospheric transports to all lands are available from any hub on the planet, as are hyperloop trains. Hyperloop stations are indicated on all park directories by a train icon."

A loud clank announced the release of the car from the orbital station.

"Brawndo?" Clinton asked.

"Off we go," Jax said as the car moved. The drop caused several passengers to gasp as their stomachs lurched. Somewhere, little Tammy giggled and shouted, yay.

Naomi nodded. "Buying planets ain't cheap, even when you're the biggest media and entertainment conglomerate the human race has ever known. Opening right before a civil war breaks out doesn't help."

Jax turned in his seat. "How'd you know?"

Naomi shrugged. "I read." She continued, "In an effort to recoup the costs of putting this all together, UniDis leases the various islands to other brands. Brawndo has West World. Space Tech has Marvelia, and so on. The Wizarding World one is run by a deodorant company at the moment. They just took it over a few years ago."

Rudy made a noise, his optics whirring. "I have downloaded all of the available maps and point of interest data available."

Clinton nodded to the small droid and looked out the window. The curve of the world was still in the distance. The stars were washed out by the glow of the atmosphere. "So, where to?"

Jax grinned. "There's a bar."

"Of course, there is," Baxter said from where he was standing.

Jax looked up, making a face. "The Stumbling Pony has a four and a half star rating."

Rudy beeped twice. "Confirmed."

Jax shook his head. "It wasn't my idea. That Sanchez guy suggested it."

Clinton cleared his throat. "You know. I could just, go to a different transit hub. I'm sure I could bribe someone to take me out of the system, drop me somewhere out of the way. I could probably even stow away. No paper trail."

"And what? You live the rest of your life with your lunch box stuck on your wrist." Jax shook his head. "Plus, it's too late. I sent our friend the details already." He saw the looks on Clinton's and Naomi's faces. "I did some thinking the other night."

"Did it hurt?" Naomi quipped.

Jax made a face. "We're here first, we're setting the stage."

"Except that he picked the stage," Baxter said.

Jax made a face. A hidden speaker crackled to life, cutting off whatever he was going to say. "Attention, passengers. We're passing through the upper atmosphere now. In a moment, you'll get your first look at West World and several neighboring islands."

The families sharing the second level of the elevator car all moved to the curved windows. A moment later, oohs and aahs, mixed with several gleeful giggles, filled the space.

Once outside planetary transit hub Eastwood, Naomi and Baxter went around a corner where there were fewer park guests and vendors.

While UniDis ran the infrastructure, the moment you set foot outside a hub, you were at the mercy of the lessee of the island.

Jax looked around, thankful that UniDis Four catered mostly to the rich and super rich. That meant that droids were commonplace. The emperor might have hated them, made droids the enemy of the entire Humanity First campaign and all that, but the rich couldn't be without their trusted metallic companions. Especially if they had children that needed minding.

Clinton watched Naomi and Baxter vanish around a shrub, then turned to Jax and Rudy. "What's going on?"

"Nothing," both said at once.

Baxter and Naomi returned, saying nothing. As far as Clinton could tell, neither looked any different than a moment ago.

Rudy said, "The Stumbling Pony is two kilometers, that way." He extended a hand, pointing in a direction entirely like every other. Nothing in West World was more than two stories, and all of it was made of wood.

Naomi pointed. "Think the horses are real?" Several were tied up outside what looked like a general store but was actually a souvenir shop. A lustrous palomino whickered as a child came too close.

"Real," Clinton answered.

They'd made it a quarter of a kilometer when a pair of actors, a man and a woman, intercepted them on the dusty street. The former said, "Howdy, folks, you look lost. New here?"

Jax looked down at Rudy. "No, we've got a map." He rapped a knuckle on the rust-colored droid's head once before a thin metal arm swatted his hand away.

The woman grinned. "And what an adorable little map he is."

Her colleague's eyes pulsed blue. "Well, if you need anything, just look for one of us. We're here to make your stay as enjoyable as possible."

Jax nodded.

The man tapped the edge of his brown Stetson. "See ya 'round, partner." He gestured for his counterpart to continue down the street.

As the pair passed, the gynoid's eyes pulsed blue as she smiled. "Have a good day."

Naomi turned to Jax and Clinton. "Androids?"

"And gynoids," the taller of the two offered. Jax looked at him. "What? That's the technical term."

Jax sighed.

Naomi consulted her gPhone. "Wow, nearly ninety percent of the workforce planetwide is androids." She looked at Clinton as he opened his mouth. "We'll just use that as a non-gendered term." He shrugged.

"Good for us, at least," Jax said, rapping a knuckle on Baxter's chest plate.

A family rushed past the group: two haggard adults, three young children, and a pale pink assistant droid trailing behind them. The droid was flailing its arms as it shuffled along repeating, "Oh, my."

Naomi shook her head. "Weird to see so many droids."

Jax nodded. "Guess the emperor's anti-droid thing doesn't apply when profits and rich assholes' preferences are at play."

Clinton nodded. "Tale as old as time."

"We should get moving," Baxter said. "I would like to get set up before the meeting."

Jax nodded. "Yeah, they should be arriving any time now. Let's go."

Naomi looked around as they walked. The emperor and his cronies had made droids the enemy of humanity for years before the war. Yet here, where it cost a fraction of what human labor would, everyone seemed perfectly okay with droids. She shook her head.

The group stopped short as a stagecoach trundled by in front of them. Naomi moved up next to Jax. "What's the plan?"

"I told you." The stagecoach passed, and they continued down the hard packed road.

She sighed. "Yeah, but you left out what you want Clinton and me to do. What you want the droids to do. What the actual nuts and bolts of the plan are. I assume you weren't thinking he'd be sitting next to you?"

"Oh. Uh..."

This time her sigh sounded like it came from as deep within her as possible. "Yeah. So, we won't let on how bad you are at this."

From behind them, Clinton said, "I can hear you, though."

Jax's shoulders bunched. "Whatever. We can find a spot nearby for you two to camp out."

Clinton looked up at the cloudless sky. "This is how I die."

The inside of the Stumbling Pony was more or less what Jax had expected: a mix of androids and humans, most in period-appropriate clothing, though some were dressed similarly to Jax and the others—guests that hadn't had time to check into their lodgings, likely.

The walk to the bar had been like walking through a Wild West town on Earth, assuming Wild West towns were dozens of square kilometers in size, and every few blocks the businesses repeated themselves, with slight variations. They had passed the Prancing Pony and the Prolific Pony already. The name of the latter they agreed to not look too deeply into.

A few heads turned as Jax and Rudy entered, all with blue, sparkly eyes. The humans were too busy ogling their surroundings and trying to keep their children under control. Rudy spied a small gaggle of droids in the corner and made his way over to them. Jax watched him go and then made his way to an empty table near the center of the room.

An android server sauntered up to his table. Resting a

hand on her hip, the other hand balancing a circular tray, she said, "Hi there, stranger. What can I get ya?"

"Something strong." Jax looked around suddenly. The occupied tables were populated by both adults and children. "I can get booze here, right?"

The server's bright blue eyes pulsed as she grinned. "Of course, honey." She winked. "I'll be right back." She turned and sauntered off, stopping at a table with more children than adults.

"I think your friend is here," Baxter said in Jax's earpiece.

Jax wasn't sure where the combat droid was but trusted him. He had split off from the group a block from the Pony.

Jax tapped the commset in his ear. "Copy that. He alone?"

"No."

"No?" Naomi cut in from wherever she and Clinton had hunkered down.

"That is what I said," the big bot replied. "I count an even dozen. All strapped, but casual."

The waitress returned with a single tumbler on her tray. She deposited it before him with a wink. "Enjoy."

Jax was about to say something when Baxter said, "Incoming."

The door to the bar swung open to allow a well-dressed older man to enter. The same man from before. Jax nodded, the man returned the gesture, letting the doors swing shut behind him.

In Jax's ear, Baxter said, "Two on each side of the door. Four across the street. I don't have eyes on the rest."

The—if Jax was being honest, handsome—BioTek man was halfway to Jax when the buxom waitress intercepted him. They talked, he pointed at Jax, she nodded, and he continued on.

Jax didn't get up or offer his hand as the man sat. "I'm Jefferson Sanchez."

Rudy watched the older man sit down. He turned his large optic sensor on a blue and white droid the same size as him, an even older model than he was. "Hello."

The droid's chrome and blue domed head turned as a single optical sensor whirred, focusing on Rudy. It warbled a reply.

Rudy made his own beep, remembering that model didn't have a vocalizer. He accessed old files, pulling up the binary audible transfer translation matrix. He warbled and chirped. The other droid replied, and several indicators on its barrel-shaped body lit up.

"Good to know." Jax inclined his head.

"And you?"

Jax smiled but said nothing.

"Fair enough."

In Jax's ear, Skip said, "Captain, they came in a cruiser that is...well, it looks mean. Two shuttles went down to the surface." After a second, the *Osprey*'s SI continued, "I was able to find an unpatched back door into the space elevator hub station's operating system. From there, getting into the rest of the park's systems was embarrassingly easy. The RI that ran things was three versions behind on its firewall. I should be able to keep tabs on things from up here."

Jax nodded, unable to respond. He looked at the man opposite him. "So?"

"You know we'll track your ident down eventually, right?"

Jax shrugged.

"Fine. Let's get down to—"

"Here you go, cowboys," the waitress said, setting a tumbler on the table in front of Sanchez. She turned to Jax, sliding a tumbler like the one he already had toward him. He downed the contents of the first and grinned, handing the empty to her.

She looked at each man again. "I get you two anything else?"

Sanchez didn't look up. "We're good. Thank you." When she was out of earshot, he said, "So, about our stolen property."

"He's property?"

The older man cocked his head. "He? The messenger?" He waved a hand. "Like I said, he's immaterial. I don't give two shits about him."

"You know he's a messenger?" Jax took a slow sip of his drink. Thinking. Clinton had mentioned his handler burning him. Whatever the waitress had brought him burned pleasantly going down, calming him. This man knew more than Jax expected.

Sanchez took his own sip, his eyes never leaving Jax. "You think BioTek has never used the messenger service?"

Jax clucked. "Does everyone know about these secret high tech delivery boys but me?"

Sanchez smiled a wholly unfriendly smile. "You couldn't afford one if you sold that old relic you fly in and then won the Imperial lottery."

Jax clucked and waved a hand. "Secret society... matching lunch boxes." He shook his head and finished off his drink. "Not surprised BioTek works with them." He honestly did not know that much about BioTek specifically but lumped most big corporations together into a single group.

"Only secret to those without the means." Sanchez shrugged again. "And by no means a society. A company, like any other. Secretive to be sure. Priding themselves on not taking sides or prioritizing one client over another."

He took another sip. "Of course, that only applies in certain situations. It took two calls to get his biometrics and get him burned." He held up a finger. "Me calling my boss." He ticked another finger. "Her calling...well, I have no damn clue who she called. But that call, burned your new friend." He finished his drink. "You win some. You lose some." He smiled.

Jax squeezed both hands into fists.

CHAPTER 12

Baxter had no idea how faithful this theme park was but knew that he did not like the "old west." The buildings were too short and apparently poorly constructed. Twice since reaching the roof of the building opposite the Stumbling Pony and making his way to a vantage from which he could provide overwatch, he had nearly fallen through the roof. Where this company got so much thin wood was beyond him.

After watching the corporate recovery team arrive, he activated his full combat suite. One of his shoulder-mounted railguns deployed along with this forearm blasters. He looked down at the restraining bolt on his chest, nothing more than a decoration after Naomi used her special talents on it. The eight visible members of the recovery team were outlined in red and tracked by his targeting system. The whereabouts of the other four were still unknown. He saw them split up and continue down both sides of the street but lost them after that.

He watched the street for several minutes. Over the

wireless network Rudy sent, *I met a nav droid older than me.*

Baxter was motionless on the roof. *Yay?*

I seem to recall someone who wouldn't stop going on about the droids on the dreadnought.

Down on the street below, the four BioTek agents on either side of the door moved. In pairs they entered the bar.

Kind of busy, now, Baxter beamed. He switched communication modes so that he could warn Jax.

In his ear, Jax heard Baxter's deep voice. "They're moving in."

"Need us?" Naomi asked.

"No," Jax said loud enough for the commset to pick up. Sanchez raised an eyebrow. Jax met his gaze. "So that reward, off the table then?"

The man opposite him shrugged. "Doesn't seem as if you earned it." Jax saw three men and a woman in tailored suits enter the bar, two each moving to either side of the door.

Jax was thinking up a witty retort when Sanchez flinched. He reached for his ear. "Repeat last." His eyes shot to Jax, who shrugged a split second before he stood, bringing the table up with him to flip right into Sanchez's face.

There was a moment of silence as everyone in the saloon stared open-mouthed at the well-dressed man and overturned table. Then the screaming started as a blaster round burned through the thin wooden wall at the front of the building.

The four agents spun toward the door. One flew backward, a minuscule hole punched in the wall.

Jax was already halfway across the room when Sanchez spotted him. He turned and waved before sprinting for the back door.

As he burst into the back alley, Jax tapped his earpiece. "Rudy, Bax, cover our exit?" He got two distinct beeps in reply. He was about to call Naomi when someone shouted from the corner of the building.

The shout was enough warning for Jax to drop to the dirt as a blaster bolt shot overhead. "No fair! You get guns!" he shouted.

The back door burst open as a rust-colored tornado burst into the alley. The sun reflected off of a pair of steak knives. In a flash, one of the blades shot past Jax to embed itself in the nearest BioTek agent's chest. With a grunt, the man collapsed.

Jax got to his feet and charged the man next to the one with a knife in him. The shocked trooper stared at his colleague, then looked at Jax before being tackled.

Rudy, still spinning and dodging blaster fire, let his second knife fly, taking out one of the two agents on the opposite side of the alley. "I should carry more knives," he shouted.

"No, you shouldn't!" Jax shouted back. He looked down at the agent he tackled. "Sorry." He punched him in the face, twice. "Naomi, we'll meet you and Clint outside in a minute." He looked both ways, orienting himself, then took off in a run. "Rudy!"

Rudy was still spinning, chasing the other two agents out of the alley. He stopped, turned, and rolled after Jax, slowing his spin to a stop as he reached the end of the alley.

At the front of the building, BioTek recovery team members were shouting and firing blindly as railgun rounds tore through knees and shoulders. Moving around the edge of the roof proved difficult for the big metal bot. Eventually, one of them spotted him. The return fire dialed in on him, shredding the haberdashery he was on the roof of. Several fires broke out. He fell back, moving to the next building over so he could drop to the ground.

Jefferson Sanchez stepped out of the Stumbling Pony. Seeing half of his force immobilized, he sighed. He tapped the earpiece attached to his gPhone. "All units report in." In the distance, sirens were wailing and getting louder. "Shit," he hissed.

After meeting up with Naomi and Clinton in a clothing shop catering to big and tall cowboys, Jax looked out the window to the dusty street outside. He waved to the door. "Okay, let's go." The three of them exited and walked as fast they could up the street, away from the mounting commotion in the direction of the Stumbling Pony.

Clinton stopped short. "Where are we going?" Jax and Naomi stopped, exchanging looks.

Jax looked around. "Well…"

Clinton threw his arms up. "Oh, this is the 'no plan' part."

Naomi shook her head. "We gotta get off this

island." She pointed behind Jax to the metallic thread that reached up to vanish into the clouds. "We can't take the elevator up. Jax's new friend's agents will be there."

Jax snapped his fingers. "The hyperloop!" Naomi and Clinton nodded, remembering the announcement from the ride down from the elevator station. Jax looked around. "Do we know where it is?"

They all looked around. "Where's Rudy when you need him?" Naomi mumbled.

"Never admit to saying that," Jax scolded. He looked around, spotting an approaching couple. "Hi, sorry to bother you. Our map is currently making his way here. Would you mind sharing yours? I didn't download before we left the hub." One of the women smiled and swiped on her gPhone screen. Jax's device chimed. "Thanks, so much."

"Why can't you be that charming all the time?" Naomi wondered as he joined her and Clinton.

"Because it causes me physical pain." He made a face. Holding up his gPhone, he pointed. "Thataway."

In no time, they were standing outside the hyperloop station. Every island on the planet was connected by a network of hyperloop tubes. Guests had their choice of transportation between the planet's theme islands. The network was cheaper than the atmospheric shuttles often used by the park's more affluent guests, with several stations on each island. They were also faster. The hyperloop trains ran a tight schedule.

Before heading into the underground complex, Jax opened an app on his gPhone. "Attention non-human teammates. We're boarding a hyperloop, destination unknown. Skip, you okay up there?"

"Affirmative. I believe the BioTek people are attempting to locate me. I have been feeding them false data through the park network, randomly assigning our parking spot to different groups. It should take them a while to search all these Lagrange holding lots. As a precaution, I am currently latched on to the underside of a large people mover out of Aswan. I should be fine for a while."

Jax smiled. "Good job, buddy. Bax, Rudy?"

"We went the opposite direction. We'll catch up to you when you get where you're going."

"Copy that." Jax nodded and looked at the others. "Let's go."

They made their way into the station. Naomi leaned close to Jax. "Where to?"

Jax looked at the schedule over the entry way. "Americana." The next hyperloop car to depart was heading there. They boarded with several dozen park goers, several with "Capable Avongers!" emblazoned on their t-shirts.

Back at the Stumbling Pony, Jefferson Sanchez was being berated by the local head of security for UniDis. He held up his hands. "We'll cover the damages, of course." Three fire suppression droids were hovering over the smoking remains of the store across the street from the Pony, spraying flare-ups with fire retardant foam.

The irate woman, a head shorter than him, was fuming. Her hands were firmly planted on her hips. "Mr. Sanchez, your people put UniDis guests and employees in danger." She gestured around them. "Not to mention our lessee, Brawndo." She glared. "That doesn't just get brushed away."

"Employees? You mean your droids?" His expression soured.

She shook her head. "Yes, expensive ones. You know what androids and gynoids of this quality cost? Let alone cost to repair?" She pointed to the server that had waited on Jax, her arm dangling by a few fleshy milky-white bits of synth flesh. "You think Brawndo won't demand reimbursement?"

"Need I remind you, Ms. Erickson? Your park allowed a combat droid to set foot on the surface. One that clearly was unrestrained."

She stiffened and produced a tablet from somewhere inside her blazer. "According to my staff, the droid was issued a restraining bolt when the group reached the surface. How they bypassed it, I don't know."

Sanchez nodded. "Uh huh. And the ship they came in on?" He knew the answer. His techs aboard the *Curry* had hacked the park's network and been unable to find any evidence the smuggler and his group had ever arrived.

She blushed. "As I said, we're having trouble identifying those records."

One of Sanchez's agents approached. "Sorry, sir. No sign of them."

Sanchez turned to Erickson. "We'll need access to your security setup on the ground. We have the ident biometrics for the man we're looking for."

She sighed. "Dirt side security is up to our lessee.

Come with me. I'll connect you to the local Brawndo rep."

Sanchez shook his head and turned to his agent. "Murphy, go with her. I'll stay here and see if we can catch their scent. You're liaison."

"Yes, sir."

He looked around. "Houser. Get our wounded up to the *Curry*."

A man in a dark suit, his hair tied back in a ponytail, nodded. "Sir."

Nearly a kilometer away from the Stumbling Pony, and two from the hyperloop station Jax and the others were in, Baxter turned down an alley. He looked down at Rudy. "Suggestions?"

Rudy bobbed on his smart material rollerball. "You're lucky I'm charming and personable. That older R2 unit I was talking to earlier—the one you made fun of? Told me about the service tunnels the non-human cast members use. The UniDis folks apparently prefer their droids to be unseen when coming and going." He rolled off down the alley toward the back of a haberdashery. "He gave me a map."

"Why does it smell so bad?" Jax complained as the trio left the hyperloop station in the middle of Americana. On the way, Jax had read that the entire island theme park of America was designed around a country on Earth.

Naomi inhaled. "That's bad." She pointed to an informational sign explaining that Americana was set on Earth in the early twenty-first century, a place called the United States of America. "Do you think all of Earth smelled this bad, back then? Or just this America part?"

Clinton shuddered. "Probably. All that pollution and shit back then. They were hell bent on destroying the planet, not just one country. I mean they wouldn't make it smell bad if that wasn't how the whole place smelled." He inhaled, wrinkling his nose. "Right?"

They made their way to a vendor on the street corner. Unlike West World, Americana, or at least this part of it, was modeled after a thriving metropolis. Buildings hundreds of stories tall blocked the sky. Jax wondered what was in them as he looked up at the steel and glass towers.

A red-haired man with a chrome shovel strode toward a group of children. "Lo, my friends. I am Thur, son of Aladdin!" He twirled the shovel. "Founding member of the Avongers." The crowd oohed and aahed. The big man flexed his free arm.

Jax raised an eyebrow. "Avongers? This is like a weird knockoff land."

Another android, a large purple-skinned man with a bushy mustache and green trunks, joined the first. "Bulk, smash!" The kids and their adults were gushing.

Jax tore his gaze from the knockoff freakshow taking place across the street. "Let's find a map." He headed off down the street. Naomi fell in with him, then turned and grabbed Clinton's free hand, dragging him with her.

Behind them, a woman in a black leather suit that

looked impossible to move in, leaped from a nearby building, spun in the air, and landed next to the big purple guy.

A child shrieked. "Dark Spider is here!"

They reached an intersection full of park guests. Getting through would be impossible. "What's going on?" Naomi asked a man with his daughter perched on his shoulders. "The battle of New Jersey is about to start," the man explained.

Naomi turned to Jax and Clinton, shrugging. Something exploded overhead as a man armored in yellow with red accents roared overhead, followed by a man in all black with pointed ears, swinging on a monofilament line.

A large mechanical slug creature flew overhead, raining sweet smelling water down on the crowd below.

"That's just gross," Clinton complained, running a hand through his hair.

The superheroes from up the street surged into action, joined by a dozen other costumed and armored androids.

Jax shook his head. "Surprised UniDis is okay with these knockoffs."

The trio watched as superheroes battled with what the crowd claimed to be the Hellspot Club.

Off in the distance, Jax spotted the distinctive carbon fiber thread that reached into the sky vanishing into the clouds. He pointed. "There's the space elevator."

"That does not look close," Clinton complained.

Jax nodded. "Who thought theme parks should fill entire islands?"

Rudy and Baxter were making their way through one of the underground tunnels when someone shouted. "Hey! You two!"

The pair stopped. Rudy's head spun, his optic sensor focusing on a man, an android standing in a door they had passed a few meters back. "Yes?" he said.

The android motioned for them to come closer. "You're late. I've been expecting you."

Baxter turned. "You have us mistaken for other droids."

"You're either the new pair of entertainment, or you're trespassing down here." The android led them into what turned out to be a large repair bay. Several powered down droids, androids, and gynoids lined one wall. "This way."

This isn't good, Baxter beamed to Rudy, who raised one fist, bobbing it in his nodding gesture.

"You first, big guy," the android said. "Hop on up here." He pointed to a pedestal in the opposite corner of the room.

"What exactly are we doing?" Baxter asked, stepping up onto the pedestal. Several articulated arms descended from the ceiling.

"You two can't go out into the park looking like this." He gestured first to Rudy, then Baxter. "There's a specific paint job for droids in Space Land."

As one of the arms moved to Baxter's side and a line

filled with what looked like white paint connected to the spray head, he said, "What now?"

"It looks like they boarded the hyperloop for Americana," a freckle-faced security officer said, looking up at his two-levels-removed supervisor, the intimidating woman, and a tall red-haired man in a bespoke suit. The screen he was pointing to showed Jax, Clinton, and Naomi stepping into a hyperloop car.

The Brawndo office was in the space elevator hub building, deep underground. Erickson and Mduba looked at the screen, then each other.

The BioTek man tapped his earpiece. "Sir, they're in Americana. Took the hyperloop." He turned to Ms. Erickson. "You have a shuttle?" She nodded. "Sir, UniDis has a shuttle. Recommend we regroup here." He nodded. "Yes, sir." He pointed to the door of the small monitoring room. "Let's go." Erickson sighed and nodded, pulling her gPhone out of a pocket.

The shuttle trip to Americana, bypassing regular channels, was faster than any other option to get around. The UniDis inter-park shuttle landed atop one of the tall buildings that made up the New Jersey section of the island. The battle for New Jersey was just wrapping up when Jefferson Sanchez stepped off the shuttle's ramp with his remaining agents.

He still had seven agents left. The rest had been shut-tled back up to the *Curry* for medical treatment. Stepping out of the elevator that brought them to the ground level, he looked at Erickson. The matronly woman was frowning at him. When she said nothing, he said, "Where to?" She pointed toward the dispersing crowd and a pair of women in not-quite-as-bespoke-as-his suits. "BlasTech security?" She nodded.

She looked at Sanchez. "You're racking up quite the bill here, Mr. Sanchez. What'd these people do?"

Sanchez shrugged. "The shorter two, the white guy and Asian girl? Nothing, they're collateral damage. The tall one." He looked at her. "He stole corporate property. Incredibly valuable and dangerous property." He didn't feel the need to mention that the danger was to corporate profits.

"You're loss prevention?"

He nodded.

The BlasTech women arrived. "You the big cheese?" the darker skinned of the two asked. Her hair was pulled into a single small Afro-puff at the back of her head. She nodded to Erickson. "Janice."

The stout UniDis woman nodded. "Beatrice." She turned to the other woman. "Dora."

Sanchez said, "BioTek appreciates your help in this. Three criminals have entered your park."

The woman who had been silent up until now smiled. "We'll track 'em down." She winked at Erickson. "Unlike Brawndo, BlasTech takes park security seriously."

Her colleague nodded. "They made a mistake coming to our park."

The small group left the shadow of the building with

Stark written over the door and reached the intersection fanning out in each direction. Sanchez watched his people discreetly check faces as they moved through the crowd. The two BlasTech women did the same, the first using a tablet to scan through security feeds.

This was shaping up to be one of the strangest cases he had worked. Plenty of people had attempted to steal property, intellectual and otherwise, from BioTek over the years, but this one...A messenger, innocent—albeit clever and annoying—spacers, and a race across a quarter of the Empire, with orders to terminate with extreme prejudice. He shook his head. If he was ever allowed to write a memoir, it'd be a doozy. Even the little bits he shared with his family when he visited would be tough to explain to them, and they had enough security clearance that he could share all but the darkest secrets with them.

One of his people signaled. Over his commset, the woman said, "Sir, we might have a lead."

He nodded and headed in the woman's direction. Reaching her, he asked, "What have you got, Mduba?"

She pointed. "I spoke to a guest that mentioned seeing the messenger's case. She said she thought he and the other two went this way." She pointed.

Sanchez looked down the street, noticed the space elevator in the distance. "Yeah. They're trying to get off-world." He signaled the rest of his people and Miss Erickson.

To the two BlasTech women he said, "I'll send you their images. Can you filter your feeds?" The senior of the two, he now realized, nodded. He swiped on his gPhone and her tablet chimed.

In orbit, the *Osprey* drifted underneath a mid-sized personnel transport painted with "Star Quest Tours" on the side. Opposite the transport, a shuttle with the BioTek logo on its side drifted by.

This is not good, Skip thought. He had already moved the *Osprey* to another space elevator Lagrange point parking lot, hoping to avoid the big cruiser and its searching shuttles that arrived after them.

The cruiser had stayed put for a while, hacking what passed for security on the elevator hub station. Skip was embarrassed for whomever at UniDis was responsible for InfoSec. Whatever they found or didn't find apparently meant changing orbits and launching shuttles. *They must be looking for me. Glad I already scrubbed UniDis' records.*

Using his proximity to the Star Quest Tours ship, he wirelessly infiltrated the ship's systems and sent a message to Baxter and Rudy.

CHAPTER 13

"Okay, this can't be real," Jax said, stepping over the prone form of someone sleeping on the sidewalk. They had moved from whatever part of Americana had the monsters and heroes to someplace that looked more depressing and somehow smelled even worse.

Clinton shrugged, kicking a piece of something out of the way before him. "Earth in this era was a mess. Everywhere, not just what they called the United States. Pollution had the environment on the brink of collapse." He shuddered looking at a gelatinous puddle next to the sidewalk. "Why someone thought this era warranted an amusement park, is beyond me."

A half dozen small fliers shot overhead, the whine of grav-lifts barely drowning out the screams of excited children as they flew out over something that looked like a volcano in the middle of part of the city.

Jax watched the kids as they vanished around the volcano. "Why is there a volcano in the middle of the city? Weren't we just in New Jersey?" He looked off past the volcano to a hill with giant block letters reading OLLYWO D on the side.

Naomi looked behind them. "People just slept on the streets?"

Clinton nodded. "Guess so." He shrugged. "Not exactly my area of expertise."

"These BlasTech folks have a weird sense of what an amusement park is," Naomi said, looking around whatever OLLYWO D land was supposed to be. A tall cylindrical building had a roller coaster wrapped around it. At the top, the cars shot off the track and flew two blocks unassisted to reach a nearby building where they looped and banked their way to the ground.

"And what is?" Jax wondered, shaking his head as a set of roller coaster cars shot into the air. He looked around, spotting a man in black and purple leather with a bow and arrow, jumping from one rooftop to another, followed by a younger woman in all purple, also with a bow. "Who thought up this place?" He shook his head.

Naomi barked a clipped laugh. Jax and Clinton looked at her. She pointed down a street called Radium Drive. A block away, a bright gold droid was walking toward them, accompanied by a much larger blue and white droid.

"What the ..." Jax said.

"Are those your..." Clinton asked.

"I think so?" Jax answered.

"No way," Naomi said, barely containing her laughter.

The trio watched the droids approach. Jax whistled.

"Nice paint jobs. I didn't know you were thinking of changing things up."

"Shut up," Baxter grated.

"Seriously, Bax." Jax walked up to him, patting the combat droid's white with blue accented chest armor. "R2-D2 found the gym." He chuckled. "Swole."

"Are who dee what?" Clinton asked.

Jax's mouth fell open.

Naomi sighed, putting a hand across her face. "Oh no. Now we're gonna be stuck watching them all, now."

Rudy's optic sensor whirred. As his head moved, the chrome gold paint job reflected the sun into everyone's eyes. "We took the cast member tunnels and got...waylaid."

"Waylaid?" Clinton approached Baxter, peering at the blue and white paint job.

Rudy made an angry beep. "An android down there thought we were new cast members for the knockoff Star Wars land two islands west." He shifted, sending a beam of sunlight lancing into Jax's eyes.

Jax nodded, holding a hand up to his eyes. "I'm a little confused by your choices."

Baxter canted his head, red optic sensor swishing side to side. "The android in charge of paint jobs didn't seem to know which character was which."

Jax rocked back. "I don't.... mmmm..." He shook his head.

The sound of shouting interrupted him. All of them turned to see a crowd forming down the street to the left.

"What the hell now? The battle of Olly Wod?" Clinton asked, adding, "This place sucks."

They reached the crowd to see the tail end of the mugging, the muggers, and a pair of pale skinned androids. The would-be victim rolled away from a kick, producing a wicked looking handgun.

"A mugging?" Clinton asked. "This place is too much."

"They stage an hourly mugging?" Naomi threw her hands up. "This place is horrible."

"A weapons company is the sponsor of this part?" Clinton asked.

"So it seems." Jax shrugged.

"Time to go," Baxter said. "Three of the BioTek people from before just came around the corner up the block. They're with two women I do not recognize."

Jax swore. "You see Sanchez?"

The droid shook his head.

He motioned the others to fall in as he headed away from the oncoming BioTek agents. The thread of the space elevator was a few kilometers distant.

"We've got to get off the street," Naomi said. She pointed to a building that took up the next block. Hundreds of park guests were streaming in and out of it. It was painted red and blue.

Clinton looked over his shoulder and groaned. "We're never getting off this stupid planet. BioTek is gonna kill me."

The reached the building. Letters as tall as Baxter on the front proclaimed it to be CostClub.

Jax looked at him. "Would make my job easier."

Up in orbit, the *Osprey* used its maneuvering thrusters to slide out from under the Star Quest Tours transport.

Shit, Skip thought. The shuttles had eased up on their search. He thought they had given up. The cruiser was drifting around the other side of the space elevator hub nearest him.

As the *Osprey* slid around behind another transport, Skip activated the full stealth suite. *A little more distance would be nice.*

"Wait. Is this an amusement park ride or a shopping center?" Clinton looked around. They were inside a two-story tall building that occupied an entire block. Shelves filled the entire building.

Park guests milled up and down the aisle, apparently shopping. Several families were enjoying a meal in the corner of the building, a small snack bar.

Jax looked around. "I wonder if it was like this when the Delphinos came?"

Naomi shook her head. "This place is mind boggling."

Jax and Clinton nodded their agreement.

Baxter moved off down one of the aisles. Several children giggled and shrieked seeing the droid's paint job. Rudy rolled off in another direction.

"I think this is one giant ass gift shop," Naomi said.

Clinton watched the two droids disappear as they changed aisles at the halfway point. He looked at Jax. "So, uh. That was Baxter firing on the BioTek people back the bar in cowboy town, right?" The three of them were following the droids making their way deeper into the massive building.

Jax nodded without thinking about the question or its implication.

Naomi caught on faster, but the damage was done. Clinton continued, "How? He had, still has, a restraining bolt on him."

Jax slowed and looked up at him. "Oh. Uh..." He turned to Naomi, pulling an awkward face.

She rolled her eyes. "We'll talk about it when we're a little further from the bad guys." She raised an eyebrow. Clinton nodded.

Over their earpieces, Baxter said, "We're in the back room. There's no back door. They load in from a hatch in the roof."

Jax swore. Before he could say anything, Skip cut in on their shared comm channel. "Change of plans, Captain. The cruiser was getting too nosy. I ran out of places to hide. I'm on my way down."

"Down? Down here?" Jax said. "To the planet?"

Naomi tipped her head. "Your spatial awareness is impressive."

He made a face. "Only problem, Skip. We're in a huge gift shop. No back door."

Rudy cut in. "Your friend from the bar just came in. He's not alone."

"The roof," Naomi said.

Clinton looked at her. "What?"

"If they load in from up there, there's got to be a landing pad."

"For a starship?" Clinton moaned. "Unlikely."

"Skip can cover hover," Jax said. "Right?"

In Jax and Naomi's ears, Skip replied, "Of course."

"There is a lift back here. Rudy, you come back here. I'll cover," Baxter ordered.

Jax, Naomi, and Clinton rushed to the door to the back stockroom as quickly as possible.

There was a crackle from overhead speakers. "Ladies and gentlemen. Please proceed to the exit. This Cost-Club is closing. There is another on the corner of Wilshire and Beverly."

Jax looked up. "Damn. They know we're in here."

Guests began streaming toward the front of the building.

Rudy rolled up next to the trio of humans. "They don't sell knives here."

Clinton leaned forward. "Why would they? Why do you need knives?"

"Don't ask," Jax growled.

A scream pierced the short silence. Then another. Then the sound of blaster fire and a lot more screaming.

The overhead speaker crackled. "Attention, shoppers, please make your way to the front of the store, now. This is not a drill."

Jax pushed Naomi and Clinton forward, through the

door into the storeroom. "Let's go." He looked down at Rudy. "You know where the lift Baxter spotted is?"

Rudy made his nodding gesture with one hand as he zipped ahead of the group.

"Follow that droid," Jax urged. Under his breath he added, "Never vacationing without a sidearm again."

Out in the main shopping area, Baxter had wounded the younger of the two BlasTech women and two more of the BioTek agents. His white and blue paint job was flaking off as glancing blows struck his armor. His old chassis had held up incredibly well over the years of adventures with Jax, but the forge aboard the *Goliath* had restored him to nearly factory condition, including armor that was factory fresh. Baxter felt invincible.

He stepped out from cover, loosing two railgun rounds that found targets in the knees of two more BioTek agents.

In the back room, Jax was looking up at the ceiling of the cavernous mega mart nearly three stories overhead.

Rudy, Naomi, and Clinton had spread out to find the lift controls. As yet, none of them had found them.

"You know, it might be controlled by gPhone," Clinton offered.

"Not helpful," Jax quipped.

Outside, the sounds of combat were still echoing out in the main shopping area. Over Jax and Naomi's earpieces, Baxter was giving an all-too-excited-sounding play by play. Apparently the BlasTech people had called in reinforcements.

Skip added that he'd be overhead shortly and had

picked up a few assault shuttles from the corporate cruiser on his tail.

The door connecting the front of the store to the storeroom opened as Baxter backed in, his railguns and wrist blasters barking. Return fire struck the combat droid as often as it struck the wall or went through the door to strike the opposite wall.

"Jesus!" Naomi shouted as a bolt struck the wall just over her head.

"Got it!" Rudy shouted, rolling back into view. He held a tablet that might have seen better days a decade ago and now resembled a beaten-up piece of plastic covered in stickers that may or may not have been used to hold it together.

He passed the tablet to Jax but stopped, moving to hand it to Naomi. Jax made a face, but admitted she was the best one to handle the busted-up device. Even if it was locked, her interface skills would have it unlocked in a heartbeat.

He looked over to see her turn slightly from Clinton. The bio-circuitry tattoos in her arm and fingers, and one around her eye, pulsed with blue light as data moved along them.

Baxter didn't turn his head. "Anytime now." A blaster bolt struck his hip where the blue and white paint had already been burned off. Sparks erupted from the wound.

The cargo lift clanged to the ground. "All aboard!" Naomi shouted. Clinton and Jax scrambled on to the platform, pulling Rudy up.

"Come on, Bax!" Jax shouted.

Baxter continued backing toward the lift, a pronounced limp slowing him down.

Weapons fire flared through the doorway, driving everyone on the lift platform to drop into crouches.

"Go," Baxter said.

"Bax—" Jax started.

Baxter turned, his railgun pivoting, firing three rapid shots. "Don't worry, I am not dying to cover you."

With a thought, Naomi triggered the lift. With a groan, the ill-maintained piece of equipment rose.

Baxter turned, firing several shots from his forearm blasters before turning to the rising lift. As the lift moved over his head, he reached up, grabbing on. His railgun swung around and took aim. He looked up. "Does this go faster?" His railgun clacked, sending a slug into the cement near the door. Someone shouted as scalding hot cement chips erupted in every direction.

Over comms, Skip announced, "I do not see you on the roof."

"This isn't an express!" Naomi shouted over the sound of weapons fire and shouts.

Baxter had pulled himself up onto the rising platform. His railgun was folded back into the armor on his back, out of ammunition. He turned to Jax. "This is going well."

Above them, a loud roar preceded a shadow passing over the opening of the cargo lift.

The *Osprey* flared its lift engines as it slewed over the top of the CostClub. On the sensors, Skip saw BioTek assault shuttles descending toward them. *I miss running contraband,* the Sapient Intelligence thought to himself as he guided the small craft around over the top of the big building once more. One of the ventral cameras spotted the team on the slow-moving lift, just over halfway to the roof.

From the lift, Jax watched Sanchez walk into the storeroom accompanied by two women, one short and pale, the other much taller, her ebony skin and height a stark contrast to the other woman. The latter clearly knew her way around a blaster, as did the dozen or so men and women in suits similar to hers.

The lift platform was shaking and was appreciably warmer as it took repeated blaster bolts.

Overhead, the daylight shining through the lift opening was blotted out as the *Osprey* settled in directly over them. The portside cargo door slid open. The powerful cargo arm deployed, sliding out of the side of the ship. Once locked into position, a thick cable with a powerful magnetic claw at the end descended through the opening in the roof.

"Grab on," Baxter commanded as the claw came within reach. The lift platform rattled and something gave a metallic ping as it snapped. The platform ground to a halt, listing a few degrees as one part slowed to a stop first.

Jax helped Naomi up onto Baxter's shoulders as he pointed to the big bot's leg for Clinton. Grabbing Bax's other leg, he looked at Rudy, who latched each tiny metal hand onto Bax's knee joint.

"Up, up, and away!" Baxter shouted as the powerful winch aboard the *Osprey* activated. The group shot up out of the opening in the roof. In the distance, Jax spotted two large shuttles bearing down on their position. He lost sight of them as Baxter rotated on the cable.

The moment Baxter and his hangers-on cleared the cargo hold deck, the big bot kicked both legs, sending Rudy cartwheeling through the large opening into the hold. The powerful arm began to retract, pulling them all back into the cargo hold. As soon as there was deck below him, Baxter urged his human cargo to let go.

Jax hit the ground running, taking the steps of the spiral staircase toward the bridge two at a time.

From the overhead speaker, Skip said, "I suggest everyone grab a seat."

Rudy got himself upright and cast what passed for a glare at his larger friend. Wirelessly he sent, *I am not a football*, before he rolled to the staircase. In the open center was a column of variable gravity. Reaching it, he shot straight up.

Jax threw himself into his pilot's seat. The moment he landed, it turned and slid into position. Skip had everything ready for him. The tactical display showed the two inbound shuttles.

"Shields up."

"Done," the ship's SI confirmed.

The moment Jax's hands touched the flight controls, Skip released his control. Jax pushed the atmospheric throttle forward as he guided the *Osprey* up and away from the giant gift shop and Jefferson Sanchez and his friends. As they moved, a few stray blaster bolts struck the shields, doing absolutely nothing.

"Okay, this is gonna be bumpy. Hold onto something," Jax said.

Rudy popped up from the staircase, rolling to his station.

The first of the two assault shuttles was coming into range. Both had a speed advantage as the *Osprey* was still powering up her thrusters after coming to a stop over the massive CostClub.

The *Osprey* rocked as its shields flared, taking direct hits from the first shuttle as it flashed by overhead.

"Shields at ninety-three percent," Skip announced, then added, "Second shuttle incoming."

Jax slid the power lever for the lift engines forward as he yanked the flight control to the right. The *Osprey* banked hard over, threatening to flip over onto her back. The move startled the second shuttle enough that its shot went mostly wide.

"The first shuttle is almost done with its turn," Skip announced.

Naomi came up the stairs. "Trying to break my neck?" She made her way to her station, making sure to never leave both hands unattached to a handhold.

Over his shoulder, Jax snapped, "We can stand still and get blasted to atoms if that would be better."

Naomi didn't reply.

Jax angled the ship toward a piece of sky that was, for now, clear of assault shuttles, and pushed the throttle all the way forward. The *Osprey* roared as her engines built to full thrust. From down on the common deck, Clinton shouted something incoherent.

"We're being hailed," Skip announced.

"Of course, we are," Jax quipped. "Who is it?"

"The cruiser. ID'ed as the *Curry*," Skip answered.

"Ignore it."

On the tactical display, the two shuttles were burning hot on the *Osprey*'s tail. Occasionally, the small ship would rattle as a blaster bolt connected with their shields.

"We're sure I can't take them out?" Jax asked.

"Probably best if you don't. They may bring in the Imperial authorities," Naomi warned.

"This sucks," Jax said, pushing the controls over to send the *Osprey* into a spiral.

Down on the common deck, Baxter was standing in the middle of the lounge area. Clinton was clinging to the sofa as best he could. When the ship started spinning, he screamed.

Baxter turned his swishing optical sensor toward Clinton. "I could tie you down, if that would help."

Clinton looked up at him. "It would not!" The ship tilted, causing him to lurch. The rugged metal case clattered against his leg.

Jax watched the sky fade from blue to black as the *Osprey* crawled out of the atmosphere. The two assault shuttles were still doggedly on their tail, nipping at them when they could.

"Shields at eighty-five percent," Skip announced.

"The cruiser is moving in on an intercept course," Rudy announced.

Jax clenched his teeth. The *Osprey* wasn't a warship. She wasn't even really designed for fighting. The Valerian Co-op Infiltrator was a fast scout, meant to sneak in and out of places, nothing more.

Jax's parents had installed a few after-market offensive systems, like the particle beam cannon mounted under the ship, but it had a limited firing arc and was only useful when charging toward an enemy head on.

The *Osprey*'s missiles were both offensive and defensive, depending on configuration, but even then, the ship carried only twenty of the small missiles. Everything else was either countermeasure or anti-personnel.

Jax checked the tactical display, seeing the two red triangles behind him and the larger red triangle burning for all it was worth to cut him off. He made a decision.

"Jax, is that a good idea?" Skip asked.

"No choice," Jax retorted, as he finished bringing the weapons systems online. He tapped a few configuration options for the missiles stored in launchers along the *Osprey*'s dorsal section. He double checked the settings, then flipped the cover on the launch button on his flight control stick.

"Ten away," Skip announced.

Rudy's optical sensor turned to look at Naomi, who looked across the bridge to the squat navigation droid.

All ten missiles streaked away from the *Osprey*, their

small motors powering them to speeds far beyond what the nimble infiltrator could manage. The missiles closed the gap between the *Osprey* and the *Curry*.

"Jax?" Naomi said.

"Trust me." He grinned even though she couldn't see it.

Once the *Osprey* cleared the moon's atmosphere, her true speed was evident. The two assault shuttles fell behind quickly, eventually falling off the tactical display.

Ahead of the *Osprey*, the *Curry* was twisting at full burn attempting to avoid the ten small, but deadly, missiles that were bearing down on her. The wild maneuvers had cost the larger ship, her course no longer intercepting the *Osprey*.

The *Curry* deployed point defenses that Jax was pretty sure weren't allowed on corporate owned vessels. Two of the missiles fell to point defenses. Then two more fell. The remaining six missiles closed the gap before being taken out, but instead of exploding against the *Curry*'s shields, they exploded two seconds before impact. The explosions bathed the larger ship in numerous types of radiation and exotic energy. The normally invisible energy barrier that protected ships, rippled and pulsed, flaring orange and yellow.

While that was happening, and the larger ship was blinded on several spectrums, the *Osprey* opened a wormhole and vanished.

CHAPTER 14

While it was safer to keep moving as far and as fast as possible, not having a destination made that course of action less useful. For all Jax knew, they could end up on the opposite side of the Empire as their goal, whatever that ended up being.

An hour after leaving UniDis Four, Jax brought the *Osprey* out of its wormhole, changed direction, and entered another wormhole for an hour. He did that twice more before cutting thrust. As far as Rudy could tell, they were exactly...nowhere.

No one had the energy to talk or do anything outside of shower and crash. They made Clinton go last since with his messenger case attached to his wrist, his showers took longer than anyone else's.

Baxter and Rudy retreated to engineering where they could work on the former's damaged hip armor. They also worked on scraping their temporary paint jobs off.

The next morning, Jax pulled on a clean shirt and pair of cargo pants, the type he had ten pairs of and wore more often than not. He walked to the lounge area of the common deck. He flipped the switch on the coffee maker and leaned against the counter while the machine beeped and burbled.

Naomi exited the short hallway that led to the crew berths. "Hey."

He nodded. "So, look."

"Before coffee? Really?" She dropped into one of the chairs around the small cafe table that served as the dining table. Jax nodded once.

Neither said a word, listening to the coffee maker work its magic.

Finally, Jax joined her at the table, two steaming mugs in his hands.

"So," she said before taking a sip.

He took his own sip, then said, "Kinda back to square one."

She made a noise Jax hadn't heard before. "Clearly your 'sell him back to BioTek' idea didn't pan out."

"That's not fair. I wasn't trying to sell him to anyone. That Sanchez dickhead lied to me. He swore they had no interest in Clint, just the case. Said—repeatedly, I should add—that they could get it off him, and we could go on our way."

"With a reward," she said, voice flat.

Jax sighed. "Yeah, would getting him free of the case, and getting a reward while we're at it, be so bad? You think it's not costing us hard credits running all over the Empire? That hacking into the next Imperial dock we visit to make sure to scrub any 'Be on the lookouts' for us is easy, or without risk? Why is getting paid so bad?"

"You're awfully gullible, you know."

"No. I'm...I dunno. A capitalist? Opportunist?" He rubbed his face. "Over my head."

Naomi took a sip of her coffee, leaving the mug against her lips while she thought. Lowering the mug she said, "Accurate." Shrugging, she added, "So what now?"

Jax took another sip. "Well, obviously, fuck BioTek." Both chuckled.

Naomi said, "So then what?" She cocked her head. "He's still got that case strapped to him. BioTek still wants him and clearly is willing to pull out all the stops."

Jax nodded. "What about your, you know?" He wiggled the fingers of his free hand in what had become his universal symbol for her using-your-embedded-bio-circuitry-to-hack-anything-with-a-computer-core ability.

She shook her head. "I don't think so. Normally I can feel, even at a bit of a distance, if there's anything I can access in something." She waved to the ship surrounding them. "Can feel every nook and cranny of the *Osprey*. But his case? Nothing."

He sighed. "You tried?"

She shook her head. "Directly, no. I was hoping to not add to the list of people who know about that." She cut Jax off. "But I can." He nodded. She changed topics. "You said he didn't want to involve the Imperials. Think that's still on the table?"

He shrugged. "Probably more so. UniDis and their clients have gotta be screaming bloody murder, all the damage we caused getting out of there."

She smiled. "Yeah, BioTek is spending a lot on this."

He nodded his agreement. She went on, "What the hell is in that case of his?"

Jax shook his head. "Secret to life and the universe?"

She stared at him over the top of her cup. "Cute."

Ten long and annoying hours after the still unidentified Valerian Co-op Infiltrator blasted its way out of the UniDis system, Jefferson Sanchez was watching the *Curry* pull out of orbit.

The damage to the massive gift shop in Americana had been significant. Added to the damage in West World, plus the service charges, labor fees, and dozens of other line items that all blurred together, the bill presented by Ms. Erickson before allowing him to leave the moon was more than several years of his salary.

On top of that, the missile stunt the small ship had used to cover its escape had caused minor damage to several of the *Curry*'s sensor systems, requiring diagnostics and repairs.

Conference Room 1 aboard the *Curry* was a hive of activity. Sanchez was seated at the head of the table while a mix of ship's crew and his own loss prevention agents bustled back and forth; tablets littered the table and were swapped between eager hands as people held dozens of conversations at once.

The chime sounded, and a section of the wall display activated, the face of Captain Ivano looking as uncomfortable as Sanchez had ever seen her. "Incoming call. Priority one from corporate."

Sanchez exhaled. He nodded to the screen, then turned to everyone in the room. "Give me the room." Captain Ivano watched from the wall screen.

When the last staffer exited and the red outline activated around the closed hatch, Captain Ivano nodded. "Good luck," she whispered before her face disappeared.

The wraparound view screens became a large, opaque display. A grid of twelve faces appeared. The stern visage of the chairwoman met Sanchez's eye. She scowled. "Well, Sanchez. You seem to have fucked this up something fierce."

A middle-aged man nodded. In a voice like gravel, he added, "The UniDis people are rightfully pissed. Even after we paid that outrageous bill."

An Asian man with old-fashioned glasses said, "Safe to assume, the messenger escaped."

Sanchez nodded slowly. "I'm afraid so. The accomplices seem to have more skill than I originally gave them credit for. Oh, and they have a combat droid."

"You have the full weight and power of BioTek at your disposal. Should we send you a combat droid too?" the chairwoman snapped, her eyes nearly closed, her glare so intense.

"No, ma'am," Sanchez answered.

A pale-skinned woman in the lower right asked, "Can we assume you have a plan?"

He nodded.

Another head in another square said, "Perhaps we should bring in the Imperials?"

The chairwoman nodded slowly. "Before we do that, I'd like to hear what Mr. Sanchez has planned." She canted her head. "Maybe he can regain some of the respect we had for him." Her look made it clear that she did not find that to be a likely outcome.

Jefferson took a deep breath. He had been thinking of his next move since boarding the assault shuttle to return to the *Curry*. After a slow, calming breath, he said, "We've already got the messenger's biometrics. Thanks to UniDis, we've got the biometrics for the other two as well. We're running them now through our systems, as well as those we have back doors into."

The Asian man from before said, "And if they're not in ours or any other systems? We know for certain the messenger isn't. Even with his organization burning him, his records were permanently deleted years ago."

Jefferson nodded. "Even if they're not, we'll leave their biometrics tied to a worm. They show up on any sensor or camera we have access to, and we'll know."

One of the chairs, a woman with olive skin that made her blue eyes stand out, said, "That's a solid plan, Mr. Sanchez." She inclined her head.

The chairwoman nodded. "Agreed. For now, you still have our support. Bring this whole thing to a close, Mr. Sanchez. Sooner rather than later." She smiled the most unfriendly smile Jefferson had ever seen. "While I'm sure it goes without saying, I'm going to say it. Failure here will have negative impacts on your employment with BioTek."

Jefferson inhaled. He opened his mouth, but the squares of faces blinked out in rapid succession.

He slammed a hand on the conference table. "Damnit."

Clinton entered the lounge area to see Jax and Naomi at the small cafe table. The pair looked up.

Jax nodded toward the kitchenette. "Coffee's hot."

"Smells good," the tall messenger said. He moved toward the coffee machine, grabbing a mug from the cupboard above it.

After pouring a cup, he sat down. The table had four chairs, despite being barely big enough for two people. When neither of his hosts said anything, he said, "So, yesterday was fun."

Naomi couldn't keep the laugh from escaping. She looked down at the case he was cradling in his lap. She glanced at Jax, who nodded, taking a sip of his coffee.

Clinton caught the look. "What? You two are freaking me out."

Naomi put her hand on his arm. "Don't freak out." Her bio-circuits in that hand lit up, slowly pulsing before the pale blue traces vanished into the sleeve of her shirt.

"What the hell?" Clinton jerked his arm away, sloshing coffee all over himself, eliciting a strangled scream as the scalding liquid splashed across his chest and lap. He moved to stand, which would have sent his chair clattering behind him, except that it was magnetically attached to the deck, so instead he pitched forward then twisted, falling to the side.

Jax watched the whole thing, then looked at Naomi. "Okay, that was worth being here to see." He stood up and made for the stairs, heading up to the bridge. "I'll give you two some privacy.

Naomi leaned around the table to look at Clinton, still on the deck. "Need any—"

"Nope!" he shouted. "No, thank you." He groaned, rolling over to get back to his feet. "I hear having children is overrated." He looked at Naomi. "What was that?"

Naomi smiled. "Long story." She nodded to his right arm and the case dangling from his wrist. "Longer shot, but may I?" She pointed back to the table.

The two sat down, Clinton placing the case in the center of the table. He looked at the case, then Naomi. "So..."

She ignored him, placing both hands on the case. The bio-circuit tattoos on both hands and arms lit up, pulsing with blue light. The faint line along her neck and cheeks and around her eyes began to glow as well.

"Woah," Clinton whispered.

Naomi shushed him. With closed eyes, she probed the case. It was like she had told Jax. The case was so well shielded that even touching it, she couldn't sense a single control circuit. She'd never encountered anything like this. Clearly the case was electronic; there was a display, and she spied the indentation on the lid where a gPhone would be placed to sync it with the case.

Her tattoo circuitry glowed brighter. Normally it took little effort to penetrate the control circuitry. This was different, as if the case were designed almost to thwart an Interface specifically.

She released an explosive breath. "Shit."

Clinton squinted at her. "What the hell?"

She looked at the case. "What's in there? It's like the case was made explicitly to keep people like me out."

Clinton leaned forward. "Asian?"

"What? No." She frowned then sighed. "I'm an Interface. Long story short, the emperor nabbed a bunch of kids and embedded advanced bio-circuitry and organic storage modules in us so that we could fight the independents and their droids."

Clinton's eyes were saucers. "What?"

Naomi waved a hand. "Not important. Normally I can hack any computerized system just by touching it." She tapped a finger on the case. "This...no."

Under his breath, Clinton said, "The other thing seems pretty important." He met Naomi's gaze. "So... square one?"

She nodded.

Jax came back downstairs.

Naomi looked at him. "Were you just waiting up there until we were done?"

Jax reached the common deck. "What? No, I just had Skip listen and let me know."

Naomi glared at him, then turned her glare upward.

The overhead speaker said, "Sorry."

Jax waved his hands to stop further discussion. "I think we should head for ParStor. Specifically, their station in the Liverpool system."

"What?" Clinton asked.

"Why?" Naomi added.

Jax held up a finger. "One, they're close by. Ish. About nine hours away." He held up another finger. "Two, I've got a friend there we can talk to."

"Friend?" Naomi probed.

"Well, more of an acquaintance."

"An acquaintance?" Clinton repeated.

Jax exhaled. "Okay, fine. He's a fence I've worked with a few times."

"There it is," Skip offered.

Naomi nodded and looked at Clinton. "That makes more sense."

Jax glared at the ceiling. "Traitor. Get us a course and get us moving."

"Copy that," the ceiling speaker replied.

Jax tapped his chin. "You know." He grinned. "There's not enough time for the whole run, but we could make a dent." He moved to the sofa.

"For what?" Clinton asked.

"Oh no," Naomi groaned.

"I'm thinking we do the first reboot, then the second, more recent one." He fetched the tablet from the coffee table, pulling up the ship's entertainment library. He looked at Naomi, then Clinton. "Any objections?"

"What's happening?" Clinton asked.

Naomi refilled her coffee. "Who knows. Some old ass show from a long, long time ago. Want a new coffee?"

"Yeah, I guess so?"

She nodded.

Jax finished tapping on the tablet. "You enjoyed *The West Wing*, and you know it." The wall-mounted display came to life with dramatic music.

"I'll make something to eat," Jax offered as *Lost in Space* faded from the screen.

Clinton looked over the back of the sofa. "How old is this show?"

Jax looked over his shoulder as he closed the refrigerator. "Pre-wormhole."

"Jeez," Clinton said. "How much space does this junk take up?"

"You do not want to know," Skip said from the ceiling.

"I'm surrounded by...by, I dunno, people who hate good things."

PART 3

Somewhere around the middle of season four of the first reboot of *Lost in Space,* Rudy rolled back away from Baxter, now back to matte black. White and blue paint chips littered the ground. Since they were alone in the cargo hold, he spoke out loud. "There you go."

Baxter examined each arm, then twisted to get a look at as much of himself as he could. He turned to present his backside to Rudy. "You missed a spot."

The small nav droid made a metallic gurgle. "Fine." He grabbed the wire brush and set to work. "You know. This is the first time he's acted so... so..."

"Un-Jax-like?" Baxter offered.

The big bot couldn't see his one-handed nod, so Rudy said. "Yeah." He scrubbed a tough to reach spot on Baxter's upper left leg. "You think he's okay?"

"I think he's growing up," Baxter said.

From the ceiling, Skip said, "They all do that, eventually."

"He's almost thirty. I'd have thought it would have

happened sooner," Rudy said, then added, "Stop wiggling."

There was a pause, then the ship's SI said, "Don't worry, though."

The speaker crackled as Skip piped in Jax's voice from the common deck: "No, that's Judy, she's their half sister. Her dad was the guy from the last episode. How can you not remember that?"

Clinton's voice said, "And why are they keeping that evil woman around?"

"Dr. Smith. She's integral to the story. But more than that, the original show had a Dr. Smith, so this one needed one."

"Why?"

Naomi cut in. "If you keep asking questions, he'll keep talking."

The speaker fell silent, Skip's point made.

"Fair point," Rudy said. He rolled back in front of Baxter, holding the wire brush up and out. "Your turn."

Baxter rumbled, taking the brush. "At least you're small." He squatted down and began removing the chrome gold paint from Rudy's frame.

Upstairs on the common deck, Jax was finishing up his explanation of the original TV show *Lost in Space* and its status as a cult classic among a certain group of aficionados like himself.

Clinton nodded. "Okay, okay, cool." He pointed to the wall display. "And who's that again?"

Jax made an unexpected and disturbing noise. "That's still Don West!"

The video stopped playing. The ceiling announced,

"Captain, you have a call coming in from ParStor Station Mort 3."

Jax looked at the screen, then the ceiling. "Okay." He pulled his gPhone out, tapped a few times on the screen. He swiped toward Clinton. "Here, read up." He headed for the stairs to the bridge.

Clinton looked at his phone, his eyes going wide. He looked at Naomi. "This is twenty-eight pages."

She stood up. "Told you not to open the door. I'm going to bed."

ParStor Station Mort 3 orbited a gas giant in the Liverpool system. The massive planet had eleven moons, three of which were in the final stages of their decades-long terraforming. ParStor was a small pre-Imperial co-op that bet everything they had on those three moons.

The station itself was a sphere a half-kilometer in diameter with a ring around its equator that housed cargo and docking facilities. It had been in the system for fifty years already, built to oversee the terraforming effort that would take nearly forty years to be complete enough to plant Earth-based flora and fauna.

Now that the terraforming was in its final phase, the station was a hive of activity as teams moved between the moons and the station, setting up monitoring outposts and initial seeding operations. Homesteaders that had been waiting in the wings were descending on the station in larger and larger numbers to make sure they got their plot.

"How do you know someone here?" Clinton asked. He was leaning on Naomi's bridge station, cradling his messenger case.

Jax turned in his seat. "I used to run goods through here."

"Goods?" Naomi questioned.

"Contraband," Jax admitted. He continued, "This place is a great stopover on the way to more interesting places. Several different smuggling groups have set up routes through here over the years. I'm assuming once these moons are more settled and the Empire decides to care, that'll dry up."

Clinton said, "What made you stop? Smuggling, I mean."

Jax chuckled. "I didn't. I just found better gigs that didn't need me to come out here."

Naomi raised an eyebrow, making a noise. "How much did you screw your contact out of?"

Jax shrugged. "Not sure." He turned to face forward again. "I'm sure he's over it. It definitely wasn't, like, a lot."

"We are being hailed," Skip announced.

The ceiling beeped. "*As-salamu alaykum.* Welcome to ParStor Station Mort 3," a feminine voice greeted them. "Need docking clearance?"

"Sure do." Jax put as much smile in his voice as he could.

The docking and cargo ring was forty meters tall and a hundred wide. It was connected to the spherical station by four thick struts. Open docking and cargo bays shined brightly all along the ring.

"Of course. Please wait one," the space control operator said.

Jax reached over and tapped the mute icon on the communications panel. "When we dock, I'll reach out to my contact."

Before Naomi or Clinton could reply, the speaker crackled. "Inbound craft, you're assigned docking bay 94."

"Awesome, thanks so much," Jax replied. The comm panel display lit up with the docking fees and flight path details. He accepted both, grimacing at the former. The latter was sent to Rudy's station.

"Flight path received. Updating your station," he reported.

The main flight control display updated with their prescribed path around the station to their assigned docking bay. Number 94 was almost halfway around the ring from their current position.

The *Osprey* made a graceful arc around the station to docking bay 94. The bay was on the lower edge of the massive ring. The bays that dotted the ring were all open to space, relying solely on static atmosphere barriers to keep the atmosphere in and space out. That meant all of them were a bit chilly. Static atmosphere barriers were great at keeping the atmosphere contained but did nothing for heat.

The *Osprey* slid through the barrier, the blue light that marked its boundary playing over the hull.

Jax met Naomi and Clinton in the cargo hold after

putting the ship's systems into standby. He looked at the pair, noticing a weird metal contraption around Clinton's messenger case. He nodded toward it. "What the hell is that?"

Naomi grinned. "It occurred to me that even though I can't sense anything, maybe this thing is emitting a signal of some type. That's how they keep finding us. I had Skip fab up a faraday cage."

"Looks like shit," Jax said. "It works?"

Naomi frowned. "Well, I'm not sure, but probably worth the risk."

"It's heavy too, if anyone cares," Clinton offered. Jax and Naomi both looked at him, expressions flat. "Okay, so no. No one cares."

Jax looked at the ceiling. "You three behave while we're gone." He turned to Clinton. "My friend isn't fond of parties, so it's just you and me."

The messenger nodded.

From the hatch to engineering at the rear of the cargo hold, Baxter said, "I'll cancel the rave."

Rudy made a clicking noise. "Naomi and I have an errand to run."

Jax looked at the bot, then Naomi, who shrugged. He said, "Okay, I guess. Be careful. This is isn't an indie station. Droids aren't common and likely aren't much tolerated." Naomi nodded as Rudy made his fist bobbing gesture. He looked at Baxter. "Guess it's just you and Skip."

"Okay, let's go." Jax led the others down the stairs into the small boarding vestibule as the ramp lowered, unfolding as it did. With a clang of metal on metal, the ramp fully deployed.

Stepping off the ramp, Jax looked at Clinton. "Come on club...club hand."

"Clever," the taller man quipped.

The four of them walked out of the docking bay. Jax lingered by the hatch, securing it with a code he stored on his gPhone. He looked at Naomi. "Be careful. This place is corporate, but there are still some dark corners."

"She has me," Rudy said.

Jax looked at his little friend, then Naomi. "Like I said."

Rudy rolled off down the corridor, mumbling at a volume that would be considered under his breath if he breathed.

Jax pointed the opposite way. "We'll go this way. Min's place is closer to spoke 2." Clinton nodded and followed him.

Naomi caught up to Rudy as the small droid reached the lobby space that fed into the spoke. The spoke was about five meters in diameter and consisted of a narrow walkway for people and a wider corridor for moving cargo. The personnel walkway was above the cargo corridor. Each lobby was an open space the height of the ring, with ramps and stairs that led to the central space and the opening of the spoke.

Once they had negotiated the ramps and levels to get

to the personnel corridor, Naomi looked down. "So, what's our errand?" Since she had no other plans, she'd gone along with the small droid out of curiosity. Jax and Clinton would be busy for who knew how long, so why not see where this little adventure took her?

While rolling, Rudy's head made a full rotation, taking in their surroundings. "I want to be more useful."

That wasn't what Naomi expected to hear, and she stopped short, forcing the man behind her to dodge and lob several colorful expletives at her. Rudy made a series of beeps, and she continued after him. "What do you mean, more useful?"

One of the compartments on Rudy's side opened. Naomi was pretty sure it was one of the ones that usually held a kitchen knife, like the one on the opposite side of his cylindrical body. This one was empty.

"You need new knives?"

While nodding was a gesture he could not make, shaking his head was easy. He shook his head, no. "No... well, yes, but I don't want them stored in compartments."

Thoroughly confused, Naomi gestured to a side corridor as they exited the spoke into the station proper. "I don't follow."

Rudy beeped his agitation. "Jax doesn't like me carrying the knives." Naomi nodded, having witnessed more than one argument between the two about Rudy's new affection for blades. "I want an upgrade to install blades into my forearms."

She stared at him.

"They'd be harder to detect if integrated into my

systems. Remember last time on Aswan? The customs guy took the knives from me. It was embarrassing."

Naomi sighed. It was embarrassing for sure. She remembered the scene the small droid caused and the only-a-bit-smaller scene Jax had caused, scolding the little nav droid.

This was new ground for her. She considered droids to be their own beings but had never had to deal with artificial insecurities.

She looked around, spotting a directory. "Okay, come on, then." Rudy followed, making a distinctly happier-sounding beep.

She ran a finger along the display, looking at the various businesses. "So, why do you need me? I mean, couldn't you just order the upgrades on Kelso?"

The droid made another series of noises. "I need money."

She stopped her search, looking down. "Don't you have access to Jax's accounts?"

Another series of noises, ruder sounding this time. "How much do you think he has?"

She groaned. "I should want to know, but I know that knowing will fill me with rage."

Rudy made his hand bobbing nod gesture. "It will."

Naomi nodded. "Okay, so you need me to pay to install blades in your arms, check. Weird, but sure, pal." She smiled and turned her attention back to the directory. Imperial stations—Imperial space in general—weren't welcoming places for droids, but it looked like ParStor Station Mort 3 had at least two private engineering firms in the common marketplace that, based on the icon next to the name, worked with droids. She picked the one that sounded the least sketchy and said, "Okay, little man, let's go."

Clinton followed Jax out of the personnel walkway of spoke 2 into an industrial sector of the massive spherical station. The corridors were tall and wide; powered load lifters and forklifts were moving cargo and other things around.

"Your friend—" Clinton started.

"Not really a friend," Jax interrupted.

"Whatever he is. His office is here in the industrial sector?"

"Not really an office, per se..." Jax stopped to get his bearings. It had been several years since he was last on this station.

They turned and walked for a while until Jax stopped at a door without any type of sign or placard indicating what lay behind it. He knocked.

When no one answered, Clinton asked, "You're sure he's home?"

Jax shrugged. "He said he would be?" He knocked again, adding a little more force.

Clinton leaned against the wall cradling his messenger case and its new faraday cage against his hip. "Christ, this thing is heavy."

Jax glanced at him and the contraption that may or may not have been keeping that dickhead Sanchez and

BioTek from tracking them. He wasn't convinced that was how BioTek kept showing up, but whatever.

The door slid open, stopping after it had exposed an inch of darkness. "What?" the person inside demanded.

"Dude, cut the crap. You know it's me. We spoke earlier," Jax growled.

The door slid the rest of the way open, exposing a middle-aged Chinese man in a dingy white tank top and floral print shorts. He was barefoot. "Come in."

Jax looked at Clinton and then followed the man inside.

The door slid shut behind Clinton, and after his eyes adjusted, he saw they were in a small cargo hold, likely meant to be personal or small business storage. In this case, it appeared to be a combination of studio apartment and workspace. In the corner behind a wood and paper divider, he was pretty sure was a portable toilet.

Min Chu had lived on ParStor Station Mort 3 for almost fifteen years. He started with a legitimate job as a shift foreman for one of the teams maintaining the terraforming equipment down on the moons below. He started his smuggling career by importing stuff that the ParStor Co-op routinely deprioritized on their supply shipments, mostly entertainment vids and books, usually of the adult variety. Then it was foodstuffs and other bigger ticket, harder-to-get-in items. Eventually, a regional arm of one of the crime syndicates noticed and made him an offer.

That was how Jax met him. The latter had been running cargo for various groups, coming through Mort from time to time, either dropping off or picking up. Most of the time he dealt with Min. When he decided to stop working the route, he did what he usually did: just didn't take the next job. The only problem had been that it was a drop-off, and he already had the material in his hold.

"You know, when you called, I kinda thought it was to apologize and make good on screwing me," Min said as he moved further into the small space.

"Oh, uh..." Jax stammered. "I just kinda assumed you'd be over that." Min turned, glaring. Jax added, "I heard you moved into doing tech stuff for the syndicates and station low-lives. Out of shipping and stuff."

Behind Jax, Clinton moaned. "This feels unsafe."

Min turned, grabbing a piece of equipment that looked like it would hurt if struck with. He came up to Jax, poking him in the chest with his free hand. "You know what?" He was glaring. Jax was holding his breath, hands balled into fists. Clinton took a step back, moving his faraday-cage-enclosed case protectively in front of his chest.

Min took a breath. "It's fine. Water under the bridge and all that. I've been practicing stoicism for the last few years. Being mad about the past isn't worth the energy." He grinned and turned toward a low workbench. "So, what ya got?" He pointed to the bench.

The sudden change in direction caught Jax off guard. He turned to Clinton and tilted his head toward the pot-bellied Asian man. "Well?"

"Oh," Clinton exclaimed. He slammed his case, faraday cage and all, on the workbench.

Min looked at it, then Clinton. "What the fuck is this?"

"Faraday cage?" Jax said. It was partially a question.

Min sighed. "I see that, you goober. But for what?" He looked up at Clinton. "What's the deal, Beanpole?"

After Clinton gave the man a hideously shortened history of messengers and how their cases worked, with Jax adding color commentary about the current situation, Min shrugged. "Well, that's above my pay grade." He held up a finger to stop Jax's reply short. "But I know someone." He turned and looked around until he found a gPhone on the workbench under a take-out container. He made a call, having a short conversation. He looked at his guests. "She'll be right over."

Jax shook his head. "I dunno, Min. We're trying to keep this on the down low."

Min waved the concern away. "It's fine. She's great. Much smarter than me." He held up a finger. "Plus, she's on her way already."

Clinton groaned. "Definitely feeling less safe than advertised."

CHAPTER 16

Min Chu's friend turned out to be a young woman in dark red coveralls, every pocket filled with tools and other gadgets. Her head was covered in a pale-yellow head scarf embroidered with intricate patterns. She raised a pair of goggles with all sorts of wires attached to bits of tech on the frames, placing them up on her forehead. "Okay, this is awesome."

The faraday cage was lying off to the side of the workbench. The young woman, Azadeh, had determined that there weren't any signals coming from the case.

That fact only made Jax more curious as to how Sanchez and his BioTek goons were tracking them.

She looked at Min and Jax, then pointed at Clinton. "He's a messenger. This is his messenger case."

Clinton and Jax nodded.

Min looked at them. "Is it dangerous?"

Azadeh looked at Min, sighing. "It's a case, you dummy, not a bomb." She put her hand on the case. "If I can get it off him, can I keep it?"

Jax looked at Clinton, eyebrows raised. The taller man shrugged. "I don't want it."

Before the young woman could let fly a whoop, he added, "We need the contents, though."

Azadeh looked at him. "Contents? Oh." She looked down at the case, her hand still caressing it. "I don't care what's in it."

Jax laughed. "Then it's all yours—if you can get it off him and open."

She got to work. Several times she produced a tool that made Clinton yelp in surprise.

Jax pulled Min aside. "Look, man. Whatever is in there, BioTek wants it. Like, really, really wants it. We need to find a buyer. Think you can facilitate that?"

Min rubbed his days-old stubble-covered chin. "Possibly. What's in it?"

Jax ran both hands over his head. "Well. We're not sure."

The other man angled his head. "Oh...what? How do you not know?"

Jax shrugged. "Dude, this whole thing is weird. We found Beanpole and his weird lunch box, and Naomi insisted we help him. I've never heard of these messengers before; they all carry those cases, I guess." He looked over to where Clinton was squeezing his eyes closed while Azadeh used a tool he couldn't identify on the thick flexible metal leash connecting Clinton to the messenger case.

"Kinda hard to sell something when I don't know what it is," Min protested.

Jax inclined his head. "I know. But still, can you see

who's around that might at least be interested?"

"I'll make a few calls." He pointed. "You stay over there." Jax made a face and joined Clinton while Azadeh worked. Min moved to the far corner of the space, his phone inches from his face.

"Why did you pick this place?" Rudy asked when they arrived outside Al's Engineering. He turned to Naomi. "Was Steve's Scary Bot Chop Shop closed?"

Naomi glared. "This a hill you wanna die on, Tiny?"

Rudy rolled forward and pushed the announcer button next to the door. He turned. "They have good reviews?"

She planted a hand on her hip. "Do I look like Yelp? You want this or not?"

The door slid open and someone inside shouted. "Come on in!"

The pair moved inside the dimly lit workshop.

Once her eyes adjusted, Naomi saw that the space they were in was only generously a workshop. A mix of droid parts and other bits of technology hung along all four walls and in baskets suspended from the ceiling. A half-assembled protocol droid was on a work table.

The pale-skinned technician looked like he hadn't been off the station in, probably ever. He gestured to the table. "Don't mind her. Repair job."

"Uh huh," Naomi said absently, looking around the room at the myriad parts and wondering how this weird ghost-pale man had come by so many droid parts on a station that shouldn't be that droid-friendly. In fact, she could only remember seeing two others on the way to the workshop.

"So, I'm Jacob." He offered a grease-covered hand.

Naomi made a face as she shook his hand. "I'm Naomi; this is Rudy. He's looking for an upgrade."

"Where's Al?" Rudy asked.

Jacob waved a hand. "Hell if I know. I bought this place from a guy named Mohammed."

Rudy beeped. "Did he buy it from Al?"

The scraggly technician canted his head. "I...I don't know. Is that important?"

Rudy turned to Naomi. "I don't like this."

She made a face, unsure what the small droid's problem was. "You're being weird."

Jacob turned to Rudy. "Anyhow...What ya looking for, Little Buddy?" He leaned down to inspect Rudy. He poked the little droid here and there, examining his arms, his rollerball joint, and parts of Rudy that would make a human blush.

Rudy chirped and beeped. "I want some offensive weaponry."

The greasy technician clucked as he stood up. "Cool, man. Like what? Rocket launchers? Flame throwers?"

Naomi tipped her head. "Where would you even put those? No, he wants blades."

"Blades?" Jacob looked down at Rudy, bobbing on his smart material rollerball. "Kinda pedestrian, but sure, we can do something." He motioned to an empty work table. "Let's get you up there."

"They need to be undetectable, part of my arm structure," Rudy said. The table lowered so that he could lift himself onto it. "But effective. Sharp. Oh, and detachable, in case I need to throw them."

Naomi's eyes bulged. "You are a dark little droid."

Ignoring her, Jacob nodded as he rubbed his chin. "Like a ninja. Cool, man, I get it." He moved around the table. "Okay, so you'll need new arm assemblies. Your existing ones are way too thin." He reached behind for a tool when Naomi's gPhone beeped. "Need to take that?"

She looked at the screen and the message on it, *BAD GUYS JUST AR—*.

She looked up from the phone. "Oh shit."

Rudy turned his head. "That's not good." He had gotten the same message via his internal communications suite. "I can't reach Jax."

Naomi rubbed her chin, looking at her gPhone's screen. "They must be jamming public comms."

The grease-smeared droid technician grunted. "Who? What?" He looked at his guests. "It's illegal to jam public comm channels."

Rudy turned his head to look at the man standing over him. "You're a lawyer too?"

Jacob frowned. He waved a hand. "Okay, we gonna do this or...?" He gestured to his workspace. "I've got other projects I can get back to, and frankly, you two are weird."

Rudy shifted on the table, nudging himself off of it. He hit the ground, his rollerball absorbing the impact. "Sorry. Raincheck." At a lower volume, he added, "I was looking forward to having weapons."

Naomi put a hand on his flat head. "Maybe next time." They exited the workshop, heading back the way they came. She looked at a directory as they passed. "Do you happen to know where Jax's friend is?"

Rudy's head turned left and right. "Nope. He never brought me or Baxter aboard when he came here."

"What's Baxter coming aboard have to do with it?"

Rudy beeped. "We share maps."

Naomi stopped. "What?"

"After jobs, we exchange map data. Just in case the other one ever needs to retrace steps."

She made a thoughtful face. "Okay. That...well, that makes sense." She turned and resumed walking.

"How much longer is this going to take? Can't you do... whatever you're doing, faster?" Clinton whined.

Azadeh looked up. "I'm not paid hourly, man. If I could do this faster, I would. Chill."

Clinton sighed.

Min Chu came back from making a few calls. He hitched a thumb toward the pair. "He's high-strung."

Jax nodded. "You don't know the half of it. BioTek has been chasing us across half the Empire, and all he does is moan and groan. It's exhausting." He was about to continue complaining about Clinton when his gPhone beeped. He looked at the screen: *BAD GUYS JUST AR —*. He looked up. "Shit."

Min leaned forward to try to get a peek at the screen.

Jax looked up, saw him, and pocketed the phone. "Looks like BioTek found us." He moved closer to Azadeh and Clinton. "I thought you said that thing wasn't broadcasting." He pointed to the discarded faraday cage.

The young hacker looked up from her work. "I did. It's not."

Jax shook his head. "Well, BioTek is here, so they found us somehow. If not the case, ho—"

Azadeh waved her free hand. "Probably just hacked every station they could and loaded his, or your, biometrics." She squinted at Jax. "You came through customs, ya?"

Jax blushed. "Damn."

Azadeh clucked. "Rookie mistake."

"Hey, this isn't my—"

She cut him off again. "I honestly don't care." She squinted at the case. "Come on, you little..."

Min turned Jax to face him. "I have a buyer," he whispered.

Jax's mouth fell open. "Really?" The other man nodded. "Who? How? How much?"

"A local broker that I sometimes deal with. He moves expensive and high-end stuff through here. He said if BioTek wants it as bad as you say, he's interested."

"Sight unseen?" Jax pressed. Brokers rarely bought sight unseen, especially from unknowns. Especially shady ones on out-of-the-way stations.

Min nodded and shrugged at the same time. "Guess he doesn't like BioTek."

"Understandable," Jax said. He looked at his phone again. This time the screen showed *NO SIGNAL*. That didn't happen on modern populated stations or really anywhere but the fringe. Every station was its own primary network repeater, and small satellites dotted the Empire, providing a seamless mesh for the Empire's communication infrastructure.

Even if the station's node went down, most large ships could also act as network nodes. According to his phone, there wasn't a node anywhere within reach. He looked at Min, holding his phone up.

The other man produced his own device and frowned. "That's not good." He didn't wait for Jax's reaction; he started moving around the space like a small tornado, tossing things into bags and boxes. He looked at Jax, snapping his fingers. "Well, help me out." He pointed to a half-filled duffle bag.

Jax looked in the bag attempting to discern a pattern to what was being tossed in. Coming up short, he just looked around and started grabbing things.

Azadeh threw both hands in the air a second before a loud click came from the case. "Boom goes the dynamite!"

Jax and Min stopped what they were doing and joined her and Clinton. On the workbench, the case that had plagued Clinton's life for the better part of two weeks was lying there, the cuff open and lying on the table next to it. Clinton was rubbing his wrist, a grin splitting his face.

Jax looked at the young woman, who was still beaming. "Nice work!" He turned to Clinton, who smiled at him, the relief evident on his face.

Azadeh reached over to the case. She tapped the lid

and said, "Tada!" A hiss sounded from the case as the lid separated from the body and sprung open.

Three heads leaned over to look at the contents of the case.

"Mr. Sanchez, all commercial comm frequencies jammed," the ensign at the communications console on the bridge of the *Curry* said.

Captain Ivano turned from the main display. "Thank you, Ensign Ybarra." She turned forward again. On the wide wraparound screen, ParStor Station Mort 3 was growing larger. "Lieutenant Keating, take us in."

The young man at the helm console nodded. He ran a hand over his hairless head, then said, "Aye, sir."

Ybarra cleared her throat. "Sir, I've accessed the station's mainframe with the back door our system's integrator subsidiary provided."

Ivano nodded. After the debacle on UniDis Four, the board brought the resources of several other BioTek companies to bear. Of particular use were back door codes that gave access to any mainframe sold by Compu-Tek. Thankfully, one such mainframe ran the systems on ParStor Station Mort 3.

Ybarra continued, "The tight beam uplink is stable, and all other comms are locked down. No one on that station is making a call until we say so."

Ivano nodded. After a beat, she turned to Sanchez. "Better go get ready, Mr. Sanchez. We've set up Conference 2 as a command and control for the boarding teams."

Jefferson took a breath. "Thank you." They were launching four squads of corporate security agents. Sanchez, and more importantly, the board, had lost interest in subtlety.

Conference 2 was one deck below the bridge. It was larger than the space he was using as an office and better suited to display the various video feeds and telemetry from the boarding teams.

Thanks to a well concealed back door in the customs and docking bay management software courtesy of BioTek's Security Concepts subsidiary, they knew the messenger and his friends were here on the station somewhere. The board authorized the use of the back doors across the Empire and would, without a doubt, hang any legal repercussions on Sanchez's department and him personally.

The hatch to Conference 2 slid open. The room was dim with sixteen hastily mounted displays showing the men and women across from the camera holder as the four teams waited in their shuttles.

"Report," he said, moving to the center of the room. The large conference table was sunk into the deck, the chairs were somewhere. He looked around expectantly.

"Teams are inbound now. Will dock in five," an ensign that Sanchez didn't know said from a portable work station near one set of four monitors.

He nodded. It was infuriating how difficult this retrieval was turning out to be. "Comms blackout?"

Another ensign turned in her seat. "Complete. We've

overridden the station's systems, shutting down their main node as well as closing off the local nodes. No one on that station is talking to anyone."

Naomi looked around the corner. The intersection was empty on all sides. She turned to Rudy. "Clear."

The pair darted across, continuing on their way back toward the nearest spoke and the docking ring.

Naomi looked down. "Sorry it didn't work out." She moved to pat Rudy's head, then reconsidered, her hand hovering over him. She let her arm drop.

Rudy clicked twice. "It's okay. We can try again when we're not being pursued by a mega corporation bent on killing us to keep their secrets."

"I like your optimism."

"I was thinking, I'll have Baxter help me come up with a design."

"What could go wrong?"

When they left the tech shop, the corridors were relatively quiet. Now, however, more of the station's denizens had realized that communications were down. People were moving here and there with the air of panic surrounding them. Several times Naomi heard someone say "corporate cruiser." It wasn't that she doubted Skip, but the confirmation didn't hurt.

"How are we going to find Jax?" Rudy wondered aloud.

"And Clinton," Naomi said.

"Sure, that guy too," Rudy quipped. He rolled to a stop. "We might be lost." They were at another intersection, this one wider than the last.

"You're a nav droid," Naomi said.

Rudy's head spun to focus his large optical sensor on her. "And if you'd like to cross the Empire without dealing with Tier 1 navigation hazards, I can do that, in seconds. I'm not a rolling map."

Naomi huffed and looked around. There was a display on the opposite corner of the corridor. She touched the display, waking it up. "Okay, so...we're here." She pointed to a pulsing red dot.

"What gave us away?" the droid asked.

"Just by tapping your head, I can rewrite your vocal routines so you only speak Spanish," she warned. A few swipes and zooms on the display and she said, "Okay. I think we can go—" The screen flickered. She frowned and flattened her hand on it. Her bio-circuitry pulsed along her arm, up her neck, and around her eyes.

"Always creepy," Rudy said at a low volume.

Not opening her eyes, she shushed her mechanical friend. A moment later she said, "Shit. BioTek has hacked the mainframe and is using the station's internal sensors to try and locate Jax, Clinton, and me. Looks like four different teams have boarded the station."

Rudy beeped. "Sucks for you three." Naomi kicked him, causing him to emit several angry beeps.

"Give me a second. I might be able to plant some false sightings," she said. She closed her eyes and concentrated. In her mind's eye she could see the ParStor Station Mort 3 mainframe. She could see the data pathways that the BioTek cruiser had infiltrated. She saw the search routine bot running in the station security sub-servers.

She put her other hand on the display. Lines of code cascaded down it as she pressed. She forced her way into the security server, avoiding several counter intrusion algorithms. "There we go," she murmured.

A group of station personnel rounded a corner up ahead. Rudy poked Naomi in the leg. She released the display and took a deep breath. Under her breath, she said, "Okay, I think I bought us what I could. I planted enough sightings near the lower-level reactor complex that the path to the docking ring should be clear." She smiled. "And I put the security cameras into a diagnostic. Should keep them offline at least half an hour."

"Did you find out where their ship was docked?" Rudy asked. The group from before passed them. Rudy waved. "Hello."

Naomi said, "Looks like they shuttled over in four assault shuttles. Come on, let's go."

"What about Jax and Clinton? Did you find them?"

"No. Too risky to access the feeds and woulda taken me forever to search. They're on their own for now."

They started down the corridor and stopped when four men in matching suits stretched over matching light armor rounded the corner up ahead.

"Detour," Rudy said. He grabbed Naomi's hand, dragging her down a small side corridor before she had a chance to process what she was seeing.

CHAPTER 17

Min Chu grabbed the small oblong box from inside Clinton's open messenger case and shook it. "Rocks?"

Jax clucked. "Why would it be rocks?" He held his hand out.

Min offered the case.

"Sounds like rocks," Clinton offered.

"Better be damn important rocks," Jax said.

Not looking up from her newly acquired messenger case, Azadeh said, "Seeds. Sounds like seeds."

"Seeds?" Min and Jax repeated. She shrugged.

Jax ran a finger along the seam until he felt rather than saw the small latch. The case popped open.

"Told you so," the young woman crowed.

Inside the case were eight small glass cylinders, each containing what looked like identical seeds.

Min Chu said, "BioTek is predominately agri-tech stuff, right? Maybe these are some kind of wonder seeds?"

Jax shrugged. "Anything is possible." He pulled one of the vials out and held it up to the light.

Clinton took the vial. "No logo or anything."

Min watched the two men, then sighed, "I dunno, man. The client I mentioned? I dunno if they want seeds. They're not in agri-tech."

"You know," Azadeh said, breaking all three men from their respective reveries. "I kinda thought it would explode."

They turned to her. "What?"

Min shook his head. "You said it wasn't a bomb."

She wiggled a hand. "I went with the odds."

Jax stared at her. "Explode?" He turned to Clinton. "Was that something that coulda happened?"

Clinton shrugged. "Not that I know of. This was only my second run. If those things," he pointed to his now-open-and-not-locked-to-his-wrist case, "explode, it'd be news to me."

"If it helps, I figured it was only maybe twenty percent likely," Azadeh offered.

"It doesn't," Jax replied.

Clinton turned to her. "That's not a reassuring percentage."

She shrugged, then looked at her phone. "Who cut the comms?"

Clinton and Min Chu said, "What?" at the same time.

She held up her gPhone, screen out.

Min turned to Jax, his expression speaking volumes.

Clinton reached over to the case and picked up the shiny oblong box from inside. He turned it over and over, ignoring the others.

"How am I supposed to call the buyer?" Min whined.

Jax looked at the ceiling. "Where were you meeting them? Let's just go before...Let's just go."

"Before what?" the portly Asian fence demanded.

"Guessing his BioTek friends shut comms down," Azadeh said, absently turning Clinton's case over in her hands. "So shiny," she whispered as she ran a hand over the top of it.

Jax snatched the seed case out of Clinton's hand, turning to Min. "Come on."

As the hatch to Min's workspace opened, Azadeh shouted, "I'll show myself out!"

"Where are we going?" Jax asked Min.

"Market District 2," Min replied, stepping out into the corridor and right into the path of a woman in a station security uniform. The pair made a loud whiffing noise as they collided and fell to the deck.

The woman got to her feet first. "Min, you clumsy—"

"Maggie, gimme a break!" he said, rolling over to get his feet under him. "What's going on?"

The woman eyed Min Chu, then Jax and Clinton, through a wrinkled brow. "A corporate cruiser arrived a bit ago, and now we're being boarded."

"Boarded?" Jax and Clinton echoed. She looked at the two men and nodded.

The gPhone strapped to her arm beeped. She consulted the screen, then said, "Stay indoors." She hurried off the way she'd been going before colliding with Min Chu.

"I don't like this," Clinton said.

For once, Jax agreed with the lanky pain in the ass. What was going on? If the station was being boarded, there should be an alert or something. The corridors weren't empty, but they certainly weren't bustling. Had BioTek done something? Wouldn't the station management resist?

The trio reached a corner, and as Jax rounded it, he stopped dead in his tracks, pushing the other two back as he stumbled backward.

"What's wrong with you?" Min asked.

Jax's gaze met Clinton's.

"Maggie was right. BioTek agents. Four of 'em," Clinton moaned.

Jax turned to Min. "I don't think your buyer is waiting for us. At least not if they're smart."

Min threw his hands up. "Man, you still managed to screw me."

Jax shrugged, smiling. "Stoicism?"

"Man, fuck that! The obstacle is you, you turd." Min swung on him. Jax dodged, raising one arm to block while the other shoved the smaller man aside.

"Dude! Relax!" Jax said, grabbing Min from behind.

"Can you two cut it out!" Clinton hissed.

Jax shoved Min away and patted the air between them. "I'll make it up to you. Promise. Line up a few runs, and I'll do them for half my normal rate." He inclined his head. "Fair?"

"A third your normal rate. And I go with." He smirked. "Ensure you don't cut and run."

"A third? You crook."

"Takes one to know one."

Jax huffed, then met Min's gaze. "Fine."

"You better not screw me. Again," Min added.

Jax held both hands up, palms out. "Would I do that?"

This time it was Min's head that canted to the side. "You just did. Literally, just now, on this job."

"Got you there," Clinton said without turning to look at the two men, his attention fixed on something down the corridor. Jax scowled at the back of his head.

Clinton said, "Let's go." He didn't wait for Jax heading down the corridor.

Jax looked at Min and nodded. The other grudgingly returned the gesture and headed off in the opposite direction.

Naomi and Rudy came up the boarding ramp.

"I'm glad you made it back. Have you seen the Captain?"

"And Clinton," Naomi groaned.

"Him too," Skip said.

Naomi shook her head. "No, but we weren't in the same area. Anything to report?" She nodded to Baxter, who was standing guard near the stairs. After that, she made her way from cargo hold to common deck to bridge. Rudy was well ahead of her, having zipped up the center of the staircase.

Skip waited until she reached the bridge. "I am afraid not. I'm not tied into the data network of the station. I only know that all commercial comms were jammed a few minutes before my sensors detected the BioTek cruiser outside. I was able to track their shuttles with my sensors, but they went around the other side of the station, so I'm not sure where they docked." Skip sounded apologetic. "My sensors are limited while inside the docking facility."

Naomi fell into her seat, bringing her station online. "Don't sweat it, you did great. Okay, at least they're not nearby." She looked over her console, pulling the various sensor feeds onto her display. She noticed a blinking icon. "What's this?"

Rudy looked over from his station. Skip said, "Did I not mention that docking clamps activated when the BioTek ship arrived?"

"You did not," Naomi groaned, rubbing her face. "Why is ParStor doing something for BioTek? Especially something like locking down every ship in the ring?" She shook her head. "Can you get around it?"

"I'll need you to connect me to the station data network. Rudy can show you how."

Naomi got to her feet. "I know what to do." She headed back off the bridge.

Wirelessly, Skip sent, *I do not think she does*, to Rudy. The small rust-colored nav droid disengaged from the specially designed cradle that kept him in place at his console and followed Naomi.

Rudy caught up to Naomi under the *Osprey*. She had several hatches open and was peering at them. He rolled out from under the ship toward a meter-wide pillar with several thick cables and conduits hanging from it on spools.

He pulled one of the thick cables free and returned to

the *Osprey*. "I wouldn't presume to step on your toes, you knowing what to do and all." He held the end of the cable out in front of him.

She took the cable and paused, looking at the various panels she had already opened. Rudy beeped. "That one." He pointed. She slotted the thick data cable into the exposed jack.

She looked over her shoulder. "I woulda gotten it."

"And I'd have turned to rust in the meantime." He rolled back toward the boarding ramp.

Naomi followed, muttering to herself. Once up on the cargo deck, she said, "Skip, you good?"

"I am accessing the network now," the Sapient Intelligence that ran the *Osprey* said.

When he said nothing more, Naomi turned to Rudy, who bobbed up and down on his rollerball, the best he could do for a shrug. Naomi opened her mouth to check on Skip when the SI said, "This is interesting."

Naomi looked at Rudy, who made a point to turn his main optic sensor away. She sighed. "What's interesting?"

"There is another presence in the network. It used a back door into the system. I believe it is likely the BioTek cruiser. They activated the lockdown. I am not sure that the station managers even know."

"I think it's just around that corner," Jax said, peering down a corridor that looked exactly like every other corridor on ParStor Station Mort 3. Crowded and dingy. Word had gotten out, which turned out to be both good and bad news. Good, because it was making it easier for the two of them to blend in with the crowd. Bad, because the crowd had twice now pulled them off course down a corridor they didn't want to go down.

"You said that the last time," Clinton replied.

"I mean it more this time."

"That's not how it usually works."

Jax made a rude gesture. "You got us lost four times already. Shut up."

Clinton poked him in the chest, right where Min Chu had. It hurt more than it should. He winced, batting Clinton's hand away. "You know, I kinda thought you'd be less whiny without your special lunchbox."

"Why? You thought it came from that?" He smirked.

Jax clucked. "Come on." He headed down the corridor, shoving a man in greasy coveralls out of his way, ignoring the colorful insults hurled at him.

Clinton fell in behind him. "You know, you're kind of a prick, like, all the time."

"I'm told I grow on people." Jax didn't look back.

"Doubt it."

Jax reached an intersection, turned left, then right, then left again, and headed that way.

"You have your ship, a business partner who makes up for all your shortcomings, and two droids who... well, they're okay if you're into that. What's your problem? You live a damn charmed life."

Jax spun so fast that Clinton backpedaled, losing his

footing and falling backwards into a woman in a business suit.

"Charmed life? Charmed life?" Jax growled. "You don't know me. You don't know jack about me, about Naomi, about anything, you privileged asshole." He sneered. "Boo-fuckin-hoo, you grew up on New Terra and it was so boring." He took a step toward Clinton. His voice was a harsh whisper. "You didn't lose your parents to this," he waved his hands, "authoritarian nightmare we live in. You don't take whatever job you could find just to eat and keep your ship in the air." He scowled, looking around to make sure no one noticed what was going on. The steady flow of station personnel was barely slowing around them. "You wouldn't know the first thing about anything! Let alone trust, or knowing who your friends are, or..." He turned and headed down the corridor, melting into the crowd.

"Jackson, wait!" Clinton shouted. He trotted after Jax, dropping his hand to Jax's shoulder. Jax spun, arm cocked back. Clinton held both hands out in front of him, one still clutching the case with the seeds in it. "I'm...I'm sorry."

Jax wanted to hold on to his anger, use it like a shield. But he couldn't.

Growing up, he had always resented the kids with families. The kids with money. His parents had left him with a ship and two droids. That was it. They hadn't been rich, and what money they had went to the cause. His adoptive aunt lived on a station administrator's salary. He never wanted for food, but many of the luxuries enjoyed by the other kids, especially the Delphinos, were not an option.

He resented the Clinton from the moment Naomi forced him to bring the messenger aboard the *Osprey*. A bored kid from one of the most prosperous worlds in the Empire—the capital, no less—who got in over his head.

Jax took a deep breath. "Look, man. We don't have to be besties or anything, but we do need to work together to get off this station." He grabbed Clinton's elbow, guiding him into the flow of the crowd. "I have no idea how many of Sanchez's goons are on the station."

Clinton nodded. "Fair." He looked around. "I still don't know where we are."

Jax looked around, spotting a directory. "Come on." They reached the directory and Jax pointed. "Son of a nutcracker!"

"What?" Clinton was squinting at the display.

Jax tapped the pulsing red dot that represented their current location. It was one corridor away from the lobby that connected to the spoke they were looking for. Jax looked from the display and swore. "We're less than a hundred meters away." He looked at Clinton. "How many times do you think we walked right past the corridor we needed?"

"I don't want to think about it," the other man said, beaming. He tilted his head in the direction they needed to go. "Shall we?"

Jax nodded.

The screens in Conference 2 were a jumble of people coming and going. The four teams were about the station, moving from deck to deck. They all had the messenger's biometrics and photos of the two spacers. As yet, none had laid eyes on the trio.

Before any of the analysts in the room could spot her, the *Curry*'s RI matched the spacer woman's face to the biometrics on file. By the time Team 2 followed, she was nowhere to be seen.

"Team 1, report," Sanchez called out.

"Nothing yet, sir. We're heading for the reactor center now."

He nodded, taking in the other displays. "Copy that." He turned to the assorted analysts. "The RI hasn't spotted them? I thought we had complete control of the station's mainframe."

A young man, barely out of college, turned, his cheeks crimson. "Unfortunately, no, sir. Shortly after the teams arrived, the security system went into a diagnostic. We lost the cameras and sensors. Just before they went offline, the RI spotted the two spacers near the engineering levels."

Sanchez swore softly. "Fine. Stay on it." The young man nodded. He moved to the far end of the conference room and pulled out his gPhone. He tapped a few icons.

"Go ahead, sir," the leader of Team 1 said in his earpiece.

"You have the package?"

"Of course, sir."

"You know what to do."

There was a pause, then, "Yes, sir."

Sanchez hated that he might have to use his Plan B but wasn't going to take a chance. He knew that the messenger, the case, and the ship he was on were aboard the station somewhere.

This was his Plan B, and only the man in charge of Team 1 was in the know. Not even Captain Ivano was in the loop. His career depended on it staying that way.

He moved back into the crowd of analysts and displays. He spied the Team 1 feeds. They were making a slow circuit around the engineering space. He watched the other displays. The remaining three teams were scattered throughout the station, trying to not look like an invading army.

The ceiling chimed. Captain Ivano's voice said, "Reinforcements have arrived."

Sanchez looked up. "Thank you. Please ask them to surround the station."

"Will do."

One of the analysts turned. "Sir. Station personnel has stopped Team 3. The administrator is demanding to speak to someone."

Jefferson looked around. He knew it was bound to happen. Cutting the station off, sending in boarding teams. It was bound to be noticed. "I'll take it."

He moved to one of the unoccupied stations and took a seat. He tapped an icon and found himself face to face with a man easily pushing seventy. "I'm Jefferson Sanchez, BioTek loss pre—"

"I don't give a fuck who you are." The man cut him off. "You have no jurisdiction here, no authority."

"We're here in lawful purs—"

"You're not listening to me, son. I don't care why you're here." The wizened face leaned toward the camera pickup. "What I do care about is how you hacked our computers. I care about why you boarded this station without authorization."

"Sir. I'm trying to—"

A grizzled hand passed in front of the camera. "When we get our systems back online, I'm filing a complaint—many of them, actually. First with your board, then the Imperial authorities."

Sanchez opened his mouth to reply, but the screen went blank. He swore. "I wish you hadn't said that." He pulled out his gPhone and placed a call. "We're proceeding with Plan B. Return to base."

Standing, he said, "Okay, pull the teams back. Don't release our hold on their computer yet, or the lockdown on docked ships."

"Yes, sir," some said.

Jax peered around the edge of the hatch. "I don't see anyone." Clinton started past him, but stopped when Jax grabbed his arm. "Wait. There." He pointed.

A team of four, two men and two women in crisp

business suits, was moving from ship to ship, checking the docking terminal in front of each ship. They must have arrived just before Jax and Clinton. They were at the ship farthest from the hatch, moving to the next in line. There were five other vessels in this bay. The *Osprey* was second to last.

Clinton leaned back. "That's not good."

Jax nodded. "No, it isn't." He pulled his gPhone out of his pocket. "Still no local comms."

"Can you tell if the others are aboard?" Clinton asked, leaning to look into the docking bay.

Jax shook his head. "Can't be sure, but I think so. Skip sealed up the ship when we left. Now, the boarding ramp is down. I hope that means that they're aboard, waiting for us."

Aboard the *Osprey,* Naomi watched the BioTek security team inspect the ship at the end of the row. "Glad they started at the ship farthest from the door."

"Agreed," Skip said. "Though that buys us only a few more minutes."

Rudy, at his bridge station, turned his optical sensor to Naomi. "And when they reach us?"

Naomi shook her head. "I don't know."

"I have already altered the records on the docking console, but that may only slow them down," Skip offered.

Jax and Clinton were still standing at the hatch leading to the docking bay, watching the BioTek team.

"Any bright ideas?" Clinton asked. The BioTek team was moving to the next ship, the one next to the *Osprey.*

Jax shook his head. "Honestly, no." He turned to look

Clinton in the eye. "They're armed, we're not. They're all trained shooters. Since the *Osprey* is in front of them, there's no way to sneak aboard without them noticing us."

"What about a distraction?" Clinton offered.

"Like what? There are two of us. Safe to assume the others are either onboard or still somewhere in the station. Neither helps us. Unless you want to sneak in and start screaming while I get aboard, which, for the record, I'm okay with."

Clinton sighed, nodding his agreement.

Jax was about to suggest they run for it and wish for the best when eight spacers in mismatched coveralls shoved their way past the pair. They made a straight line for one of the ships in the bay and weren't at all quiet about it.

The security team spun at the sound and rushed to intercept the frantic freighter crew.

Jax watched the four well-dressed operatives stop the spacers, brandishing firearms to get their attention. "Go!" He pushed Clinton.

Naomi watched the BioTek team turn and double-time it to stop what must have been the crew of one of the ships with them in the docking bay. "That's weird."

"Indeed," Skip agreed.

Outside of the ship, the four agents were in a shouting match with the freighter crew.

"Look!" Rudy was pointing to one of the displays mounted near the top of the transparent

forward window. It showed the feed from the camera mounted under the ship. Jax and Clinton were making their way straight for the ship using scattered cargo modules as cover.

Jax and Clinton walked up the *Osprey*'s boarding ramp. As they reached the cargo deck, the sound of the ramp sealing shut echoed through the ship.

Clinton looked over to Baxter and said, "That was fun."

"Sounds like." The droid slanted his head. "No case."

Clinton held the seed case up. It rattled softy.

Baxter inclined his head. "Rocks?"

"Seeds," Jax said.

"This was all for seeds?" the big bot asked.

"Looks like," Jax said. He started up the stairs to the common deck.

Baxter turned to Clinton. "Are they magical?"

This time, the lanky ex-messenger tipped his head. "What?"

From the opening in the deck, Jax shouted, "Come on, Beanpole!"

Clinton turned to the stairs, then looked over his shoulder at Baxter. The big droid was watching him. He shook his head and followed Jax upstairs.

Naomi looked up as Jax stepped off the staircase onto the bridge. "Hey," she said. "You didn't die. That's a plus, I guess." She looked at Rudy. "I was starting to plan what I'd rename the ship."

"Excuse me," Skip said from the ceiling.

Jax walked past Naomi's station, dropping into his chair. "Let's get the hell out of here." He started going through the pre-flight checklist.

The freighter crew was nowhere to be seen, likely

aboard their own ship. Jax noticed that the security people were also gone. "That's weird. Where'd they go?"

"Do we care?" Rudy asked.

"We have a problem," Skip said. The *Osprey* was still connected to the station network.

"Because we didn't have enough of those already," Jax quipped. He flipped a few more toggles, watching the reactor power come up to full.

"Do you want to know what is going on or not?" Skip replied.

Naomi clucked and said, "Yes, please."

"According to the station's network, two more corporate cruisers have arrived," the ship's SI said matter-of-factly.

"What?" Jax asked, stopping what he was doing.

"I did not stutter," the obviously annoyed Intelligence replied. He went on. "Looks like both are light cruisers. The station personnel are attempting to regain control of the computers. As yet, they have not succeeded, but likely will soon."

"Wonderful," Naomi sighed.

"Any idea why Sanchez called off his goons?" Jax asked.

"Negative," Skip answered.

"Five will get you ten they aren't withdrawing for a good reason," Naomi said.

Outside the ship, another large group of people flooded into the bay, splitting into two groups, heading for other ships in the bay.

"Getting a little crowded in here," Jax said under his breath.

"All the more reason to leave," Clinton said from the back of the bridge.

"About that," Skip said. "The docking lockdown is still in effect."

"Damn," Jax said. He looked over the displays before him. "Can you bypass it?"

"Yes, I just thought it would be fun to leave myself secured to the deck," the SI replied. "No. I cannot. At least not quickly."

"I got this," Naomi said, standing. "Bax, I could use your help."

Clinton watched her leave, then said, "She can, you know...What'd you call it? —"

"Whammy," Jax offered.

Clinton nodded. "Yeah, whammy. She can just whammy the docking control holding us to the deck?"

Jax nodded. "Yeah, usually."

Naomi and Baxter were standing next to the control pedestal for the *Osprey*'s docking slip. The noise level in the bay was becoming deafening as ships powered up.

"This looks promising," the big combat droid said loud enough for Naomi to hear.

Naomi eyed the terminal. Taking a deep breath, she put both hands on the sides of the pedestal. The bio-circuitry along her arms and neck and up around her eyes pulsed a glowing blue.

"That is never not weird," the droid said.

"Sshh," Naomi hissed.

The screen on the pedestal flickered, then went dark. After a second, lines of code started scrolling down the screen.

Several loud clicks sounded from the decking beneath the ship. Naomi turned to Baxter. "Let's go."

Following her up the ramp, Baxter asked, "Why did you make me come with you?"

She shrugged. "Protection."

"From?"

"No idea, but you're good to have around. Just in case." She winked as she continued toward the bridge.

The *Osprey* rumbled as Jax fed power to the lift engines. "Good job, Naomi!" Jax shouted.

Down below on the common deck, Clinton was jury-rigging a strap to hold the seed case down on the sofa.

"What are you doing?" Baxter asked, coming up the stairs with Naomi.

Clinton turned. "Oh. Well, I figure these things are important. We should probably keep them safe."

"With a bungee cord and the sofa?" The big combat droid tilted his head.

Clinton shrugged.

"We have a vault," Naomi said, heading up the stairs. "Oh?"

Baxter held out his hand. Clinton undid his work, offering the seed container to the big bot. Baxter said, "Turn around. Close your eyes."

"Really?"

Baxter said nothing, staring at the man, his red optical

sensor swishing back and forth. Clinton sighed and did as the big bot asked.

He could hear Baxter move around, then heard his heavy footsteps vanishing down the stairs. "Why did I have to turn around and close my eyes if he was just going to go downstairs?"

The ship shook.

Up on the bridge, Jax said, "What's this now?" Outside the forward windows, red lights were strobing.

"The station's reactor just exploded. Cascade failures and secondary explosions are ripping the lower levels apart. We have to leave," Skip said, no hint of urgency in his electronic voice. To punctuate his warning, the *Osprey* shook as the bay rumbled.

"Don't have to tell me twice," Jax said, spinning the *Osprey* around to face the opening of the docking bay. With the station exploding, the lockdown on the other ships failed. A mid-sized freighter was pushing off the deck, drifting in front of them.

Jax waved a hand. "Watch out, asshole!"

Before he could dodge the other ship or escape out into space, the docking bay tilted around them.

"Oh, shit!" Jax grabbed the flight controls, using the maneuvering thrusters to keep the ship centered in the bay. "I think the ring, or at least our part of it, just broke free."

"Confirmed," Skip said.

Naomi looked at her console. "Holy hell." She looked up, but Jax was busy, his attention on one of his displays. She looked back down at her console. "They're gonna kill everyone here."

"They already have," Jax growled. Outside the bay, space was spinning by the opening. The freighter that had blocked their exit shot out into space, only to run right into a piece of debris twice its size.

"Damn," Naomi whispered. The other ship, wisely, was still sitting on the deck, likely watching the *Osprey* for its next move.

Loose cargo crates were now drifting freely around the bay. One clanged against the top of the ship, ringing like a gong.

Using the maneuvering thrusters, Jax kept them more or less centered in the remains of the bay. Outside, the still exploding station passed by. A large section erupted in flames, sending several hundred meters of hull and decking spiraling out into the void.

Jax swore. "That fucking bastard. All for some damn seeds?"

The captain of the other ship lost their patience. It rocketed out of the bay toward open space.

"Looks like they'll—" Naomi started, but fell silent when a missile streaked in and destroyed the ship.

Jax inhaled.

The section of docking ring they were in continued to drift, slowly twisting after several pieces of debris struck it, sometimes hard enough to change their trajectory. By this point, the remains of the station never passed in front of the bay's opening. Jax had set the ship back down, magnetizing the landing gear to hold her to the deck. Occasionally, a BioTek ship would slide into view before vanishing again.

Twice, one of the remaining ships in the bay drifted

into the *Osprey*, ringing the hull like a bell. Jax was glad the remaining ships were about the same size. The *Osprey*'s hull would need some repairs, but the ship wasn't at risk of being flattened.

"Why don't you raise the shields?" Naomi asked.

"They'd see them," Jax answered, pointing out of the bay. "They're almost certainly scanning every piece of debris." He turned his chair. "Our best hope is that they ignore this chunk of station as we drift far enough to slip away."

Fifteen minutes later, after one of the BioTek ships, much smaller now, passed by the bay's opening, Jax guided them out of the bay. One of the drifting ships got in one last clipping blow as they slipped out the remains of ParStor Station Mort 3's docking ring.

"That was louder than the others," Naomi observed.

Using the maneuvering thrusters, Jax guided the *Osprey* further from the docking ring. With the sensors offline, he relied on the camera feeds. When he was sure they were out of the path of the piece of docking ring, he powered down the rest of the ship's systems except life support and artificial gravity.

"Should we kill the grav-plating?" Naomi asked.

"It wouldn't hurt, but I plan to have a beer or twelve, and I hate drinking in free fall." He unclipped his harness and stood.

Skip said, "We should look like a piece of debris until we are far enough away to open a wormhole."

Jax nodded as he reached the staircase. "All those people," he whispered. "For seeds."

CHAPTER 18

Clinton dropped onto the sofa with a groan. "So, we'll die out here?" He rubbed his now free wrist.

"Probably," Rudy said.

Jax scowled at him. "We're not going to die." He looked at the ceiling. "Skip is running a full diagnostic."

"The good news is that the BioTek ships haven't seen us," Naomi offered.

"But they haven't left yet, either," Rudy pointed out. "I wonder why?"

"So long as they stay over there, I don't care," Jax said.

"Captain, I have completed the diagnostic," Skip said, drawing all eyes to the ceiling. The two droids had no idea why they did that, but all did it, so it must be a thing. Baxter met Rudy's gaze and shrugged.

"How bad is it?" Jax asked.

"It is...not terrible and not great. As far as I can tell, there are several pieces of the station stuck in me. Most are not a problem, but at least two have caused damage to the wormhole generator system."

"Is the generator—" Naomi started.

"As far as I can tell, the generator itself is fine," Skip interrupted. "However, the main power bus is throwing low voltage faults, which is why our first attempt to leave this system failed. There is also a reading from a primary matrix stabilizer that is concerning."

Jax looked at Naomi. "Do you know what that last thing was?" She shook her head.

He opened his mouth, but stopped when Skip said, "I can walk Baxter through it." Jax let out a breath. "Rudy will need to assist him," Skip added.

Jax nodded. "Okay. Anything else?"

"A great many things. However, those are the most pressing. I believe when those two items are repaired, we will be able to at least leave the immediate vicinity."

Rudy added, "We're currently still on a ballistic course out of the system with the rest of the station debris. We're angled slightly down from the ecliptic. The fact that they haven't spotted us by now leads me to assume we're in the clear. We should be outside their main sensor range."

"I'm still worried about what they're still doing here," Naomi said. "Why loiter at the scene of the crime?"

Clinton clucked. "By crime, you mean murder of what? Three? Five hundred people?"

Under his breath, Jax said, "I hope Min and that nerdy girl got out."

"I am afraid that even if they escaped, the *Curry* and her support ships made thorough work of destroying every lifeboat and shuttle that fled the station," Skip said, hearing Jax.

"No witnesses," Baxter said. His ruby red optic sensor silently swished back and forth. "BioTek can control the narrative now."

Clinton rubbed his until-recently-encumbered wrist. "You know, I'm going to be in the head for a bit." He stood and went straight for the small head at the forward section of the ship.

When the door to the head closed, Naomi looked at Jax. "Do I want to know what he's doing?"

He shook his head. "He's had that case on his wrist for almost a couple weeks now. No, no, you don't want to know what he's doing in there." He looked at the door. "Glad he's not doing it in his berth..."

Naomi made a choking noise.

After Rudy and Baxter went down to the cargo and engineering deck to work with Skip on fabricating parts for the upcoming repair, Jax and Naomi grabbed a beer and sat down. Clinton was still in the head. They hadn't talked much since before UniDis Four.

Jax took a breath. "So."

Naomi shook her head. "You're not good at this."

He inclined his head. "No argument."

She smiled. "Seeds, huh?"

He nodded and took a sip. "Yeah. A lot of them. Not sure if that matters or not."

"What kind?"

"No idea. Beanstalk, carrot, rutabaga..." He shrugged. "No labels. Also, no stamps or serial numbers."

Naomi leaned back, taking a sip of beer. "That is interesting. I'm pretty sure a company like BioTek stamps every seed they produce." Jax nodded. "So, someone, I'm guessing disgruntled BioTek science types, hired Clinton to smuggle seeds. Seeds that their company... what? Didn't create?"

When she didn't continue, Jax looked up from his beer. "Oh, that wasn't rhetorical?" She shook her head. "Maybe they aren't BioTek? Maybe they stole 'em?"

Naomi sipped her beer, thinking it over. Why would a mega corporation, one of the biggest in the Empire, steal seeds from a competitor? She shook her head, then snapped her fingers. "What if these seeds are pre-production?"

"Pre- what?"

"Do you not read anything?" She shook her head. Sometimes dealing with Jackson Caruso was infuriating. Most of the time, really. Whenever she thought about finding someone more reliable to work with, though, she remembered how few questions he asked. For better and worse, most of the time.

"Not about seeds, no."

"The guys that hired Clinton probably developed these seeds. Whatever they do, it must be valuable."

Jax's expression revealed that he was catching on. "And they didn't want BioTek to take their work and sell it."

"Or hide it away where no one would see it, yeah," Naomi agreed.

The door to the head opened. Clinton stepped out, spotted the two of them, and stumbled to a stop. "Oh. You're still here."

Jax turned, putting his arm over the back of the chair. "It's a small ship." He winked. The other man's cheeks turned a deep crimson.

Naomi sighed. "Men."

I wish there was a topside hatch, Rudy wirelessly beamed as the *Osprey*'s boarding ramp lowered, stopping halfway to form a horizontal platform.

Making his smart material rollerball magnetic, he rolled out to the end of the platform. Baxter, his feet magnetized, followed.

Ready? the big bot asked.

For indignity? No, Rudy replied.

Baxter reached down and plucked the nav droid from the platform. Turning him upside down, he raised him to the hull, letting the rollerball attach.

Rudy rolled up and out of sight toward the *Osprey*'s dorsal section.

Baxter reached up to grab onto the hull. He demagnetized his feet, pulling himself up and around to plant them on the hull. *We're moving to the wormhole generator,* he sent to Skip.

Rudy was waiting for Baxter on the section of the

hull behind the mechanical hump that housed the worm-hole generator. He looked at Baxter as the combat droid rounded the hull. *Skip, you were right.* He pointed to a large piece of metal that had pierced the *Osprey*'s hull.

Quite the splinter, Baxter quipped. He joined Rudy, handing the smaller droid the bundle of parts he was carrying.

Rudy took the tools and parts, moving away from the jagged piece of metal. Baxter grabbed the offending hull fragment with both hands and pulled. *Really stuck in there,* he beamed.

I am well aware, Skip replied.

Baxter adjusted his grip, lowering into a squat.

Use your legs, not your back, Rudy offered.

Baxter turned to look at the small droid, his optic sensor swishing. *I do not even have muscles or a spine. Also, shut up.* He locked his finger joints, feeling his fingertips dig into the thick metal. With a single fluid motion, his leg and hip actuators powered up to over one hundred percent.

Inside the ship, a loud screeching pierced every deck. Outside the ship, Baxter heaved the large piece of debris up and out of the *Osprey*'s hull. He turned and tossed the offending piece of metal away from the ship.

Rudy set about probing the equipment inside the tear. Skip narrated the small droid's progress.

While the droids finished making repairs, Jax, Naomi, and Clinton were still at the small dining table.

"Now that we know what they are, we can more easily look for a buyer," Jax said for the second time.

"A buyer?" Naomi spluttered. She waved a hand. "They just destroyed a space station. A station full of people. Likely thousands of people. Innocent people!"

Clinton pointed to her. "She's got a point."

"You said that already," Jax fumed. He looked at each of them in turn. "What do you suggest, then?"

"Put them in an airlock and open it," Clinton offered.

Jax made a face. "And what? Just send an email to BioTek? 'We don't have the special seeds you're willing to kill thousands for anymore. You can just forget all about us. We won't tell a soul, promise.'" He smirked. "How likely do you find that to work?"

Naomi sighed. "Yeah, that wouldn't happen." She took another sip of beer, realized the bottle was empty, and sat it down with a clunk. "He killed that station. Ensuring we're silent has to be a given."

Clinton looked at each of them. "Then what?"

Jax rolled his eyes. "We. Sell. The. Seeds," he said, slowly, hoping that it sunk in the third time. They'd been burning reactor fuel, food, air, water, and more on this little adventure. BioTek wasn't going to stop chasing them. He held up a hand. "The hacker on Mort 3. She—"

"Azadeh," Clinton offered.

"Ahem," the ceiling speaker said.

Jax nodded. "Yeah, her. She said Sanchez was likely using Clinton's biometrics. Uploaded them to every station and customs checkpoint he could, gets alerts when you show up." He pointed to Clinton.

"Ahem," the ceiling speaker said again.

Naomi nodded slowly. "That makes sense. BioTek has other divisions—probably military goods and services, mainframes, you name it. Likely have back doors in all of it." She shook her head. "We'll never be able to stay ahead of them."

This time Skip didn't opt for polite. "This might be a novel idea." The three humans looked up. "My sensor logs and the seeds themselves would be quite damning. No?"

"So, what? Go to the Imperials?" Jax asked. "Just like that. 'Hey, space fascists, care to crack some corporate skulls? They're breaking the law, after all.'"

"I would not phrase it that way," Skip replied, his voice clipped.

Jax shook his head. "What makes you think the Imperials would even care?"

Naomi's face made it clear she didn't have a good answer to that one. She rubbed her face, then looked at Clinton. "He's not wrong. The Empire has never seemed to care about what corporations are up to, as long as they pay their taxes."

Clinton sighed. "Okay, so we can't toss them." He gestured to the case in the center of the table. "We can't involve the authorities." He took a long, slow breath. "What's that leave us? I'm not built for running the rest of my life."

"Got that right," Jax agreed, eyebrow raised at the other man. "Too scrawny and you lack survival skills."

Clinton made a rude gesture, eliciting a laugh from Jax.

Naomi undid her ponytail, raked her fingers through her hair before pulling it back into a new, tighter ponytail. "We go to the public."

Before either man could respond, Skip said, "I have good news and bad news." All three people on the common deck looked at the ceiling. The ship's managing SI continued. "The good news is that Baxter and Rudy were able to make repairs to the wormhole drive equipment."

"That's good," Clinton said.

Skip ignored him, continuing, "The bad news is that we have at best one trip before the entire thing needs an overhaul."

"At best?" Clinton asked.

Skip continued, "The starboard forward thruster quad is damaged. So is the starboard ordinance panel."

"We can't fire missiles?" Jax asked.

"Not from the left side, no," Skip answered. "Oh, and engine 2's thrust nozzle is cracked. I did not know about that. Baxter spotted it."

"At best?" Clinton repeated.

PART 4

CHAPTER 19

Clinton leaned over Jax's shoulder. "That doesn't look safe."

Jax reached up and palmed the other man's face, shoving him back. The *Osprey* was approaching a station that was nearly three kilometers long and one wide, a massive cylinder floating at the Lagrange point of a mid-sized world that looked like it was mostly ocean. Originally a deep space colony run by a bottled water company, the O'Neill cylinder was sold to a private co-op when the company moved its colonists to floating cities on the planet Voss-Dasani 2 below.

The first thing the co-op did was install artificial gravity and stop the massive structure's spin. After that, they invited colonists to resettle in the massive cylinder. People came from other colonies and all across Earth. Within a decade of being under new management, the colony was back to full capacity and served as a trading depot for several nearby star systems. The Voss-Dasani

corporation rented a significant amount of space from the
co-op to have offices outside the gravity well of the planet.

"I am afraid this was the closest station that had
docking facilities we could use," Skip answered. He
added, "It only looks old and run down. Second Chance
is quite safe and modern. According to the WikiGalaxia,
the owners take great pride in both the station's cleanliness and lack of crime."

Clinton looked at Jax. "They hate crime. No wonder
you've never been here."

"You need me to show you to the airlock?" Jax asked,
watching the station approach.

A light on the comm panel lit up. Jax accepted the
incoming call. A face appeared on the display above him.

A middle-aged woman with skin as dark as the
surrounding space looked at him. "What can we do for
you?"

Jax was taken aback by her bluntness but composed
himself. "We're looking to effect some repairs if there's a
mechanic aboard that can work on a Valerian Co-op
Infiltrator."

She looked down at something, then said, "One
moment." The screen went dark.

Jax looked over his shoulder. "I guess cleanliness and
a lack of crime make bluntness okay?"

Before Clinton or Naomi could reply, the woman
reappeared on the screen. "I'm sending you docking coordinates now. The Macklemore ShipWorks has space for
you."

Another indicator lit up on his console. Jax smiled.

"Thank you." The woman nodded and cut the connection.

"I've got the coordinates. Sending you the nav plot," Rudy said.

On the main display before Jax, ghostly green arrows appeared, guiding him under the station toward the end where massive solar collectors connected to the station like sparkling petals.

The Macklemore ShipWorks docking bay could have held three, maybe four ships the size of the *Osprey*. At the moment, only one other ship, a blocky medium-sized freighter with a missing engine, occupied the far end of the bay.

A pale-skinned woman with equally pale hair met them at the bottom of the boarding ramp. Her hover chair came to a stop before the trio. She looked at Jax, then Clinton. "What's wrong with his face?"

Knowing that the BioTek man, Sanchez, was likely using Clinton's biometrics to track them, they had applied geometric patterns to his face with what Jax assured him wasn't shoe polish. He was also wearing a wide-brimmed hat that Naomi bought on their last trip to Sandusky.

Naomi looked up at him, then turned to the woman. "Skin condition." It was partially true now. The patterns on his face were taking on a splotchy red halo. She was certain that it was shoe polish Jax had given the lanky messenger. Too late to say anything now.

The other woman tutted. "Sorry to hear that." She looked the three of them over. "Who's the owner?" Jax raised his hand. "This isn't elementary school." She motioned for him to lower his hand. "Looks like you got in a fight in with a Justicar class and lost."

Jax followed her as she guided her chair out from under the ship and around the rear of the craft. "Something like that. How long do you think it'll take?"

She hitched a thumb over her shoulder. "I gotta finish getting the engine on that heap refurbished and mounted. Then you."

Jax sucked at his teeth. "What would it take to move us up the line?"

The mechanic looked up at the *Osprey*'s damaged engine nozzle, then up at the ceiling. Jax followed her gaze, realizing that, in between structural supports and the gantry for a heavy crane, were mirrors. He shuddered, hoping there was a perfectly good, non-creepy reason for them.

"Damn," the mechanic said. Her gaze stayed fixed on the mirrors and the dorsal section of the *Osprey*. "You try landing on your back or something?" She pointed. "Is that a piece of someone else's hull?"

"It's complicated," Naomi said.

Jax waved a hand to bring her attention back to him. "So? Bumping us to the top of your list?" When the woman didn't immediately answer, he leaned forward. "Ms. Macklemore?"

The mechanic rubbed her chin. "Name's Nilsson. Macklemore is my ex."

Clinton made a face. "Then why—"

"Costs too much to change the business license." She cut him off. She looked at the three of them. "Ten K, on top of parts and labor."

"Ten?" Jax shouted. "Do we look rich?"

Nilsson shook her head. "You look desperate." She winked. "That's even better. You probably don't have time to be choosy." She added a polite smile for effect.

Jax looked at Naomi, who gave a minute shrug, raising an eyebrow. He sighed. He was about to agree when Baxter stomped down the boarding ramp.

Nilsson spotted the combat droid and gasped.

"It's okay." Jax help up his hands, turning to glare at his mechanical friend. "He's friendly."

"I'm smiling, you just can't tell," the combat droid replied. Naomi cocked her head, looking at him. She shrugged and turned back to the mechanic.

The mechanic guided her hover chair past Jax, nearly knocking him over. "He's in pristine condition."

Baxter nodded. "I am. Thank you."

She stopped in front of the droid. "A Mark IX..." She turned to Jax. "I'll get started on your ship if he stays here."

"Forever?" Jax stammered.

She shook her said. "No, stupid. Just while I work. I want to hear everything he's been through." She looked up at Baxter, her eyes wide. "I bet he's got stories."

Jax looked at Naomi and made a vaguely sexual

gesture. She made a disgusted face and shook her head. Clinton watched them both and sighed.

Jax turned to Baxter. "Bax?"

The big bot looked down at the mechanic. "No weird stuff."

She nodded.

He shrugged. "Okay."

Jax clapped his hands once. "There we go." He looked at Nilsson. "So, how long?"

The strange, droid-obsessed mechanic rubbed her chin. "Two days."

"Too long," Jax replied. He raised his eyebrows. "We have a nav droid. Wanna talk to him too?"

From inside the ship, Rudy shouted, "Are you pimping me out?"

Nilsson made a face. "What? No. Why would I?" She waved him off. "Two days. More if you annoy me."

Jax sighed. "Fine. There a place we can crash that you recommend?"

The *Curry* and her two sister ships were still drifting among the remains of ParStor Station Mort 3, surrounded by two Imperial Lightfoot class corvettes and an Adjudicator class battle cruiser.

Jefferson Sanchez was on the bridge next to Captain Ivano, looking at the main viewscreen and the stern face of Captain Lucy Scanlon of the *Hammer*. He nodded.

"Yes, ma'am. We arrived shortly after the station exploded."

The Imperial naval officer nodded along. "And there was no indication of the cause?"

Captain Ivano took that one. "We detected elevated radiation levels in the debris. My science teams believe the reactors crashed in a cascade that took the station personnel by surprise."

Scanlon frowned. "No survivors?"

Both BioTek employees shook their heads. Sanchez said, "I'm afraid not."

Captain Ivano added, "We're happy to make all of the sensor data available."

Captain Scanlon canted her head. "Thank you. We'll also need you and the other ships to remain on station while we continue our investigation."

"Of course," the pair said as one.

The screen went black. Captain Ivano turned to Sanchez. "Welp."

He slowly adjusted his suit and tie before saying, "Yeah."

"I don't know what the plan is here, Mr. Sanchez, but it now involves three ships." She shook her head. "The board is not likely to appreciate—" she waved her hand "—the cost."

He nodded.

An ensign at the communications station turned and motioned for the captain's attention. She nodded, then turned to Sanchez. "Guessing that's them."

He took a deep breath. "Probably. May I?" He

gestured to the hatch that led to the short corridor and the offices and conference rooms connected to it.

"Be my guest," the captain said, extending a hand toward the hatch.

Conference 1 was much like he'd left it an hour ago. He had watched the attack on ParStor Station Mort 3 from this very room, directing the boarding teams and supervising the ship's intelligence team as they hacked the station's mainframe, searching through the security feeds, such as they were.

He knew destroying the station was a bold move but was running out of moves, bold or otherwise, to contain the problem. How the messenger and two low-life spacers were keeping one step ahead of him, he could not believe. Destroying the station, and every shuttle and lifeboat that launched, had seemed like the only option left on the table.

His boarding teams had barely made it off the station. He'd have to promote and bonus every one of them to ensure their silence.

He sat down as the windows turned opaque and became display screens.

The face on the screen wasn't the twelve faces of the board. A single face was looking at Jefferson. His boss, the CEO of BioTek. "I need just one reason to not fire you, Jeff. The board wants your head. First that business on UniDis Four, now this?" She sighed. "Hundreds, if not thousands, of innocent people, Jeff?"

He made a show of looking down at his clasped hands on the table. Looking up, he said, "Ma'am. I believe this was it. We confirmed they were on the station. After eluding the boarding teams, I made the call. By destroying the station, I ensured that the stolen goods were neutralized."

She stared at him. "No chance of recovery? Those seeds were worth more than that ship you're on."

"Seeds?"

When Monika Jones came to his office weeks ago, she had not known the contents of the cryo-transport case her employees stole. His boss nodded. Clearly, the board knew more than he did. He supposed it made sense given the department but wished his bosses had been more forthcoming. He shook his head. The contents of the case weren't really important to him.

"I didn't like the odds," he said. "The teams that went aboard were unable to pick up the trail. They had to know we were here. I couldn't risk them rabbiting. They'd done it before."

His boss nodded, taking in what he'd just told her. "You're certain? That they're dead. That the seeds are off the board?"

Sanchez nodded. What kind of seeds could be worth all this? His job was his job, no matter what—but seeds?

"Good. The Agri-Tech Symposium, where we presume the seeds were headed, ends in four days—"

Sanchez cut her off. "Symposium?"

"We believe the employees that stole the case, and the seeds, meant to present them at the symposium."

"To what end?"

She shrugged. "We've had teams pouring over security footage since you left. We also set the corporate SI on both employees' email. All we know right now is that they were working with someone but did their best to keep that person's identity hidden." She frowned. "But it doesn't take an SI to know that if these seeds get to that symposium, it won't be good for us."

Sanchez nodded.

The CEO of BioTek said, "Stay there. Smooth over whatever you need to with the Imperials." She looked off screen, then turned back. "I'll do what I can with the board." The screen went dark.

As the windows returned to their regular transparency, he ran a hand through his closely cropped hair. "Ag-Tech Symposium," he murmured.

After grabbing go-bags and ensuring Baxter would keep an eye on the mechanic, Jax, Naomi, Clinton, and Rudy left the spacedock facility, venturing into the station. Rudy and Naomi wanted to see if they could find out what Clinton's clients had intended. Jax wanted to get a drink. Clinton went with Jax.

The first bar they found, one level up from the mechanical section, was Sir Tipsy's. The interior was a mix of old Earth sailing ship and Arthurian knick knacks.

Jax found a booth near the door and sat down. "Well, this is... something." He gestured to the decor. A suit of armor stood between their booth and the next.

Clinton slid into the opposite side of the booth and looked around. "Wouldn't be my first or second choice of themes." He shrugged. "Knights on Earth didn't sail on ship, right?"

Jax shrugged, staring at his gPhone screen and the menu displayed on it. "Not a historian."

A rail thin man, his skin bordering on translucent, arrived. "What can I get ya?" He was wearing some kind of period appropriate outfit: canvas pants and, over them, a tunic that looked like it was handmade. He held a ruggedized gPhone in one hand.

Jax looked up. "We'll have two Only Bad Options."

The man grunted. "That kind of day, huh?"

"That kind of week," Jax replied. The server nodded and walked away.

The pair watched bar patrons come and go in silence until the server returned with their drinks. Clinton took a sip of his and choked. "What is this?" he wheezed.

"Vodka. Mostly," Jax said, downing half his drink in one go. He raised a hand to get the server's attention and nodded toward his half empty drink, then held up two fingers.

"Why does it have a name if it's just mostly vodka?" Clinton wondered, now a bit more composed. He took a cautious sip of the drink, ready for the taste this time.

"Because 'big glass of vodka' sounds bad," Jax replied. He took another drink, emptying his glass as the server arrived with two new glasses. He took the full and offered the empty glass to the man. Nodding to Clinton's side of the table, he said, "He'll catch up."

The server smirked and left without a word.

Clinton eyed his one and a half drinks, took a deep breath, and downed the remainder of his first glass. He slammed the empty glass to the table with more force than intended, causing a few bar patrons to look in their direction. He blushed. "Sorry." He pushed it toward the end of the table. Jax watched without saying a word. Clinton met his gaze and said, "Thank you."

"The drinks are going on your tab," Jax replied.

Clinton clucked. "Of course." He shook his head. "I meant, well, for everything. I know you don't like me and want nothing to do with me."

Jax cut him off. "It's fine."

"It isn't," Clinton replied. "I get it. You came up considerably differently than I did. We're not friends. I'm not your client. You don't owe me anything." He took a sip of his drink, the effects of the first beginning to warm his cheeks. "But I do owe you."

Jax looked down at his drink. "Did she tell you I shot her when we first met?"

Clinton's mouth fell open. "What? Her? Shot? Naomi?"

Jax nodded. "I didn't know her yet. But yeah. She got better, though." He grinned. "We've been working together..." He made a face. "Two years? Before that, it was just me and the droids." He took a sip. "I wasn't looking for a business partner. I certainly wasn't looking for friends."

"You don't have any friends?" Sure, Clinton hadn't seen any of his friends from university in a while, not since becoming a messenger, but he occasionally traded emails with them. How could Jax not have any friends?

Jax shrugged. "I mean, sure, I have some friends back

on Kelso: the Delphinos, Laz, Lucas." He looked at Clinton. "Bartenders count, right? Oh, and Sandor."

Clinton wasn't sure how to respond. He had no idea who any of those people were or what or where Kelso was. He opted to say nothing, letting Jax continue.

"Sure, the Delphinos are kinda mad at me, over the whole Nemesis Fleet thing, and I think I still owe Laz a few grand..." He trailed off as he reached for his drink. After a sip that almost emptied the glass, he said, "I do better alone."

Clinton waved to the server. "Can we get two burgers?" The man nodded.

Jax looked at Clinton. "Thanks. I think I drank those," he motioned to his now almost empty glass, "a bit too fast." He looked Clinton in the eye, his gaze lingering.

Clinton looked away. "Uh, yeah. I think you did." He looked around, spotting the server. "Two waters, too. Please."

"And another round!" Jax shouted. When Clinton turned back to him, he winked. Clinton blushed.

CHAPTER 20

After leaving the docking level, Naomi and Rudy stopped at a restaurant that advertised the best sushi in the sector. She was reasonably sure that was a false boast but figured it would at least be the best sushi on the station.

She ate slowly, enjoying the better-than-mediocre sushi, and more importantly, the silence. At the best of times, Jax could be a bit much, but adding Clinton to the mix had made him unbearable of late. She knew he had attachment issues but also knew it wasn't her job to fix him.

As a piece of toro melted in her mouth, she sighed. "Okay, this is good." She looked at Rudy, patiently waiting next to the table. "Maybe they are the best in the sector."

"Statistically unlikely," he said. "There are two water worlds in this sector: Oceana and Frisk Vand. Both worlds are known for the quality and variety of sea life."

Naomi plucked another piece of sashimi from the plate. "Don't ruin this."

After a meal that stretched out nearly two hours, during which Rudy mentioned the urgency of their research project only three times, they found a data cafe a few levels above the docking complex. Each terminal was in its own small alcove. After finding something sticky on the seat of the first alcove, they tried moving to another, and Rudy and Naomi were hard at work.

She looked at the screen. "An accident?"

Rudy bounced on his smart material rollerball. "BioTek has deep pockets and lots of influence."

On the screen was a news blurb, barely more than a mention, regarding the presumed reactor failure at ParStor Station Mort 3.

She shook her head. "Evil bastard." She shook her head, dismissing the article. "Okay, so we know the case was full of seeds. We're as sure as we can be that Clint's clients on Freeground were BioTek defectors."

"Thank you for that concise recap," Rudy quipped.

She turned to look at the small droid, squinting. "You could have stayed aboard the *Osprey*."

"With that weird, droid-fetish mechanic? No, thank you," the nav droid replied. He pointed to the terminal. "Don't forget to spoof your searches."

She nodded, placing a hand on the top of the small processing core behind the display. Her bio-circuit tattoos glowed and pulsed. "Okay. I routed the network traffic for this terminal through the sticky seat alcove." She turned to Rudy. "I also logged our user account as

Dorothy Zbornak." She chuckled at her own joke. Rudy said nothing.

Naomi turned her attention back to the terminal's display. "Okay, so seeds."

"Yes, we've covered that."

She scowled, holding up a hand, blue bio-circuits glowing. "I will make it so you speak only Italian and roll in reverse."

Ruddy beeped and sank down a few centimeters, changing the density of his rollerball.

Naomi turned back to the screen. "He's a messenger. Where would they want these seeds to end up?" She tapped the screen, scrolling through news feeds.

Rudy pointed to the screen. "What's that?"

Naomi stopped. "Huh." She leaned closer to the screen. She read for a minute, then looked at Rudy. "Have you been to Bustamonte before?"

Rudy swiveled his head back and forth. "No. Jax avoids the Phase 1 colonies when he can."

Naomi clucked. "Not a bad strategy, for sure." She tapped the screen with a fingernail. "The Imperial Agri-Tech Symposium. Held every five years, bringing the best and brightest in the agricultural sector together on one of the Empire's most productive ag-colonies," she read. A moment later, she added, "Started yesterday, ends in four days."

Rudy made a happier beep. "Sounds like a likely destination. They'll certainly have the means to analyze the seeds for...well, whatever it is seeds can do."

Naomi looked at him. "You know plants grow from seeds, right?"

"Of course!" His tone was shrill. "I just don't know what you would analyze a seed to determine."

She shrugged. "Fair enough." Standing, she said, "Let's go find the boys."

Rudy projected the time on the alcove wall. "They are likely incredibly drunk or passed out," he offered.

Naomi sighed. "Drunk Jax is not someone I have the energy for. Let's find a place to crash." Rudy made his nodding gesture and led the way out of the data cafe.

Naomi and Rudy were the first pair to return to the docking area. The *Osprey* looked as good as new, or at least as good as it ever looked. The mechanic Nilsson guided her hover chair toward Naomi. "Morning."

Naomi smiled. "Looks good." She nodded toward the ship's wing over her head.

"You all got a nice little ship." The mechanic smiled. "A little routine maintenance wouldn't hurt, though."

Naomi clucked. "Tell that to her owner."

From the speaker in the boarding area, Skip said, "I have. Repeatedly."

The mechanic chuckled. "Those two are a hoot. I don't think I've laughed as hard as I have the last day and a half in my life."

"Surprised you got it done so fast, then," Naomi said. Rudy rolled up the ramp, vanishing inside the ship.

"That was all Baxter," the blonde-haired woman said. She guided her chair around one of the landing legs, wiping something off of a hydraulic strut. "He was exceptionally helpful."

Naomi smiled. "Good to hear. Did he or Skip get you paid?"

The other woman nodded. "Sure did. You're all set. Just call for departure clearance when you're ready." She drifted back toward the freighter that the *Osprey* had preempted repairs on when they arrived.

Naomi turned at the sound of the hatch grinding open. Jax and Clinton walked in. When they reached her, she eyed each of them suspiciously, eyebrow raised.

Jax leaned in. "The room had two beds. Both were slept in...Mom." He winked. She scowled. "Ship looks great," he added, heading up the boarding ramp.

Clinton fell in with Naomi as she followed Jax up the ramp. She turned to him. "I think I figured out where you were supposed to go."

Convincing the Imperials that ParStor Station Mort 3 suffered a catastrophic reactor cascade failure had proved to be harder than Jefferson expected. Unlike most things, the company's wealth was not able to smooth over the issue. Captain Ivano's people, as well as the crews of the two other ships, had been working long hours to fabricate sensor logs and readings to share with the captain of the massive battle cruiser still hanging over the small cluster of corporate cruisers.

Jefferson had moved to the small office set just off his

VIP quarters. Mrs. Loreda, BioTek's CEO, mentioned a symposium as the likely destination for the messenger and his case. He was scrolling through the details page for the Imperial Agri-Tech Symposium taking place on Bustamonte, a colony in Phase 2 space settled by humanity in the early days of expansion. Humanity had barely touched Phase 1 space when Phase 2 opened up at the behest of corporations and smaller governments wanting in on the gold rush of planets.

He looked at the list of attending and supporting companies. BioTek, of course, was one of the main sponsors. He didn't recognize any of the names, but that wasn't surprising.

Jefferson was taking a sip of an expensive whiskey the captain had offered him, when a pop-up appeared in the corner of his display. The alert opened to a notice from one of the smart routines he had set loose. This one wasn't looking for the messenger. It was the one looking for any mention or sighting of a Valerian Co-op Infiltrator.

He leaned forward. "Interesting." Using the various backdoors that BioTek's weapons and computer subsidiaries had access to, he'd launched Rudimentary Intelligence search routines into the internex to scour every security feed, customs database, and sensor log to look for the messenger's biometrics or that unidentified ship he was on.

If this was them, they had to have set down for repairs. That station was too remote for any other use. Could they know about the symposium? He took a sip, letting the whiskey burn its way down his throat. It stood to reason that the traitors that hired him would have told the messenger where he was going.

Jefferson closed the terminal down and tapped an icon on the desk. "Mduba, get the team together and prep a gunship. I'll be right there."

"Copy that, sir."

After disconnecting, he tapped the icon for the bridge. "I'm going to take a gunship and check on something. Can you keep the Imperials busy?"

Captain Ivano made a noise on the other end. "I thought this was over?"

He nodded, though she couldn't see him. "Probably, but I need to be sure."

"Will the board like that?"

He tapped the icon closing the connection. By now, Mduba and the rest of his reaction team were assembled. He opened up the terminal again, pulling up a star chart. "Hmm." Bustamonte was not far. If they were on that station making repairs and left soon, or had already, they'd make it to Bustamonte before that symposium was over.

Jefferson got to his feet.

Naomi finished telling Clinton and Jax about the symposium she and Rudy discovered. She looked at Clinton.

He shook his head. "I've never heard of it. Like I told you. The gunfight happened before those guys could finish the sync, let alone tell me where I was supposed to go." He was standing next to her bridge station.

The *Osprey* had left Second Chance ten minutes ago. Jax had them on a course to get clear of the gravity well of the station's parent planet. While it was technically possible to open a wormhole in orbit, the effects on the planet below, and the ship opening it, were such that no one did it. He turned. "So, what? We go there?" His face made it clear what he thought of that idea.

Naomi held up a hand. "Hear me out."

Jax looked over his shoulder at his flight console. "We're ten more minutes from safe wormhole distance." He looked up. "Skip, keep an eye on things."

"Of course," the ship's SI replied.

Everyone filed off the bridge down to the common deck and lounge space. Once everyone was seated, Naomi powered up the large entertainment display on the bulkhead. The internex page for the Imperial Agri-Tech Symposium.

"Bustamonte?" Jax said, reading the screen.

Clinton nodded slowly. The shiny metallic case of seeds was on the coffee table before them. He looked at the display. "Makes sense." He shrugged. "I mean, the timing is pretty spot on. If that greasy loser and his friends hadn't barged in, I'd be there already, offloading to whomever is waiting for the seeds."

He looked back down at the seeds. "But we don't know who's waiting for them."

Baxter came up the stairs from the cargo and engineering deck. Everyone turned to look at him, causing him to stop. "What?"

Jax tilted his head. "I dunno. I kinda thought maybe she bot-napped you."

There was an awkward silence, then the big combat droid said, "And you didn't look before we took off?"

Naomi and Clinton turned to look at Jax, who was just then realizing the trap he set for himself.

Jax coughed. "What's that, Skip? We're ready for wormhole? Great, be right there." He jumped up off the sofa and bounded for the stairs.

Clinton, Naomi, and Baxter watched the ship's captain retreat. The former turned. "So, uh...What did that mechanic lady want with you?"

Baxter moved to stand near the small kitchenette. "None of your business, you weirdo."

Clinton looked like he'd been struck. "That's not... No. What I—" he spluttered.

Naomi watched the exchange with interest, knowing the big bot's sense of humor.

Baxter shook his head. "Too easy. She's a Sapient Intelligence fangirl. Especially loves the processing cores that were created just for combat droids." He put a hand on this armored chest. "The Mark IX design was the last, and we were fitted with specially designed cores, capable of more nuanced thinking."

Clinton smiled. "I see. That's—"

Baxter cut him off again. "Plus, she was super freaky and wanted to have sex, a lot of it."

Clinton's eyes went wide.

Naomi discreetly put a hand over her mouth, biting her lip.

"Super freaky stuff. Would make Jax blush," Baxter continued.

Naomi looked at Clinton, who was now beet red, both hands held out in front of him, waving frantically.

Baxter made a rattling, laugh-like sound and headed for the stairs. "I'll be downstairs."

Naomi looked at Clinton, who was staring at her. She couldn't contain her laughter any more.

Up on the bridge, Jax looked over his shoulder at Rudy. "What the hell's going on down there?"

"You do not want to know," Skip said before the small nav droid could reply.

Jax shook his head, then said, "Course ready?"

Rudy beeped. "Yup. All set. Looks like thirty hours travel time."

"Cutting it close," Jax said, accepting the nav plot on his flight console. He powered up the wormhole generator, hearing the powerful machine's hum through the ship's hull.

"Off we go," he said, pushing the controls forward, driving the small ship into the rip in space-time directly ahead of them.

CHAPTER 21

"It's pretty," Jax said as the *Osprey* approached Bustamonte. Kelso station was in the middle of Phase 3 space, and most of Jax's work kept him in that region. The Unification War, while affecting the entire human sphere, had been fought mainly in Phase 1 and 2 space.

Bustamonte was one of those early worlds that humanity stumbled on that was just waiting for them. Next to no terraforming had been required, but even better, the bacterial landscape was hospitable to Earth crops. Wheat, corn, sorghum, and dozens of other grains took to the planet naturally. Animals also proved to have few, if any, issues. The planet became one of humanity's first bread basket planets, providing foodstuffs for almost all of Phase 2 and a large portion of Phase 1 worlds.

Naomi was busy looking at her console. She sighed. "I hate these bougie-ass planets." She looked up at Jax. "Two hours wait before we can even get an orbital insert."

Jax growled. "You tell them we're in a hurry?"

She clucked. "Surprisingly, they weren't that interested. Go figure."

Clinton, standing near Naomi, looked past Jax out the forward windows. There were dozens of ships visible between them and the planet, mostly science vessels of the Imperial variety, but there were plenty of corporate logos to be seen on hulls as well.

Hanging silently like massive ogres in high orbit were two Adjudicator class battle cruisers.

Clinton whistled. "Those aren't at all intimidating."

The kilometers-long ships, like mushrooms on their side, were just sitting there, gun ports closed, looking ominous and powerful, each ship a projection of the emperor's might.

"Ugly mushrooms," Jax said under his breath.

"We are being scanned," Skip announced.

Everyone tensed. After a moment, Skip said, "Why were you holding your breath?"

Naomi and Jax turned to Clinton. The taller man made a face. "I don't know. I've never been scanned before."

Jax sighed. He released the controls to Skip and turned his chair. "So, what now?"

Naomi looked at her screen, then said, "We're 84th in line for orbital clearance. Estimated wait, just under two hours now."

"Beers, then," Jax said, standing. He eyed Naomi. "Maybe Mario Kart."

She smiled. "I'll wipe the deck with you, you—"

"A BioTek gunship just arrived," Skip interrupted.

Jax spun his chair back around, locking it into position in the same motion he reclaimed flight control.

"Is it him? That Sanchez guy?" Clinton asked, leaning over Naomi's shoulder.

She shoved him away. "It looks like it's registered to the *Curry*. So yeah, probably him."

Jax swore and powered up the sub-light engines. He looked out the forward windows at the nearest Imperial battle cruiser. "Stay put." Studying the tactical display, he added, "Has he spotted us?"

"Unknown," Skip replied. "We are not being targeted."

"Oh, no," Clinton whined. "Should we call the Imperials?"

Jax looked over his shoulder, his smirk half hidden. He turned back to the tactical display, watching the gunship approach. It was still a way out.

Jax turned again. "Declare an emergency. See if they'll bump us up."

Naomi nodded and tapped on her console.

"Take it easy. Be cool," Rudy said.

Jax made a noise. "Should I roll the window down, hang my arm out?"

Naomi turned to the nav droid's station opposite her, making a face.

"What?" the droid snapped.

She shook her head.

"He's going to spot us before we get our chance to land," Naomi warned. The three humans and one droid on the bridge had their eyes and optic sensors glued to the tactical sensors that were passively watching the approaching gunship.

Naomi's entreaties to the space control operator had gotten them bumped halfway up the queue of ships waiting for landing clearance. The BioTek gunship was still making its slow and unassuming approach to the planet.

"At least they haven't alerted the Imperials," Rudy offered, pointing out through the window to one of the massive battle cruisers still in view.

"That we know of," Clinton said. Everyone turned to glare at him. He took an involuntary step back. "Sorry."

"They may not have alerted the Imperials," Skip said, breaking the silence. "But I believe that they have alerted several other ships." The tactical display that everyone was staring at updated. Several icons changed positions and were on tracks to intercept the *Osprey*. "I am currently tracking two BioTek vessels and a Tellus ship. None are military, all are armed."

Naomi looked at one of the screens on her console that wasn't showing the tactical feed. "The Tellus and one of the BioTek ships left their place in the queue. The other BioTek ship is parked in orbit."

"I believe they are attempting to box us in," Skip

warned as he updated the tactical display with the projected courses of the three ships.

Jax goosed the thrusters a bit, guiding the ship closer to the one in front of them and slightly below it. He twisted the control stick, bringing the *Osprey* under the freighter. A press of a button and the landing gear unfolded, the powerful electromagnets activating to lock the small ship to the larger one.

The *Osprey* was about to latch on to the freighter when Skip said, "The gunship is accelerating."

Jax swore. He slapped the control to retract the landing gear. "Guess hiding is out." He pushed the throttle control forward.

"That's got people's attention," Naomi said. One of the displays on her console was monitoring local comms traffic, and suddenly that screen was awash in frantic broadcasts.

Jax glanced at the tactical readout on his console. It did not present a pretty picture. It seemed the gunship had spotted the *Osprey*, based on its targeting of them. The ship he was about to hide under was accelerating away from the *Osprey*, along with several other ships, all bolting in different directions.

"Oh no," Clinton moaned.

Jax brought the *Osprey* up and around the fleeing freighter, putting it between them and the gunship. As the nimble scout ship rose above the freighter, Jax used the foot pedals and flight controls to swing the ship around, bringing its nose to bear on the inbound gunship.

"Don't fire!" Naomi and Rudy shouted as one.

"I wasn't going to!" Jax shouted back. "Jeez!" He

gunned the sub-light engines, closing the distance between them and the oncoming gunship.

The smaller ship opened fire from a top-mounted turret. The blasts splashed against the shields. Clinton screamed as the gunship raced past the *Osprey*.

"He gets to fire," Jax complained, bring the ship around in a tight arc.

Before anyone could reply, the overhead speaker crackled. "All vessels in the Bustamonte orbital space, stand down immediately." After a pause, the voice continued. "There will be no further warnings. All ships in the Bustamonte orbital area are to cut thrust and power down."

Jax reached over and cut the comms. "That isn't happening."

"The *Jupiter* is moving," Skip announced.

Jax glanced up. "The planet?"

The overhead speaker made an exasperated-sounding noise. "No, the INV-1223 *Jupiter*. Adjudicator class battleship. Directly overhead."

Jax looked up and out of the forward window. "Oh."

True enough, the massive mushroom-shaped vessel was slowly angling toward the mad scramble of freighters. Jax looked at the tactical display to confirm that the *Jupiter*'s sister ship, the *Justicar*, was still where he'd last seen it. Thankfully, the *Justicar* had not fired up its engines. He did a double take, finally noticing the ship's registry. "Shit, the *Justicar*."

"You just now realized it was them?" Skip said.

Jax didn't deign to reply, his attention fully back to what was directly ahead of him. Namely, a lumbering bulk freight flagged out of New Egypt.

"Friends of yours?" Clinton asked. He had braced himself in the space between Naomi's and Rudy's stations.

"You could say that," Rudy answered.

The *Osprey* banked around the massive freighter, bringing the aggressive gunship back into view. Jax slapped the weapons console.

"I don't think that's a good—" Naomi started.

He held up a finger to silence the objection. Before Rudy could add his warning, Jax rotated a small selector on his flight control stick, then squeezed the trigger.

A loud clunk echoed through the ship.

"Did you just fire a—" Rudy started, stopping when a small missile streaked from the top of the forward window.

"Dude!" Clinton shouted.

The missile struck the shields of another freighter, a mid-sized hauler. The impact was a fraction of what the missile was capable of but had the desired effect. The terrified ship's captain pushed his engines to max thrust, driving his massive vessel directly into the flight path of the onrushing gunship.

As the *Osprey* angled around under another ship eight times her size, Clinton said, "That was actually pretty clever."

Rudy made his nodding gesture. "Indeed. Quite clever. Did you see it on a vid?"

"Hardy har har," Jax grated as he steered them back toward Bustamonte.

"Not out of the woods yet," Naomi said. She nodded toward the tactical display on Jax's flight console. He looked down, seeing that the two BioTek ships were still bearing down on them from their respective places in orbit. The nearest was only two minutes away.

"Oh, and the *Justicar* is adjusting course," Skip added.

Clinton swore. "What now? Even you're not insane enough to go up against two Imperial battle cruisers!"

Jax didn't turn. "You're damn right I'm not." He tapped a few icons on the weapons control panel. "But we can do what we do best."

"Oh, boy," Rudy said.

Jax spun the selector on his flight control stick and squeezed the trigger. Four *ca-thunks* echoed through the hull just prior to four missiles streaking past overhead. Each missile split off, arcing toward individual ships.

Jax had picked each target specifically. The moment each ship realized a missile was coming for it, they lit their engines off at full thrust on whatever vector they could think of.

One of the larger freighters accelerated right into the flight path of the *Jupiter*.

The local comm channels were now flooded with freighter captains, shouting in shock, dismay, and confusion, depending on whether a missile was coming for them or not.

One of the missiles found its target, exploding harmlessly on the ship's meager shields.

"The *Justicar* is closing," Rudy said.

"So are the BioTek ships. The Tellus ship has slowed but is still angling to block our route to the planet," Naomi said. "Must be getting cold feet," she added.

In the midst of the confusion, one of the freighters being pursued by a missile steered right into the path of the much larger *Justicar*. Both ships had too much momentum. The warship's shields took the impact, flaring brightly as the freighter buckled against them momentarily. The force of the freighter striking the shields blew out several emitters across the wide domed front of the battlecruiser.

"That's our cue," Jax said. He lined up on the small science vessel from Tellus that was still burning, albeit slowly, to intercept them. He pushed the sub-light throttle forward, driving the *Osprey* toward the planet at breakneck speed.

"Entering the atmosphere at this speed is not recommended," Skip warned.

"Yippee Ki—Oh shit!" Jax shouted.

The BioTek gunship swung wide around one of the scrambling freighters ahead of them, lining up to fire.

Jax pushed the foot pedals and pulled his flight control stick hard over, forcing the *Osprey* into a tight corkscrew. Blaster bolts splashed across their shields.

The bridge lighting flickered as the smaller ship raced past.

"They are not pulling their punches," Skip announced.

"Gimme a route down to the planet!" Jax ordered. "We don't stand a chance up here once those two heavies get everyone calmed down." He yanked the controls hard over again, forcing the ship into a tight turn, the gunship doing its best to keep up after making its own tight turn after passing the *Osprey*.

"This is the best I can come up with," Rudy said. A display on Jax's console updated with a flight path. "You'll need to get that freighter out of the way, ideally along the vector in yellow."

The lights flickered again as the tenacious little gunship continued to fire on their aft shields.

"Got it." Jax brought up the missile control panel, selecting two and increasing the yield on their warheads up from the twenty percent he had been using to scare the other freighters to forty percent. "That should do it." He grinned, selecting the freighter Rudy flagged. He squeezed the trigger twice. The telltale *thunks* echoed through the ship.

One of the missiles streaked toward the targeted freighter to a point off its starboard side, where it exploded just close enough to flare the ship's shields and spook the captain. The other missile was heading straight for the freighter, which was more than enough to sell it. The ship's engines flared to full power, sending it straight toward the nearest Imperial ship, the *Jupiter*. Unlike the *Justicar*, the *Jupiter*'s captain wasn't willing to risk her ship. The massive warship's weapons flared to life, shredding the freighter, creating an ever-growing cloud of cargo modules, luckless crew members, and other debris.

Jax pushed the throttles all the way forward. The *Osprey*'s shields flared as bits of the now dead freighter impacted on them. "Let's try this again!" He spared a glance at the tactical readout, getting a lay of the land. The debris cloud had the *Jupiter* blocked for the moment, and the gunship was falling back, its engines nowhere near the *Osprey*'s in output.

"We are coming faster than is advisable," Skip warned. Jax ignored him, following the nav plot Rudy provided. It was continually updating as they got clear of the confusion.

"Jax?" Naomi asked.

The nav plot updated as Rudy added more data. They did not have landing clearance from orbital space control, but Rudy and Skip were accessing the local planetary net.

"Captain, the planetary air traffic controllers are being quite vociferous in their displeasure at our approach."

"They'll get over it. Do we know where we're going?"

"I'm working on it," Rudy replied.

"Faster would be better," Jax said through gritted teeth.

The *Osprey* was just reaching the outer atmosphere. The gunship was still on their tail but out of weapons range. The two Imperial warships were still doing their best to corral the frantic freighters and other assorted vessels in orbit.

Jax glanced at the tactical readout again. There was no sign of the other two BioTek ships. They likely fled back into the confusion.

"I thought we agreed. No more dying," Clinton said from where he was holding himself steady between Naomi's and Rudy's stations.

CHAPTER 22

The bridge was lit by the flickering light of plasma streamers deflecting off the *Osprey*'s shields.

"Skip," Jax said.

"On it. Angling deflectors," the ship's SI replied. The color of the plasma streamers changed slightly. "That is the best I can do. One of the gunship's shots overloaded the starboard ventral emitter."

"What?" Clinton shouted over the roar.

"Calm down," Skip said. "The emitter is still functional, and we will be through the worst of our reentry momentarily."

The ship jolted.

"Oh, good," Clinton quipped.

The forward view cleared, revealing a beautiful world of pastures, farms, and cities.

Jax reached out and flipped first one switch, then another. "Cutting over to atmospherics," he said as he pressed a button next to the last switch. The hum of the sub-light engines faded until the concussive boom of the atmospheric engines igniting—pushing everyone into their seat backs and Clinton to the back of the bridge, a few steps short of falling down the staircase—drowned them out.

"I'm okay," Clinton said.

Ignoring the messenger, Naomi just said, "Wow." After looking up from her console to glance past Jax out the forward windows, she added, "So much open space."

"The locals are attempting to override our flight controls," Skip announced.

"Can you stop 'em?" Jax looked down at his console, not noticing anything wrong.

"No, I thought I would let you know. They're in full control." Before Jax could reply, the SI continued, "Of course I am blocking them."

"They're also yelling at us on every available channel," Naomi said.

Outside the *Osprey*, the landscape was flashing by below. Square kilometer after square kilometer of assorted grain crops interspersed with small stands of trees to provide windbreaks for the farms. In the distance, the towers of the nearest city were coming into view. The buildings were a mix of steel and glass winding around each other like they had been grown.

"Rudy..." Jax said as they roared over another tract of farmland.

"So, uh, now what?" Clinton asked.

"Now you go grab your seeds, maybe a backpack, and get ready," Jax said. He glanced at the tactical screen. The gunship, no doubt that prick Sanchez at the helm, was being joined by a half dozen smaller atmospheric interceptors. He groaned. The gunship wasn't a threat at their current speed, but the interceptors were not only coming from the city ahead but could easily keep up with the *Osprey* in an atmosphere.

"Found it!" Rudy said.

Jax looked over his shoulder at Clinton, then at Naomi. "Go get ready. This is the easy part."

"The easy part?" Clinton moaned, only to be silenced by the ship rocking back and forth as low-powered blaster fire splashed against the forward shields as the interceptors raced past.

Naomi stood. "Come on, Green Bean, let's go." She pushed him toward the stairs.

Jax looked at the ceiling. "Baxter, get ready to go. We're gonna need an escort."

"When have you known me to not be ready?" the reply came back.

Jax shook his head, bringing his full attention back to the city ahead, now much closer.

The interceptors were already making wide arcing turns to make another run on the *Osprey*. The gunship was still on their tail.

Directly ahead of them, the city of Roanoke was visible. Closer now, Jax wasn't sure that the dozens of steel and glass towers spread out directly in front of them hadn't, in fact, been grown. Two of the tallest towers seemed to lean against each other, each holding the other tower up. Everything looked so organic. Hard angles were in short supply.

"Where to, pal?" Jax pressed.

"There," Rudy said as Jax's nav console updated. The

convention center complex was on the opposite side of the city in a sprawling campus that abutted another section of the ever-present farmland that surrounded the city for hundreds of kilometers in every direction.

Jax took a deep breath, then pushed the atmospheric engines to full power. The small ship roared as it closed the distance to Roanoke. Jax guided the ship in a wide arc around the cluster of towers that made up the downtown core. The interceptors were hot on their tail.

"Captain, you need to reduce your speed by eighty percent, at a minimum, in order to land," Skip warned.

Jax toggled their countermeasures package and pressed the activation switch. A series of thuds echoed as small canisters popped out of their compartment along the *Osprey*'s spine.

Once clear of the ship, each canister activated. Some exploded into expanding clouds of reflective confetti. Others burst like small suns, emitting a blinding light in all directions. Yet others fired an electromagnetic pulse that distorted sensor readings for several seconds.

The countermeasures were doing their thing. Jax pushed the flight stick forward while angling the *Osprey* around toward the sprawling convention center complex. At the same time, he pulled back the atmospheric engine throttles, cutting their speed enough to force him forward in his seat.

Ahead, he spied a landing area, meant for personal and commuter shuttles. "That'll work," he said, then added, "Full stealth!"

"That landing area is far too small for us," Skip warned.

"Stealth systems activated," Rudy announced.

"Nah, it'll be fine," Jax assured the ship's managing Intelligence.

"It will not," Skip insisted.

Even though the ship's aft sensors were still a bit scrambled by the countermeasures, the rear camera spotted the interceptors shooting by in a straight line out over the farmland beyond.

"That bought a few minutes," Rudy said.

Jax nodded as he pulled the atmospheric throttles back further. He slapped the landing gear controls as the ship continued to drop. The slap of another control panel powered up the lift engines. Jax eased up the power to the lift engines as he continued to reduce their airspeed.

"This will not work," Skip said.

Jax had his eyes glued to the sensor screens, especially their airspeed and altitude. Without warning, he pulled the *Osprey*'s nose up, flared the lift engines beyond their rated maximum thrust, and killed the atmospheric engines.

Their speed nearly zeroed out before Jax pushed the flight stick forward to level them out. The *Osprey* hit the ground at an angle, causing the ship to skip off the ground as her landing gear dug into the permacrete. They skipped two more times before the nose settled lower and clipped the side of a commuter shuttle, leaving a sizeable scratch in the *Osprey*'s paint.

The *Osprey* came to a stop teetering on her birdlike landing gear. Sparks fell from several overloaded pieces of equipment on the bridge.

"That wasn't so bad," Jax groaned, releasing the latch to the harness that kept him in his seat.

"Should I read off the list of damaged systems?" Skip asked.

"No."

By the time Jax and Rudy made it to the boarding room, Naomi was suited up and helping Clinton into one of Jax's long overcoats. On the taller man, it was closer to a regular coat that was just slightly too long. Jax grabbed a pair of pistols from the locker. He looked at the other man. "I want that coat back when this is over."

"I'll do my best," Clinton quipped.

Baxter was already waiting on the permacrete at the base of the lowered boarding ramp. "We should go now," he called out.

Jax grabbed two spare power cells, shoving them into pockets in his cargo pants before rushing down the ramp. The others were right behind him.

"Seal up, Skip. Deploy defenses. Non-lethal," Jax ordered as they headed toward the entrance to the convention complex. "Oh, and keep as much of your stealth systems active as you can," he added, looking over his shoulder.

Their landing had drawn a moderate amount of attention, mostly in the form of shuttle pilots waiting with their vessels—many of which were now damaged or ruined after being landed on by a ship much larger than them. By the time the crew was moving, the area had cleared out. Furious or not, none of the aggrieved pilots wanted to mess with an angry-looking combat droid in a cloak.

Behind them, the sound of small anti-personnel blasters deploying from the *Osprey*'s wing roots was barely audible over the pings and pops of the hull cooling off.

The landing area was one of many, all of which emptied into a grand multistory foyer. According to the map on the wall outside, there were five other landing pads arrayed around the main foyer and ten smaller pads two levels up. Jax remembered seeing the small pads flash by on their way down. He ushered everyone into the building.

"Damn, this place is fancy," Naomi said, looking around. "We should come to Phase 1 space more often." The domed foyer hall was ringed by hanging banners in concentric circles. Every other banner was the Imperial logo; the rest were the logos of the many worlds of the Empire. A gracefully curving ramp connected the doorways to the smaller landing pads. The ramp met up with the level Jax and the others were on a few meters away. The floor of the foyer was two levels below them.

The commotion from the landing area was only beginning to reach those meandering the great hall. As people murmured to each other and looked toward Jax and the others, the sight of Baxter was the final catalyst. Shouts of surprise and terror punctuated the background noise of conversations.

Clinton looked up at the big bot in his dark cloak. "I don't think your disguise is as effective in daylight."

Jax looked around. "We should go before whatever passes for security here gets moving." He started off toward a corridor but stopped when Rudy made a loud noise. He turned to see the small droid pointing toward a different wing than the one he was heading for. Their level had four enormous staircases that brought visitors down to the main floor and the branching corridors of conference space beyond.

Jax winked. "Look at you, pointing the way. Navigating, as it were."

"There's a directory right over there," the droid replied, adding, "asshole," at a lower volume.

Baxter put a hand on Clinton's shoulder, turning him the correct way, then set off leading the way, his cloak billowing behind him.

A hundred meters down the corridor, a group of people dressed as animals surged out of the ballroom ahead of the team. They were laughing and petting each other as they filed out of their wing of the conference space. Baxter's arms snapped up, taking aim at the group. It took the group a moment to realize what was happening. One of them looked over, spying the combat droid and his arm blasters pointed at them. The man screamed and fell backward, tripping over his skunk tail, knocking over a basset hound next to him.

Two women, both dressed as squirrels, pointed toward Baxter and shrieked, stumbling over each other as they ran back toward where they came from.

Baxter lowered his arms. "Please. You are not in

danger. Clear the hallway." When the rest of the group didn't move, he doubled his volume. "NOW." They scrambled back into the room they came from.

"Guess the seed nerds aren't the only ones having a convention," Jax quipped.

"According to the local network, there are five concurrent events taking place this week: the symposium we're looking for; the, uh, furry gathering; a conference for software developers; an agri-tech sub-function around farm equipment; and what I can only describe as a poorly disguised pyramid scheme beauty product company's annual gala," Rudy offered.

The group continued past the main door to the wing the furries were using.

"I tried one of those schemes before signing up as a messenger," Clinton said.

Jax and Naomi turned to him. The former said, "What?"

"Pyramid scheme. I knew what it was, but," he shrugged, "I was looking for direction."

Jax clucked. "No offense, dude. I wouldn't buy makeup from you."

Clinton made a face. "It wasn't makeup, asshole. It was health and fitness stuff. You know—protein supplements, vitamins, health nanites, that kind of stuff. You'd buy a bunch of stock, then entice your friends and—"

A trio of convention center security officers rounded a corner up ahead, stopping Clinton from elaborating further.

"Drop your weapons," Baxter boomed, his arms snapping up to take aim.

The three women gaped a moment, then sprang into action: two drawing their stunners, one leaping for cover, her hand reaching for the gPhone secured to her sash.

Baxter was faster. Both of his arm blasters barked as stun blasts lanced out, dropping the two women who drew their weapons. One of them got off a shot that went wide as her fingers went numb a moment before she collapsed.

Without missing a beat, Baxter charged toward the corner the third woman was behind. She leaned out, spotting the charging droid, and fired. Her stunner's energy blasts rippled off of Baxter's armored hide. He fired a single blast that dropped the woman.

He turned to the others, pointing to the third woman's hand, her gPhone clutched in numb fingers. "Good bet they know where we are now. More will be coming."

Jax nodded. "By now Sanchez and his goon squad are here, too."

From all of their earpieces, Skip said, "You are correct. The gunship landed two pads over. I am certain they saw me as they made their approach."

"What about those interceptors?" Jax asked.

"They circled once and departed. I do not believe their angle allowed for a visual spotting of me."

Jax nodded. Better news than he had hoped for. He motioned everyone to keep moving.

Clinton took a deep breath, hitching his backpack up, tightening the straps.

Naomi stopped at an information kiosk, placing her hand on the screen. The display flickered and then went blank as lines of code scrolled from the top. Her bio-circuitry tattoos lit up all along her arm. The faint tracery of blue along her cheeks and around her eyes pulsed similarly.

"Naomi?" Jax pressed.

She shushed him, then turned to Jax and the others. "Yeah, the entire convention center is on alert now. The locals are coordinating with what they're calling 'outside experts.'"

"BioTek," Rudy said. Everyone nodded.

"I think Sanchez is trying his comm blackout trick, too," Naomi added.

"Then they haven't called in the Empire?" Clinton wondered.

She shook her head. "Not that I could see."

Jax nodded slowly. "Okay, that's good, -ish."

"Is it?" Clinton wondered. He had no particular love for the Empire, but surely, they'd put an end to BioTek's maniacal manhunt.

Jax shook his head. "This is whole adventure is borked enough without adding shock troopers stomping everywhere in lockstep." He angled his head. "Plus, this time, we're ready for his tricks. With Rudy and Baxter here, Skip can keep a local mesh connection for us open."

Baxter made a noise. "Well armed antenna reporting

for duty. We should find the seed nerds, and fast." He turned and continued down the corridor.

Everyone nodded and fell in behind him.

"This place is gigantic!" Jax said as they reached another wide intersection. He'd accompanied his aunt to a few conferences around the Empire over the years. Usually as her valet, but he never cared. None of them had ever been held in a facility as gigantic as this one.

Naomi was about to reply when a quartet of convention security personnel rounded a corner up ahead. The security people pointed and began running toward the *Osprey* crew.

"They're in a hurry," Jax said, head cocked to one side, watching the four earnest security personnel rush toward them, stunners in hand.

Baxter waited until the security folks were one hundred meters away, then raised his arms and opened fire. Stun blasts lashed out, striking all four security people multiple times. He turned to look at the others as four unconscious bodies hit the ground, sliding into furniture. "Shall we?"

Jax grinned. "You're enjoying this way too much."

The big bot shrugged. "Most of our jobs, I don't get to shoot people." His cloak fluttered.

"Do you have a fan tucked under there?" Rudy asked. He rolled ahead of the group, pointing to a wayfinding sign. "The midday general session is getting started." He bobbed. "Big crowd."

Everyone followed the small droid as he set off down the hallway, dodging unconscious bodies. Clinton accidentally nudged one of the knocked-out security people with his foot. "Oh, excuse me." He blushed and looked around.

"Heard that," Jax shouted over his shoulder.

Despite the ruckus that was following the crew as they moved through the convention center, the authorities were not alerting the building as a whole. Twice more on their way to the main hall for Wing B, groups of attendees came out, shocked at the sight of the combat droid and, often, stunned convention security littering the carpeted hallways.

"Here we are," Rudy said as they reached a pair of doors that looked exactly like every other door in the massive building. A digital signboard next to the closed doors read "Imperial Agri-Tech Symposium: Midday General Session: New Developments in Fungiculture."

Jax read the board. "Not sad we're interrupting this. Eel nuggets were bad enough. No way I'm eating fungus."

Clinton looked at him, then Naomi. "Eel nuggets?"

"Hate to break it to you," Rudy said.

"Long story. The short version is never go to Themura," Naomi said.

He paled. "Eel nuggets?"

Jax looked at Baxter and nodded. The big bot pushed the pair of doors open. They swung in, slammed against the wall, and swung back shut loudly in the big bot's face. Baxter turned slightly. "Too hard."

"You think?" Jax replied.

Naomi was nodding.

Baxter pushed the doors again, more gently this time. By the time Jax and the others stepped in, every occupant in the room, all three thousand or so of them, had turned in their seats to look at the door and the new arrivals.

"I've had nightmares that start like this," Clinton said. He gave the crowd a sheepish wave.

Jax nodded. "At least we're clothed." He looked down to be sure.

"Saw that," Clinton said with a smirk.

Naomi sighed.

Jax led the group into the conference hall. After a few steps, he raised his pistol, setting it from stun back to normal mode. He fired two shots at the ceiling, causing the room to burst into gasps and cries of shock. Those nearest him leaned back in their chairs, and several scrambled out of their seats.

He was about to speak when glass rained down on them from above. He swore, looking up when it was over to see the ruined skylight overhead. Several people near him were glaring as they brushed glass off themselves.

"Smooth," Baxter quipped.

Naomi pushed the doors closed, placing a hand on the locking mechanisms. Her bio-circuits pulsed, then the locks clacked into place. She moved to the other set of doors and did the same thing. She looked into the room. Jax, Clinton, and Baxter were making their way to the stage. Every eye in the room was tracking them, including the eyes of the woman on stage. Looking at Rudy, who had stayed with her, she said, "Guess we'll wait here."

He held up a small fist, bobbing it up and down.

The woman behind the podium watched as the two men and what looked like a droid wearing some type of cloak approached. When they were almost to the stage, she said, "I'm sorry. Who are you?" She pointed to the massive display mounted on the wall behind her. "I'm in the middle of—"

"Trying to convince people to eat fungus, yeah I know," Jax interrupted. He looked over his shoulder at the assembled symposium guests. "They'll thank us."

"Why, I never—" she spluttered.

In the back of the room, Rudy said, "Do you think we should tell him how many meals are fungus-based proteins?"

Naomi shook her head.

Jax waved a hand. "We've got something more important than fungus." He turned to Clinton and nodded toward the stage.

Several loud thuds came from doors behind Naomi. She jumped and looked at Rudy, who bobbed on his rollerball, then rolled a few feet farther from the doors.

A man in the last row turned to look at Naomi and Rudy. "What's going on here?"

Naomi smiled. "Just exposing massive corporate corruption and criminal wrongdoing."

"At an agri-tech conference?"

She shrugged. "The furries weren't interested."

The door behind Naomi exploded inward, sending

her and Rudy sprawling to the ground. The man she was speaking to released a startled yelp and scrambled over the person in the chair next to him.

Jax and Clinton spun, both of their mouths falling open as Jefferson Sanchez walked in surrounded by his BioTek agents and a dozen convention center security officers.

Jax turned to Clinton and shoved him toward the stage. "Go! Get up there!"

Sanchez took a few steps into the room and raised the pulse rifle he was carrying, taking aim at Clinton. He squeezed the trigger.

Jax watched the corporate security man raise his rifle. Saw where it was being aimed. Saw that Clinton had his back to the new arrivals. Jax spun and dove toward Clinton as the rifle barked.

Jax tackled Clinton to the ground. The pair landed with a thud next to the stage, Clinton shouting in alarm.

"What the hell, man! You said go up on stage!" Clinton shoved Jax off of him.

Jax rolled away and sat up, patting his body all over. When he couldn't find a singed spot, he looked up.

Over him and Clinton stood Baxter. His cloak was sporting a new scorch mark, smoke still wafting from it. "Downright heroic," the bot said in his deep voice. He shrugged out of the now-ruined cloak, offering a hand to each man. "I liked that cloak," Baxter said. Once Jax and Clinton were on their feet, he spun toward the oncoming security forces.

"Stay back," he boomed. His arm blasters snapped into place a moment before his twin railguns rose out of his back, swiveling into place over his shoulders. He moved slowly back down the aisle toward the middle of the spacious room.

Jax shoved Clinton toward the side of the stage and the steps up to the lectern.

Naomi rolled onto her back, looking around.

The convention security people that came in with Sanchez had her and Rudy surrounded, weapons aimed at the pair. Both slowly raised their arms.

At a low volume, Rudy said, "I wish I had my knives." Naomi sighed and shook her head.

The commotion and gunplay sent the speaker woman to the back of the stage to hide behind a row of chairs left over from the panel earlier in the day.

Jax got to the lectern and looked out at the crowd. Hundreds of people were on their feet nervously milling about, putting as much distance between themselves and the two threats, Baxter and Sanchez, and his people still near the back of the room.

"Everyone, sit down!" he shouted. No one moved. He glared around the room. "I said, sit down!" This time, people moved. No one wanted to get close to Baxter or Sanchez, so they found seats far from either of them or stood against the walls on either side of the room. To his surprise, no one tried to run for the exits.

He turned to the woman who had been speaking. "Who's in charge?"

She stared at him, mouth hanging open.

"Ma'am?"

At his tone, she blinked. "What?"

"Who's in charge?"

Baxter made his way closer to the stage, stopping halfway. "Remain where you are," he barked at the security forces. Each of his railguns tracked back and forth.

"Stand down!" one of the security people shouted back. "This is an illegal activity."

"To say the least," Baxter replied. He turned toward the stage. "This chassis is new. Don't screw up."

"Thanks, Bax!" Jax shouted, giving him a thumbs up. He looked around. "We..." he nodded to Clinton, "he's got seeds, and a lot of people have died to make sure they made it here." He looked around. "Seeds that we're guessing will change quite a lot in the agri-tech space." He shrugged. "That part's a guess. We're hoping someone here can help with that."

"Enough!" Jefferson Sanchez roared. He shifted his rifle to a one-handed grip and, with his free hand, pointed at Clinton. "Arrest that man!"

Several people in the audience leaped from their seats, rushing to the stage. They formed a human wall. One of them, a middle-aged man in a floral print shirt made for a much smaller man, said, "We want to see what he's got."

Baxter looked at Jax, who shrugged.

More scientists came forward, surrounding the stage, forming an even deeper human wall.

Jefferson looked to the back of the room at Naomi and the convention security personnel. "Watch her."

He stormed down the walkway toward Baxter. By now the entire auditorium was in chaos. Those still seated were frantically tapping their gPhones and tablets, shouting for information, order, transparency, and several other things. Those not seated were crowding around the stage shouting to see the seeds, to hear more about them.

"I'm in charge," a small voice said from the rear of the stage.

Clinton and Jax turned to see an elderly man in a bespoke suit coming out from behind the stage, a tablet in one hand.

"I'm the chair of the symposium," he said.

CHAPTER 23

The old man approached Clinton. "I'm Chad Belvedere."

Clinton coughed, wiping sweat from his brow. "Clinton...Uh." He took off his backpack and thrust it toward the elderly man. "Two men hired me to bring these to this meeting."

Belvedere looked at the bag, his brow wrinkled, leaning back a bit. "A backpack? By whom?"

"Weren't you listening?" Jax quipped. "Seeds." He pointed. "Inide the backpack."

The man turned to Jax. "Listen up, Sparky." He waggled a finger at Jax, who backed up, hands held up in front of him.

Clinton watched, then said, "Well...I don't really know. You see, I'm a messenger—well, I was. The guys that hired me. They were killed on Freeground station."

Belvedere gasped, taking a step back.

Clinton put his hands up, one clutching the metal seed case. "Not by me!"

Jefferson Sanchez and his agents, trailed by a few of the convention security people, stopped in front of Baxter, near the stage. Behind the big bot, symposium attendees now in the hundreds were milling around, filling the space between the bot and the stage.

"Get out of the way," Jefferson growled. He still had his rifle held at the ready, as did his people. The security officers were looking around. Several had their stunners drawn and pointed at Baxter.

"Okay." The big bot turned to allow them to pass.

At the back of the room next to the ruined doors, Naomi looked at the two security people standing guard next to her. "So, we saw those furries down the hall. Weird, right? I mean, to each their own, but seems like it'd get hot in those costumes. They cause many problems?"

Neither security officer replied. She spied the woman to her right giving her side-eye as she fought to suppress a smirk.

She continued, "What's the weirdest thing you've seen here? I mean, gotta be some wild stories: dentists getting drunk and having orgies, accountants setting the stage on fire, that sort of thing."

The security woman turned her head enough that Naomi couldn't see her smile. Naomi looked at the man on the other side of her, eyebrow raised. He stared straight ahead.

Sanchez was shoving conference attendees out of his way, ignoring the shouts and angry retorts. The still-unsure-what-the-deal-was local security folks and his own people were in his wake, doing their best to keep up and keep the angry executive from being surrounded.

Up on stage, Jax watched Clinton try to explain the situation. He had pulled the metal seed case out of the backpack and was gesticulating at it. The elder scientist looked skeptical. He looked out at the crowd to see Sanchez pushing and shoving his way toward the stage. It wouldn't be long before the man reached them. With the local security people trailing behind him, Jax wasn't sure he or Clinton would get a chance to tell their side of the story.

Jax looked around. He spotted the woman who had been presenting her fungus propaganda and rushed over to her. She screamed when he reached her.

"I'm not gonna hurt you. Calm down." He patted the air between them. "Sorry, sorry. I just need your mic."

She shook her head. "My what?" Feeling less afraid, she stood up from behind the chair she had been cowering behind. Jax pointed to the small device clipped to the lapel of her jacket.

"Oh. Oh. Here." She unclipped the device and handed it to him. "Who are you people?"

"We're...No one, nobody. Don't worry about it." He turned, then turned back. "Thank you." He turned again and rushed back to the podium while clipping the small device to his own lapel.

He reached the podium and shouted, "Everyone. Calm down!" The overhead speakers rang with feedback and static. The room fell silent. All eyes turned to the stage and Jax.

"Uh. Hi." He waved.

At the back of the room, Naomi sighed. "Idiot." The two convention center security officers chuckled.

Jax said, "Look. BioTek," he pointed to Sanchez, "killed a bunch of people to keep us from bringing these seeds here." A ripple of shock spread through the room. Half the eyes in the room stayed focused on Jax. The other half turned to Sanchez, who visibly shrank a little under the scrutiny.

Sanchez straightened. "They're transporting stolen property!"

Jax didn't stop. "He killed the people who hired Clinton. He blew up a space station. He—"

Clinton raised his hand. "Actually, a tweaking spacer on Freeground killed those guys." He hitched a thumb toward Sanchez. "I don't think he or the company had anything to do with it."

Jax waved a hand. "Anyway. These seeds are something special. He," he jabbed a finger into the crowd at Sanchez, "killed to keep us from getting here, and oh yeah, tried to kill us. More than once."

Someone shouted, "Asshole!"

Jax pointed in the voice's direction. "She gets it!"

Clinton leaned toward Jax's chest. "The guys that hired me said there'd be someone here for me to meet." He straightened and looked into the crowd.

Belvedere joined him at the podium. "Is there anyone here who can vouch for Skippy here?"

The three men on stage looked around the crowd. A light brown arm in a short-sleeved blouse rose into the air.

Jefferson Sanchez's head snapped over to gaze at the woman, who was now standing up, her arm still raised over her head. He glared, muttering, "Traitor," under his breath. He looked to one of his people. "Identify her." The man nodded.

He handed his rifle to the woman next to him. Raising both arms, he shouted, "I'm with BioTek loss prevention." He pointed at Clinton. "That man has stolen goods. BioTek property." He shifted his finger to the woman who was standing. "And she's complicit in that theft."

The woman made a face. "No, I'm not!"

Sanchez watched the woman make her way to the stage. He growled and started shoving his way through the crowd.

Jax rushed to her side when she reached the stage. "Hi. So, you know what those things are?" She nodded, her brown eyes alternating between being fixed on the floor and glancing at Sanchez fighting his way toward them.

She looked at Belvedere. "I'm Beverly Rehman. I..." She looked again at Sanchez, who hadn't stopped staring at her. "They sent the seeds to me." She held up her phone, the screen showing a complex code. Clinton suspected he was the only one that understood what it was or meant.

"What are they?" Belvedere asked.

Sanchez's agent leaned in. "Beverly Rehman. Works in the agri-tech division under Monika Jones."

"Worked," Sanchez grated. He looked at the man onstage and shouted, "They're proprietary property, that's what!"

A heavyset man in a cardigan who did his best to stay in Sanchez's way stopped him. He met Jax's gaze and winked.

Beverly accepted the seed case from Clinton. She gave him a shy smile, then turned to the symposium chair. "They're modified wheat."

The older man scoffed. "That's not interesting." He turned toward the podium, intent on putting an end to all this excitement.

Rehman shook her head. "You're wrong. We cracked the code. It's everything we've ever wanted. Strong stalks. The Gluton proteins don't trigger immune responses, they're completely bio-inert. It can grow in high- and low-PH environments. It's even capable of growing in thin atmosphere and zero gravity."

Belvedere stopped and turned, staring at her a moment. He rubbed his chin, then turned to the crowd. "This needs validating."

"No!" Sanchez roared. He shoved past the man blocking him, pushing a small Asian woman down on his way closer to the stage. "Those are proprietary BioTek intellectual property, goddamnit!" He turned to one of the convention security officers. "Do something!"

A portly Asian man approached the stage. "I have a portable analyzer." He pulled a device from a satchel he had over his shoulder. "It's for a meeting I had at lunch."

Jax reached down. "Thanks, dude." He turned to the old man next to Clinton and the woman scientist, what was her name? Mabel? "Here."

The two scientists set about setting up the portable unit on the lectern, connecting it to the BioTek woman's tablet.

Rudy made a soft beep, catching Naomi's attention. She didn't react, still standing between the two convention security people. He beeped again, louder. All three humans turned to look at the insistent droid.

"Excuse me. I think my droid might be about to explode," Naomi said, kneeling down. "What?"

He put grabbed her hand, placing it on his head. *Can you hear this?*

Her eyes went wide. She nodded.

I didn't think it would work. Neat.

Naomi raised an eyebrow.

Oh. I guess it only goes one way.

She scowled.

Okay. Okay. We need to get out of here. I don't know what Jax is doing, but the longer we're here, the better the odds I'm melted down into a decorative paper weight.

Naomi made a face as she thought, then nodded. She tipped her head toward the front of the room, then drummed her fingers on Rudy's rust-colored head. Then she stood up.

Rudy turned to look toward the front of the room. He accessed the convention center's wireless network, then reached out to Skip.

Up on stage, Clinton moved next to Jax. "Thank you."

The two scientists were busily babbling to each other over the portable analyzer.

Jax turned, looking up. "For what?"

Clinton tilted his head. "You know, trying to save me." He gestured to the spot in front of the stage where Jax had dove to intercept a pulse rifle blast. Baxter blocked the shot, but to Clinton, it was the thought that mattered.

Jax nodded. "Oh. That. Don't sweat it."

Clinton shook his head. "All that grief, and then you try to take a plasma round for me. That's not nothing."

A flush crept up Jax's cheeks. "I said, forget it."

Clinton was about to press the issue when the doors that led to the service corridor exploded inward.

Roanoke Police flooded into the ballroom, weapons up and ready. An authoritative woman with a pair of yellow metal bars on each of her shoulders shouted, "I don't know what the hell this is, but cut it out." She pointed at Baxter. "You better stow all those weapons!" She looked around. "Who brought a combat droid up in here?"

"Uh, that'd be me," Jax said from the stage.

She waved her gun at Baxter. "Well, make it stand down and go, I dunno...Stand in the corner." She turned to glare at the combat droid. She held two fingers up to her eyes, then moved them to point at Baxter.

Jax looked at Baxter and inclined his head. The big

combat droid stalked to the back of the room to stand near Naomi and Rudy.

Sanchez approached the woman. "I demand that you arrest," he pointed at Clinton, "him," then moved his finger to Beverly Rehman, "her," then waved toward Jax, "and him, too."

The police captain looked Sanchez up and down. "And you are?"

"Jefferson Sanchez, BioTek loss prevention. These people are in possession of stolen property." He waved a hand. "We need to secure this room. Take all of them into custody. Then we—"

She held up a hand. "I'm sorry, no."

Sanchez leaned back. "What?"

This time, she was the one waving a hand. "I'm not doing any of those things you just said." She held up a finger. "I need you to step back." She turned to the stage. "I need you all to stop doing whatever it is you're doing up there."

"Excuse me, officer, uh..." the old man on stage, Belvedere, said.

"Captain. Captain Kipkemei."

"Captain Kipkemei, we're analyzing seeds that could very well change how the Empire feeds its citizens."

"Can I eat 'em now?"

"No."

"Then stop."

Jax and Clinton each took a step back from the lectern and the little device neither understood with its blinking lights and soft beeps.

The woman from BioTek put a hand on the older

scientist's shoulder, easing him away. Before they took two steps, the device made a happy little singsong noise.

Every face in the room turned back to the stage.

"What was that?" Captain Kipkemei asked.

"Nothing!" Sanchez shouted. He turned and started for the stage. Kipkemei nodded to two of her people, who rushed over to intercept Sanchez.

From a seat in the front row, the man who provided the analyzer said, "It's finished the analysis."

Everyone was staring at the lectern.

Jax's gPhone buzzed in his pocket. He looked at the screen, then up at the crowd. He spotted Baxter in the near corner. The big bot nodded. He turned to Clinton, grinning.

Sanchez struggled in the grip of the two police officers. "Damnit, these people have committed a crime!" Captain Kipkemei made a face. "What? Theft of corporate property is illegal."

"It's not BioTek property!"

Everyone turned to Beverly Rehman, standing next to the lectern. She had the portable analyzer in one hand. "See." She held the tablet connected to the device in her other hand, screen out. Belvedere took the tablet.

"I don't believe it." All eyes moved from Sanchez to the two scientists on stage next to the podium. Belvedere turned to Rehman. "You really did it."

She nodded.

Rehman turned to Sanchez. "BioTek did not develop these. My friends didn't. I didn't." She took a deep breath. "My niece developed them. On her own. She gave them to me to vet."

She turned to the police captain. "The company has no claim to these. She designed them in her garage. When our boss got nosy, we agreed to bring our findings here to the symposium so that there was no chance of the company hijacking them." She glared at Sanchez. "We'd seen it happen too many times before."

In the back of the room, Naomi smiled. "Boom."

Sanchez scoffed. "I don't believe you. Your boss came to me and turned your two conspirators in."

Rehman's face fell. "She was wrong. I told them they were being too weird about sneaking around, but they didn't trust her. I guess they were right on that part." She snuffled loudly, the weight of her friend's deaths catching up to her.

Captain Kipkemei watched all this, then turned to Rehman. "So, your niece made these magic seeds, but you gave them to your coworkers, to hire that skinny fella to transport...to the place you were going?" She cocked her head.

Beverly inhaled. "Yes. Malcolm and Leonard weren't attending the conference. I was. I couldn't bring them. We're scanned more than once by BioTek corporate security. They'd have seen them and taken them from me."

Kipkemei turned to Sanchez, who continued to stare at the stage, not turning to meet her gaze. She clucked. "I see."

Jax tapped a few icons on his phone, looking for the processing core that ran the wall display that was still showing the other woman's fungus slide. "There we go." He swiped.

The wall display flickered, then began playing the

Osprey's feed of the destruction of the ParStor Co-op station. The entire ballroom fell silent.

Jax poked Clinton in the ribs. "Time to go."

Clinton looked at him. "What? Why? Where?"

Jax shrugged. "This is when people like us," he put a hand on his chest, "bow out. Shit's about to get real. We didn't exactly do legal things to get here and no matter how appreciative the nerds are..." He pointed to the police captain woman standing next to the stage. At the moment, her gaze, like everyone else's in the room, was on the wall display.

"She won't have a choice. She'll arrest us to be safe. They'll maybe drop the charges once they sort things out, but until then..." He pointed to Sanchez. "He's going to prison, but BioTek will get nothing but a slap on the wrist. Hell, they'll probably just throw him to the wolves." He shrugged. "So now, we vanish."

"What happens to me?"

Jax pulled him toward the back of the stage while all eyes were on the display that was now showing the destruction wrought on UniDis Four.

"You vanish with us. We'll set you up somewhere. I know some folks. We can get you a new identity or something. How do you feel about the Resistance?"

"The Resistance?"

Jax shrugged. "Yeah, you know: tight pants, hate the Empire. Fight for the people or something like that."

"Tight pants?"

"Never mind. Not important." Jax tapped his earpiece. "Bax, can you get Naomi?"

"We're good," Rudy replied. "On our way to the ship. With Baxter."

"What?" Jax looked around the room. "You left us!" he hissed. He looked to the back of the room, spotting two convention security officers slumped against the wall.

Jax looked up at what he thought was the skylight he shot earlier, expecting a shaft of daylight to be stabbing down into the middle of the room. "Wow, that thing was super realistic." The room was now completely dark, except for two ceiling panes that were crackling with intermittent static, throwing random shadows everywhere.

Jax grabbed Clinton's shoulder. "Come on."

Clinton shrugged and allowed Jax to guide him from the stage amid shouts and screams. The local police captain did not sound happy.

Clinton and Jax came up the stairs from the *Osprey*'s boarding room to see Naomi, Baxter, and Rudy waiting for them in the lounge space. Naomi had three beers ready in her hands. She smiled. "On our way out, I took the liberty of wiping the convention center's mainframe. Parking control, security data, all of it. There's zero trace we, or five thousand other people, were here." She smirked, eyebrows raised.

Jax took a beer and looked at the ceiling. "Skip, are we safe?"

"Safe is a relative term, but for now, yes. The moment

we set down, I powered down what I could except our stealth systems. I cannot be certain but would put credits on those fast movers having reported our location. From what I have been able to gather from local comms, whatever you all were up to inside the convention center was more interesting than tracking down where we landed, at least for the moment. That said, we should get moving. Those Imperials overhead are bound to take an interest."

Nodding, Jax took his beer to the staircase leading to the bridge. He turned to Rudy. "Come on."

The small droid turned his large optical sensor from Naomi to Jax, then rolled to the staircase.

Naomi made room for Clinton on the couch. He accepted his beer and said, "So, you all are in the Resistance?"

Naomi choked on the sip of beer she was taking. She wiped her mouth. "I'm sorry, what?"

"Jax said you all could hook me up with the Resistance. New identity, all that."

Naomi made a face. "Huh. Didn't see that coming." She took a sip of her beer. She squinted. "You into that?"

"I'm into not dying, yes."

She tipped her head. "Fair."

He stared for a moment. "So?"

"Oh." She shook her head. "No, we're not. We do some work for them from time to time, though."

Clinton nodded slowly, taking that in. Who worked with the Resistance but wasn't with them? Was that even possible? He shook the thought off and asked, "What'd you think was gonna happen?"

Naomi kept the bottle at her lips, raising an eyebrow.

"Oh...No. No. No?" He looked toward the spiral staircase that connected the small ship's decks. A flush crept up his cheeks. "I don't know. I mean, he's—"

Naomi shook her head. "Don't. He's not worth the trouble. Believe me," Naomi interrupted.

He blinked. "Oh, were you...? I didn't pick up on—"

"God no!" Naomi blurted. She couldn't hold in her laughter. "No. No. No."

The deck rumbled as the lift engines powered up. Everything tilted slightly. Then the sound of metal scraping against metal reverberated through the ship.

Clinton looked around, then shrugged and took a sip of his beer. "Okay. Just making sure. I mean he's attrac—"

Naomi reached over, pressing a finger to his lips. "No. Thank me later, but do not entertain the thought a second longer." She removed her finger and was quiet a moment, then looked at the ceiling. "I owe you ten credits, Skip."

Clinton raised an eyebrow but said nothing when Skip answered, "Yes, you may deposit it in the ship's account, where I will hope it is used for repairs and watch as the Captain uses it for beer."

Clinton watched the exchange, then said, "So, now what?"

"Well, I have updated our list of planets to avoid for a while to include Bustamonte," Skip offered.

Clinton smiled. "How long is that list?"

"Bustamonte was the 23rd entry," Skip answered.

The ship juddered, and something down below in the engineering space groaned. The overhead speaker crackled. Jax's voice said, "It's okay. We're fine, that's fine.

We should be in a wormhole in thirty minutes. Had to squeak by one of those big bruisers from before, but I think I shook 'em." There was a pause. "Well, shook 'em enough that they'll spend a few weeks looking for the *Sea Sprite*."

"*Sea Sprite*?" Clinton repeated.

Naomi leaned her head back on the couch and sighed. "I sometimes think I picked the wrong ship to hitch my future to." She reached up and took a long pull on her beer.

When she didn't say anything more, Clinton said, "Is this one of those times?"

The overhead speaker crackled again. Jax said, "We'll be rendezvousing with our... friends in a week. Someone think up dinner."

She closed her eyes. "Nope."

The End

Clinton approached the Osprey, parked near the edge of the Goliath. Looking up at the open cargo bay, he spied two sets of legs dangling over the edge.

"Hey!" He called out.

The legs vanished to be replaced by Jax and Naomi looking down at him. The former smiled. "Hey, man."

Naomi grinned. "You're looking dapper."

Clinton looked down at himself and his uniform. Looking back up, he said. "Thanks. Still getting used to it." He picked at an imaginary piece of lint on one sleeve.

"Be right down," Jax said as the pair disappeared from sight.

They stepped off the boarding ramp a moment later, followed by Rudy and Baxter. The latter said. "Fancy duds."

Clinton nodded to the combat droid. "It's not an intimidating cloak, but I'll make do."

Baxter made a rattling sound. "I never liked you."

Jax offered his hand, and Clinton took it. "How you been?"

Clinton smiled. "Good. Better than I expected." He made a slow turn, hands raised to encompass the cavernous landing bay of the Goliath. "Never in a million years would I have thought I'd be part of the resistance."

"Let's hope it goes better than your stint as a Messenger." Naomi quipped. She looked down to Rudy, who offered a little metal hand for her to slap.

Clinton laughed. "Be hard for it to go worse."

Rudy made a series of beeps. "We should go. He just jinxed it."

Clinton shook his head. "Anyhow. I've got to get to work, but I heard you all were making a cargo drop." He smiled as he looked at the landing bay deck. "Wanted to say hi, and thanks again." He looked up, blushing. "I owe you both my — "

This time it was Baxter that made a metallic gargling sound.

Clinton glanced at the menacing combat droid. "I owe all four of you my life."

"Don't mention it," Jax said. "It was the right thing to do."

Naomi turned to Jax, arms crossed over her chest. "Really?"

He just grinned.

ACKNOWLEDGMENTS

Thank you so much to my dedicated Beta Readers. Without their help these stories wouldn't be as good! You rock and I can't thank you enough!

Rick Lindsay

Chris Boyd

Marcus Zarra

Mitchell Schneidkraut

Roger Gilmartin

Andy Canning

Felix Muller

Jim Stiles

Want to stay up to date on the happenings in the Grand Human Empire?

Sign up for my newsletter at

johnwilker.com/newsletter

Visit me online at

johnwilker.com

You can also join my Patreon page for all sorts of awesome goodies!

If you like supporting things you love by sporting merch or buying direct, well you're in luck! I've launched a shop, take a look. **Use, discount code "Osprey" and you'll save %15!**

As they say, there's no harm in asking, so here we go.

If you can help connect me with someone who can get The Grand human Empire on a screen (Big or Little) I'll cut you in for 10% (Up to $10,000) of whatever advance is paid.

Send me an email and we can discuss.
rights@johnwilker.com

The Space Rogues Series. Wil Calder and a bunch of alien misfits somehow keep finding themselves in the thick of it. No one ever checks qualifications when it comes to saving the galaxy!

The Grand Human Empire Series. Jax, Naomi and the droids are just trying to get by. New droid parts ain't cheap after all.